ANGEL EVOLUTION

Book One of the

Evolution Trilogy

David Estes

ISBN-10: 1466422777
ISBN-13: 978-1466422773

Jacket concept by Adele Estes
Jacket art by Phatpuppy Art
Jacket design by Winkipop Design

This book is dedicated to my lovely wife, Adele,

for all of her wise and practical advice,

creative perspectives, and support and

encouragement. I hope that someday I can pay it back.

PART I

One

Her parched throat burned like it was on fire. She tried to swallow, but each desperate gulp seemed to have no effect. The dizzying effect of the dehydration was affecting her memory. She couldn't remember where she was or how she got there, but knew that if she didn't find water soon, Death would painfully claim her. As she tried to get her bearings, a steady fog drifted in and surrounded her in an icy shroud. Dropping to her knees in anguish, she prepared to give in to the sleep that she had been desperately fighting.

Out of the corner of her eye she saw a familiar slithering Evil. A snake, inky black with blood-red eyes, undulated towards her. Weakened by her thirst, she could only watch as the sharp-fanged reptile approached, without caution. She collapsed face-first onto the cold, hard ground. The snake reached her naked foot, and climbed over her heel and onto her slender ankle. Without hesitation, it moved up her bare leg, its rough scales buzzing along her exposed skin.

With her cheek pressed against the rocky earth, she saw what had to be a mirage: two Beings strode purposefully toward her through swirls of mist. Despite the exhaustion that clouded her vision, she could see that both Beings were exquisitely beautiful. The first had a subtle glow about its body that cut through the fog casually, as if the weather was clear. Its glow brightened as it approached. The second was cloaked in darkness, although it wore no head covering. Surprisingly, she felt safe.

The snake reached her waist, caressing her hips like a dance partner, but the visitors didn't seem to notice.

One of them gently touched an animal-skin pouch to her cracked lips. As the lubricating water ran mercifully past her teeth, along her tongue and down her inflamed throat, she wondered who these wondrous presences were and why they had saved her. Forgetting the snake, she insatiably gulped down the cool liquid. Seconds later she cringed, as the fire returned. The second Being slid another vessel into position, and she greedily opened her mouth to receive the life-giving water. She barely had time to choke out a scream before the sand filled her mouth.

Her last memory was the black snake: its red eyes staring into hers, its mouth gaping open to reveal fiercely sharp fangs dripping with blood as black as oil. Her final thoughts could be summed up in one word: fear.

Two

One week later.

Despite the light drizzle, Taylor sat cross-legged on the lush lawn; she was patiently scouring the grass with her hands and eyes. Trying to find it. She wasn't a superstitious person by nature, but something inside her very soul compelled her to keep looking. It had become a ritual for her. A painstaking search was required in any new place where she would be spending more than a week. Every few minutes, she shifted her towel a few feet over and continued her hunt.

After one such move, her grazing hands stopped abruptly and her eyes locked on her ring—*the* ring. While she wore many rings—eight between her two hands, to be exact—only one had the ability to distract her so completely. Like now. Not the dog bone or the horseshoe or the thorny rose or the black bat or the cross. Not even the skull or the death spikes. Those rings all felt ordinary compared to the last ring—the one she wore on her left ring finger. The four-leaf clover.

It wasn't the clover itself that made the ring special. Or the four leaves, which traditionally implied luck for the bearer; rather, it was the giver of the ring that defined its value. It was the last gift her mother had ever given her, for her birthday.

"You're a teenager now," she had said. "You're going to need all the luck you can get." Taylor had laughed and given her mom a big hug.

Ever since her mother's unexpected death, when Taylor was only thirteen, she had forced herself to keep looking. Searching. To her, finding a four-leaf clover in a place was a sign. A sign that she was meant to be there. A sign that her mom was watching. A sign that she had not gone astray. A sign that her mom was proud of her. A sign that she was not alone.

Of course, she was never really alone. She still had her dad, her brother. And there was always Sam, her best friend and roommate.

Since she had arrived at The University of Trinton, or UT as the students called it, a week earlier, she had enjoyed herself like most college freshman do, especially because classes hadn't started. Yet, she had never felt fully comfortable. She was acutely aware that her lingering unease was inexplicably linked to her failed search for the Holy Grail of all clovers. Time and time again she had plucked tiny greens from the earth; with each attempt her heart had skipped a beat, only to discover that the chosen clover had a mere three leaves. Or, freakishly, the clover would have a fifth leaf, an atrocity of nature. Sometimes Taylor was tempted to remove the unwanted extra appendage, thus creating the object of her desire. But she never acted on these urges, knowing full-well that you can't force fate.

Now, wrenching her eyes from her cherished ring, she tried to concentrate. Taylor was glad for the light rain; it cooled down the muggy, late summer's day. And it generally kept other students inside and off the lawn. She didn't want any distractions.

As she focused on her task, an unwanted vision was shaken from her memory tree. In her mind she saw her dad reprimanding her. He had not understood why she got the tattoo. He had been furious with her. *How could she be so immature?* Taylor truly believed that her mom would have understood why she needed it. As long as she could remember, Taylor had had a recurring nightmare about a vicious black snake with red eyes. Many times it was the main subject of her bad dreams—she would be trapped in a room without doors or windows, with only the snake as a companion—and other times it would unexpectedly appear in her good dreams, creating chaos from beauty.

However, regardless of its form, the beady-eyed snake would eventually sink its razor-sharp fangs into her flesh, and then drip black blood from its mouth, causing her to wake up to cold sweats and blood-curdling screams. So she got the tattoo when she was sixteen. Not to be cool, or weird, or sexy; the tattoo symbolized her conquering of the snake—proof that she wasn't scared anymore. She still had nightmares, but now when she woke up she could cope. Fear of the snake no longer kept her awake at night. A six-inch, red-eyed, black snake rested on the back of her left shoulder, and was visible now because of her tank top; the serpent was maliciously cut in half by her shoulder-strap.

She hardly wore any makeup, which was lucky, because given the rain, it would be smeared and running anyway. Her slightly-wet jeans were ripped, but not in the trendy, I-bought-them-like-that way; in her case, the tears, frays, and holes were all natural. She also wore a bright red tank top, which coincidentally matched her red flip-flops.

Her choice of best friend was Samantha Collins, or Sam as her friends' called her. She was the typical cheerleader, prom-queen, date-the-high-school-quarterback, subject-of-a-school-boy's-wet-dreams type of girl. Taylor, on the other hand, hated the spotlight, dated even less frequently than she wore makeup, and had likely never been included in anyone's dreams, girls or guys. But somehow she and

Sam just clicked. She valued Sam's opinion above anyone else's, and they harbored no secrets from each other. Sam had been Taylor's shoulder to cry on when she lost her mom; she might not have made it through the ordeal without her. She hoped to be able to repay her one day.

Still sifting through the grass, someone caught Taylor's eye, in her peripheral vision. Up to this point, only a few students had walked past her, but she had barely noticed them as they hurried along the sidewalk, clutching umbrellas like lifelines. This one was not on the sidewalk, nor did he seem bothered by the rain; rather, umbrella-less, he had crossed over onto the grass, and appeared to be on a collision course with her. When she looked up, what she saw startled her. He was tall, and was wearing a tight, white t-shirt, which clung to his skin from the rain. He was muscular, but not in a meathead kind of way. More like in an athletic, Hermes-messenger-of-the-gods kind of way. With sandy blond hair and a handsome broad face with a strong chin, he might have been a Swedish celebrity that just landed on a plane from Europe. She searched his eyes for color, and found it eventually—a thin ring of blue circled his exceptionally large, black pupils. At first glance his eyes looked only black. But his well-toned physique, movie star good looks, and black-looking eyes were not what had captured Taylor's attention; instead, it was the strange glow that seemed to resonate from his body: his legs, his arms, his chest. Even his head was emanating light. Almost like a glow worm.

He approached.

"Have we met before?" he asked directly.

Taylor stared at flashlight-boy like he was an alien who had just passed through a black hole, complete with three heads, slimy tentacles, and at least fourteen eyes. "Not in this lifetime," she replied.

"Well, I've definitely seen *you* around campus."

"Congratulations." She said it sarcastically, but felt a flutter in her stomach at the thought of being noticed by the radioactive stud that stood before her.

"I'm Gabriel. Gabriel Knight." He extended a hand.

She took it and squeezed hard when she shook. It was something her mom had taught her. *Women are not expected to have a firm handshake*, she used to say. *Be different.* Despite her efforts to get a reaction from him, he just grinned at her. His grip was even firmer, like iron. Eventually she released his hand.

"I'm Taylor," she said. "Taylor Kingston." She mimicked his introduction, like a parrot.

"Nice to meet you, Taylor. What are you doing out here…by yourself…in the rain?"

She almost blurted it out, but managed to shut her mouth before her flapping gums betrayed her. Recovering, she said, "Just enjoying the day. But I'm not here by myself, you're here aren't you? And I would hardly call this rain."

He grinned. "You're unusual."

"Now that's a line you might want to work on."

Still grinning, he said, "It wasn't a line, just an observation."

"Anyway…," Taylor said, trying to end the conversation.

"Ah, I see that I've overstayed my welcome," Gabriel replied.

Taylor noticed his eyes growing blacker, as if the faint ring of blue was being devoured by his widening black pupils. He looked down at the wet grass, scanning it like a security camera detecting an intruder. Reaching down, he plucked something from the earth. "Wow, a four-leaf clover," he said. "I don't think I've ever found one of those before. It's supposed to be lucky."

Taylor's eyes widened as he handed it to her. She checked it. One, two, three, four: It was the genuine article, and the object of her futile search. She tried to hand it back to him, but Gabriel stopped her. "Consider it a gift…to match your ring." Shrugging his shoulders, he turned before she could reply. Over his shoulder he said, "See you around, Taylor."

"Bye," she murmured, watching the glow worm walk away from her. When he crossed over onto the sidewalk, she finally turned her attention back to the tiny bit of greenery in her hand. *She had found it.* Well, technically Gabriel had found it, but she would have found it eventually. For a moment, a sense of peace washed over her and seemed to enter her body through her skin. As if by osmosis, her mother's undying influence flowed through each and every pore, and then into her bones, her organs, her mind, her soul. But as rapidly as it had arrived, the sense of peace vanished, and was replaced by a sense of dread, of foreboding. *How had Gabriel known what she was looking for? And how had he found the clover so fast? His eyes had been much further from the ground than hers.*

Suddenly, his image flashed back into her mind and a lost memory was unchained. Like a wine bottle that had at long last been uncorked after an aging slumber, the memory of the nightmare was opened to her. It was as if her mind had been trying to protect her, locking the memory in a vault and throwing away the key, only to thrust it back into the open now. A week ago. The two Beings: one dark and one light. The black snake. While the snake had appeared in many of her dreams, never had it been accompanied by the two Beings that had assaulted her. She remembered what she had felt that night:

Fear. She had awakened from the nightmare in a cold sweat, issuing a terrified scream that could have startled the dead from their resting places. As she had started to separate the horrific dream from reality, her heart rate had finally slowed from an accelerated 150 beats per minute to just under 100; however, her chest had continued to heave with short and choking breaths. Wide-eyed, she had looked out the window into the darkness, half-expecting to see the two foreign Beings standing in the backyard. When she had checked the blue digital numbers on her iHome alarm clock, she had noted it was only 2:39 in the morning.

Normally, she slept on her back, like a vampire, with her arms directly at her side, her head lolled to one side or the other, but that night she had found herself curled into the fetal position, all balled up in a cocoon of blankets.

She had heard frantic footsteps in the hallway and her door had swung open.

"What happened? Are you alright? Are you hurt?" her father had questioned in one breath.

She had been unsure of which question to respond to first, but had managed to squeak out, "I think so…," which had caused her dad to rush to her side in a panic.

"You think you're hurt? Where are you hurt?"

"No, I'm not hurt, Dad. I was responding to the middle question of, 'Are you alright?' which I think I am. It was just a bad dream."

"Are you sure? It sounded like you were being tortured in here," he had replied. His forehead had been crinkled in concern for her well-being. He had looked older than usual.

"Yes, yes, I'm fine. I promise, Dad. Can I please just go back to sleep? I want to get enough rest for my first day at college."

His face had finally relaxed and he had said, "Okay, no problem. I love you."

As he turned to pass through the door, she had said, "You know, starting tomorrow you won't be around to worry about me every time I have a nightmare."

Before closing the door, he had smiled and said, "But for tonight, you are still my little princess."

Taylor couldn't help but to smile. "I love you too, Dad," she had said.

For the rest of that night, she had tried to turn her mind off, but sleep continued to elude her, as the blurry visions from the dream continued to flash through her mind. She had wondered: Who were the Beings and, more importantly, what were they? And did one of them really want to kill her? If so, which one? Although they were both beautiful, it had to be the dark one. Dark signified evil and light signified good. At least that's what she was always taught in Sunday school. Or did they both want to kill her? She had racked her memory, trying to picture which one had given her the water and which had given her the sand.

As light began to appear across the horizon, she had finally drifted off to sleep from sheer exhaustion.

Taylor sighed as the vision ended and her mind began to clear. Until now, she had managed to ignore her fear from that night, chalking it up as an anomaly, possibly due to something she had eaten—Sloppy Joe's always did weird things to her. But now she was scared again. The boy, Gabriel Knight, reminded her of one of the Beings in her dream: the one with the subtle glow around his body.

She looked at her hand, the one that held the four-leaf clover. Gabriel's gift. Without realizing it, she had plucked the four leaves from the stem, leaving it leafless, naked. She had desecrated it, destroying any luck that it might provide. Her fingers were rigid and curled, claw-like even. They looked deformed. She shuddered, finally feeling the effect of the cold, damp clothing on her skin, as icicles of rain continued to assault her.

Three

Gabriel Knight still had an amused grin on his face. He was smooth. It wouldn't be long before he had her eating out of his hand, figuratively speaking. The trick with the four-leaf clover was genius. Of course, he had already known what she was looking for. He knew almost everything about her. Because he was thorough. That's why he had been given the assignment. He was a rising star and the girl was an easy target. He would not fail.

He flipped open his phone and called the number. A cold voice said, "Yes?"

"First contact made. No complications. It won't be long." His report was direct, his sentences clipped. The key was to only give the facts.

The hard voice replied, "Good. I knew you were the right one for the job. Do not fail me, Gabriel. Get the girl. Report after your next contact."

"Yes, my lord."

He ended the call.

He smiled again. His first contact with the girl had been far more interesting that he had expected it to be. He had meant what he had said about her being *unusual*. Although to her it had probably been a strange remark, he had meant it as a compliment. Unusual-weird was bad, but she was unusual-interesting, unusual-unique, unusual-quirky. That was good. He suspected that he would quite enjoy this mission. It might even be regrettable to him if it all ended with her death, which was very likely under the circumstances.

Four

Taylor half-walked, half-jogged back to the dorms. She would have run, but wearing flip-flops made it difficult, especially on the sidewalks, which were still slick with rain. When she arrived back at Shyloh Hall, the all-girl freshman dormitory that she had been assigned to, she took the stairs to the seventh floor. The elevator was hit-or-miss—sometimes arriving in one minute, and other times not coming at all—and she was anxious to get back to her room.

Out of breath, she opened the door to room 715. Samantha was lying on her bed flipping through a fashion magazine. Despite being dressed down by her standards—wearing only blue cotton shorts and a white tank-top—Sam still looked stunning. She had probably just come back from the gym, part of her daily routine. In Taylor's mind, Sam was beautiful in all of the ways that guys liked. She had long legs and good curves, blond hair that always seemed to fall just the right way, and a dazzling smile with perfectly straight, white teeth. She usually jumped from boyfriend to boyfriend in high school, and Taylor expected college to be the same. Taylor didn't mind it though; she preferred to have someone else to take the attention away from her.

Taylor did not think of herself as pretty. When she looked in the mirror she saw a very average girl, with straight brown hair, mild brown eyes and a rather crooked smile. She dated sometimes, but couldn't keep up with Sam.

"Hey, Tay," Sam said. "Where've you been?"

"You know, the usual."

"Still trying to find that damn clover?"

"Yeah." Not knowing what to say about it, she left out the part about her conversation with the mysterious Gabriel.

"You'll find it, don't worry." Sam stood up. "I hope you don't mind, I finally finished unpacking and had to borrow some of your closet space. It will only be temporary, I promise."

Taylor shrugged. She'd never quite understood Sam's need to wear a different outfit every day of the year, or even every day of the month, for that matter. If she could find clothes that were clean and relatively unwrinkled, she was happy.

Sam, on the other hand, liked to dress based on whatever the current fad was, and would quite often give her new clothes to her younger sister after only wearing them for a few months, if at all. "Out with the old and in with the new," she liked to say. Sam didn't come from a wealthy family, but had worked through high school to fund her shopping habit.

"Also, while you were gone, I made another friend on our floor. I'll introduce you."

Taylor smiled, happy that she was rooming with "Social Sam", as she jokingly called her sometimes. Taylor liked being social and liked having friends, but didn't particularly like having to go out and make them. Samantha eliminated that need, as she had an uncanny ability to make friends and was happy to introduce them to Taylor. In a non-English speaking foreign country, with a bunch of kids at a daycare, at an adult dinner party: Sam could make friends anywhere.

"Cool," Taylor replied.

"Great." Sam tried to grab her hand but she managed to slide it away. Sam chuckled—she was fully aware that Taylor wasn't into that kind of thing. Taylor followed Sam to room 714, which was immediately next to their own room. The door was open and Sam walked in without knocking.

"Marla, I've got someone for you to...," she started to say and then stopped, realizing she was intruding. "Oh, I'm sorry, I should've knocked."

Taylor peeked around Sam and saw a tiny, sprite of a girl with her arms wrapped around a guy, clearly having been interrupted from a serious make out session.

"No, don't even worry about it," the girl said, her cheeks flushing in embarrassment. "Boyfriend is my Jennings from high school...I mean, Jennings is my boyfriend. We should've closed the door, but one thing led to another...," she managed to stammer.

"Hi, I'm Jennings." The tall, skinny, freckle-faced boy with glasses extended his hand in greeting.

Sam said, "I'm Sam and this is my best friend from high school, Tay...I mean, Taylor."

"Nice to meet you. Where are you guys from?" Taylor asked.

"We actually grew up here, in Collegetown," Jennings replied.

Marla was still rather flushed and seemed incapable of speaking. Taylor could tell right away that she would like these two. They seemed normal.

As usual, Sam filled the void in the conversation. "Has your roommate arrived yet, Marla?"

Marla found her voice. "Not yet, but when I spoke to her over the summer she said she wouldn't arrive until just before classes started, so I'm not expecting her."

"Did she seem nice?" Taylor asked.

"I think so, but she also seemed a bit strange. She confirmed about three times that we were in room 714 in Shyloh Hall." Marla frowned as she said this, clearly concerned that she might be the one stuck with an oddball roommate for the year.

"Well, you can always request a transfer if you don't get along with her, and then we can apply for a triple room for next year," Sam said.

Marla's face brightened at the prospect, and she exclaimed, "That sounds perfect!"

Jennings laughed. "We've barely been here two weeks and you're already plotting to remove your 'evil' roommate who you haven't even met yet, and replace her with two girls who we just met, no offense to either of you. You should meet my roommate, now he's an odd duck. I haven't seen him leave the room yet and every time I come in, the lights are off and he's shouting commands into his headset. I think he actually believes he's the general of an army, and not just playing a virtual reality video game. I assume that he'll leave to pee and shower and such, but he has enough packs of instant noodles to feed him for the entire semester."

Taylor laughed. "Sounds like my type of guy. Low maintenance."

"I'll introduce you," Jennings joked.

"What are you guys up to tonight?" Sam asked.

Marla shrugged. "We don't really have any plans."

"Should we go have dinner in the Commons?" The Commons, or the Common Area, was the central portion of the dormitories, where students would gather to eat, watch TV, shop, and shoot pool, among other things.

"Yeah, let's go. I could eat three horses as just an appetizer," Taylor said.

Marla and Jennings agreed to go too and, due to another elevator malfunction, they were forced to trudge down seven flights of stairs. Upon reaching the ground floor, they headed towards the Commons. As they walked, Marla and Jennings held hands quietly, while Sam kept up a running chatter in Taylor's ear as they passed various freshman boys. "He was cute, don't you think?" or "Wow, he was hot, right?" were her typical comments.

Taylor tried to tune her out and replied with, "Mmmm," or "Yeah, Sam," while she escaped into her own thoughts. Despite having friends with her, Taylor was unable to shake the feeling of unease from her unexpected meeting with Gabriel. *Gabriel Knight*, she thought. *Who the hell is this guy?* Something about Gabriel rubbed her the wrong way, like an itchy hive. Perhaps it was the confident way he had approached her, but that certainly wasn't uncommon for testosterone-filled freshman guys. He had called her *unusual*, but that didn't really bother her either. Despite her sarcastic reply, she had thought it sounded more like a compliment than an insult. More likely, her unease was due to him giving her the four-leaf clover, as if he could read her thoughts, coupled with his subtle glow and black eyes. She had to admit, the intensity of the memory had unnerved her.

Throughout dinner, her fears continued to dominate her thoughts. She knew she wasn't making a very good impression on Marla and Jennings, but she couldn't seem to concentrate on the conversation. Luckily, Sam was there to pick up the slack. When they were finished eating, Sam suggested they go shoot some pool, but everyone declined; Marla and Jennings were heading to a movie and Taylor wanted to relax a bit.

Sam headed to the pool hall alone, but Taylor didn't feel bad about it. She'd probably make ten new friends before the night was over. Taylor walked back to the dorm alone and climbed the stairs to her room.

She lay on her bed for hours, staring at the ceiling. Trying to work....*something* out. At times it felt like the answer was right in front of her eyes and yet impossible to see.

At around ten, she turned off the lights and tried to sleep. A shiver shook her spine, but she wasn't cold. She felt apprehensive, threatened. Like someone was watching her, plotting her demise. She sat up and looked out the window into the darkness. There was no one there. Her window overlooked a massive parking lot. The closest building was half-a-mile away. Someone would need high-powered binoculars to spy on her from there.

I'm probably just being silly, she thought.

Five

Gabriel watched her from across the parking lot. Even from this distance he could see her every feature. She was quite pretty. Much prettier in person than in the picture. He hadn't expected this. But he wasn't complaining, as it would make his job much more enjoyable. He also hadn't expected the tattoo. While he was aware from his *research* that she had nightmares about snakes, he would never have thought she would announce it to the world on her skin. She was interesting. And unusual. But none of that changed anything.

His instructions had been clear: Do whatever it takes to bring the girl in. His first idea was also the easiest one:

seduction. Using his good looks and charm, he would get the girl to fall for him. Then he would bring her in. He had even decided on his technique: honesty, in a manner of speaking. He certainly wouldn't tell her everything; rather, he would tell her just enough to capture her attention. *I will definitely get her attention*, he thought.

In this game, boldness would be rewarded. He needed to keep his eye on the prize. He could singlehandedly win the War for his people. His actions could change the course of history forever.

But he needed to be cautious, too. He was not the only player in this dangerous game. The dark one would try to stop him. He'd already spotted him on campus, watching, waiting. For him to make a false move. But he wouldn't. This was his destiny. Secure the girl. Bring her in. Game over.

Chapter Six

The first two weeks of school came and went uneventfully, but Taylor's sense of foreboding continued to plague her every waking moment. Time and time again while in class, she found herself startled out of a daze when class ended, or if someone asked her a question. Sometimes she found that she'd scribbled black serpents all over her notebooks, in a tangled mass of scales and fangs. She had no recollection of drawing them.

Night was not much better. For fourteen consecutive nights she had dreamed of the oil-black snakes. Thirteen of the nightmares ended with her being bitten, and each subsequent night there were more and more slithering assailants, until she was facing an army of red-eyed creatures of death. The fourteenth night was different though.

On the last night of her nightmare marathon, she was back to a single snake. But this time it was massive, a demonic night-crawler from scary movies about anacondas and pythons. No matter how fast or far she ran the monster was right behind her. When her legs turned to jelly and threatened to fail her, she saw a halo of light through the gloom. A Being approached her. It appeared angelic at first glance, but then she noticed its black eyes. Apprehension returned. She shrank from its presence, but instead of assaulting her, it stepped around her and produced a bright sword from beneath its white cloak. The giant snake hissed, spraying drops of black blood from its jaws. Fearless, the glowing Being struck first, plunging its brilliant sword deep into the snake's skin. Moments later, the fight was over, the snake's lifeless body lying cold on the hard ground. The Being turned to her, and its previously alien, genderless face became clear, like a camera lens coming into focus. It was Gabriel Knight. That's when she woke up.

Sleep escaped her that night, like it had the first night she'd dreamed of the glowing Being, of Gabriel. At the time, she didn't know it was him, but now she realized that it was. From the moment she laid eyes on him that day in the rain, something had warned her to steer clear of him. But maybe she had been wrong. The facts didn't lie. He'd found her a four-leaf clover. Initially she'd thought it was a bad sign, but perhaps she'd misread things. In her latest vision, he'd killed the snake, her greatest adversary. And in the first dream he was probably the one who'd given her the water when she needed it the most. The other darker Being was likely the one who'd choked her with the sand.

She needed to find him, to ask him the hard questions. Like why did he look like a human glow worm? And why were his eyes black? Or had he ever dreamed about deadly black snakes with blood-red eyes?

Over the next week she looked for him. Everywhere she went she was distracted, trying to take in each face that she passed, searching for the guy. Her search intensified when she realized that she hadn't dreamed of snakes since that night—that final nightmare. He'd slayed her demon, and the very least she could do was thank him for it.

Desperate for answers, Taylor went to the student registry office as a last resort. The girl behind the counter looked up at her suspiciously, her eyes narrowing and eyebrows forming a V, as if anyone that came into the office looking for information must be up to some sort of mischief, or criminal activity. She looked Taylor up and down as she approached, lingering on Taylor's necklace and assortment of rings, in particular. Taylor was glad her tattoo wasn't visible from the front.

She waited for the girl to initiate the conversation, maybe ask her how she could help her or welcome her or something. Instead, the girl continued to scowl at her. After thirty seconds of awkwardness, Taylor said, "I was wondering if you could help me."

"I can't give out confidential information," the girl replied coldly.

Damn, she's good, Taylor thought. How could she possibly know that Taylor wasn't looking for information about herself? She needed to change tactics. Intuition told her that honesty was the best approach.

"I understand, but please just hear me out. This is going to sound pathetic, but there's this guy. I know his name, but nothing else. I didn't really like him, but then he was in my dream and he kind of saved me. I really just need to find him." Silence filled the room. Pathetic. She was pathetic. Thinking back on her words, she realized how ridiculous they sounded, how desperate. But she *was* desperate.

Taylor turned to leave and mumbled, "I'm sorry I wasted your time…"

"Wait," the girl said.

Taylor turned, surprised.

The girl's face had softened. "Look, I really need this job, so I can't break any rules, but technically if I just tell you the general area that he lives in I wouldn't be giving out his address. What's his name?" She didn't ask for Taylor's name, probably for both of their sakes.

Dumbfounded, Taylor said, "Gabriel Knight."

The girl's eyes focused on her computer screen. Her fingers moved the mouse rapidly, clicking intermittently with practiced precision. She typed something, probably his name, and then said, "Freshman dorms."

"Which one?" Taylor asked, pressing her luck.

The girl sighed, as if it pained her to be hamstringed by the rigidity of the rules assigned to her post. "Starts with a J and ends with a Y. You'd better go."

"Thanks," Taylor said, grinning. She exited the office. Ignoring the crowded buses outside the registry office, Taylor raced back on foot to the freshman dorms. Her black sneakers felt light, like they'd grown wings. She was wearing moderately ripped denim shorts and mismatched socks, one black and one gray. Lately she'd felt compelled to cover her tattoo, out of reverence to the slain beast, and today was no different—her t-shirt hid all but the crown of its scaly head.

She noticed a few strange looks as she ran past, but they didn't bother her, not today.

Arriving at the edge of the freshman dorms, she slowed to a walk, striding purposefully towards her destination: Jacoby Hall. It was the only freshman dorm that started with a J and ended with a Y. Little Miss Rules at the registry office hadn't been so by-the-book after all. She'd practically given Taylor the exact location of her quarry.

Upon reaching Jacoby Hall, Taylor stopped outside the metal security doors. While each dormitory had student-ID card readers on each door to prevent non-residents from acquiring access, the security system wasn't particularly effective. Taylor only had to wait about five minutes before two boys exited the dorm, holding the door open for Taylor to pass through. This classic move was referred to by the students as *piggy-backing*, and was a generally accepted method of travel unless you looked homeless, smelled like you hadn't had a shower for a week, or were carrying a bloody knife. Girls were practically immune to the rules anyway, posing no real threat of rape, violence, or other untoward behavior. Even if Taylor had had a bloody knife, smelled like rotten fish, and was wearing a tattered, bright-orange, prison jumpsuit, she still likely would've been able to piggy-back into any dorm on campus. "Thanks," she said. As expected, the guys didn't question her motives, probably thinking she was just another girlfriend coming to see her guy.

Finding Gabriel would not be difficult. Each floor had a cork noticeboard with various news and information posted on it. There was also a listing of all residents by room number. No one lived on the first floor, so Taylor climbed the stairs to the second. Ever since she entered the building, her heart had begun hammering in her chest. She was vaguely aware of the pounding thuds, but didn't stop to think about them, afraid that she might lose her nerve if she did. The second floor's noticeboard did not include anyone named Gabriel. Neither did the third's or the fourth's.

The fifth floor listing had a Gabriel Dayton, causing Taylor to pause. Could he have given her a fake last name? While unlikely, she chose to err on the side of caution. The potential Gabriel was in room 510, only two doors down, couldn't hurt to check. She knocked twice hard. "Coming!" she heard someone yell.

The door began to open. "How'd you get through security?" a voice asked around the door. A face appeared. "Oh," the guy said. "I thought you were the pizza man."

The guy was definitely not Gabriel. At least not the Gabriel she was looking for. He had long, black hair, constructed into greasy-looking dreadlocks. His face was absurdly narrow and pale, with gaunt, green eyes and about two days' worth of stubble on his chin. He reminded her of the killer's mask in the movie, *Scream*. While not who she was looking for, he could be his roommate. "Gabriel?" Taylor asked.

"That's what my mom called me when I was born, but mostly friends just call me Silk," he replied. Taylor thought he might've been giving her some kind of a line, but the look in his eyes told her he was dead serious.

"Fascinating," Taylor said. "Sorry, wrong Gabriel." Before he shut the door, she turned and headed back to the stairwell, making her way to the second to last floor, the sixth. Jackpot. The first name on the list was him. Gabriel Knight. Room 601. No roommate was listed. He had a single room, which was very rare for freshman, who were mostly bundled into doubles and triples due to space constraints. Thud, thud. Thud, thud. Her restless heart continued to pound, the drum beat so loud now that she thought it might be audible outside of her body. It was now or never. Seize the day.

The first room on each floor was the one next to the stairwell; she had walked right past 601 on the way to the noticeboard. She knocked twice and then waited expectantly. No answer. She tried to look backwards through the peephole, but saw only black, like it had been covered by something. She knocked again. No response. He must be out. At least she knew where to find him now. She'd have to try again later.

Seven

He watched her out his window. She must know someone in his building. Probably just a coincidence. Gabriel had waited patiently for nearly three weeks. Waiting for the right time to approach her again. He had entered her dreams twice now. Saved her twice. The next time she saw him, she would trust him implicitly.

She entered Jacoby Hall, moving out of sight. A couple of nerds had let her in. He was tempted to seek her out, but acting on impulses was immature and would eventually lead to failure. Restraining himself, he satisfied his urge to act by going through each sequence of his mission plan in excruciating detail. He was nearly finished when he heard the knock on the door. Probably just another one of the idiot guys on his floor looking for someone to hang out with.

Still, with the dark one lurking around, he couldn't be too careful. Before opening the door, he put an eye to the peephole.

What he saw shocked him.

The girl. Of all people, the girl. She had found him. He watched as she put her own brown eye to the tiny glass portal, attempting to see beyond the door. For a moment their eyes locked. He held his breath. Could she see him? She pulled back from the peephole and knocked once more. He ignored her and continued watching. Then she left.

Moving back to the window, Gabriel waited for her to exit the building and then watched her walk west, back towards her dorm, Shyloh Hall. Undoubtedly, she'd be back. He needed to act faster than he anticipated. He was the Hunter, not the Hunted. Everything felt backwards. Using his computer-like brain, his thoughts spun faster and faster through his head, teetering on the edge of chaos. He analyzed every angle of what'd just happened, until he reached the conclusion. It was obvious, really. He'd given her his name and she'd inquired about him. Some careless office worker had probably given her the information she wanted: his address, maybe even his phone number.

But why had she gone to such great lengths to find him? Perhaps he'd underestimated the importance of the snake to her, considering she had it tattooed on her back. She might be obsessed with seeing him again. Infatuated by the one who set her free from fear. Yeah, that was probably it. If so, his mission was nearly complete, he'd barely have to make any effort at all to seduce her.

Even still, he preferred to be the Hunter. It was time to act.

Eight

Taylor arrived back at Shyloh Hall at five o'clock on Saturday evening. She took a shower and then dressed for dinner, wearing gray sweatpants and a t-shirt. Sam was working on a paper at her desk.

"How's it going?" Taylor asked, as she slipped each of her rings back on one at a time.

"Good. Nearly done with the first draft. I've finished enough of it to let us have some fun tonight!" Sam flashed a smile. Taylor marveled at how contagious her friend's smile was. She could almost certainly win smile contests, if there was such a thing.

Grinning, Taylor said, "Good, then you can help me find this guy…"

In the middle of typing a sentence, Sam's fingers froze. "What did you say, Tay?"

"Don't make me repeat it."

"It's just…this is a monumental day. I've never heard those words roll from your lips."

"Don't make a big deal out of it. It's not what you think. It's just a guy I met once that I want to talk to."

"Hmmm….sounds like more than that to me. But of course I'll help. Let's grab Marla, get some food, and we can plans."

They found Marla, and by default, Jennings, and took the surprisingly efficient elevator to the ground floor. They made their way along the path to the Commons.

"Tell me all about him," Sam said.

"Maybe later."

"Tell you about who?" Marla asked.

"No one."

"C'mon, Tay. It's no big deal," Sam said. Turning to Marla, she said, "Taylor just has a thing for some guy."

Taylor was about to contradict her friend, when she noticed a familiar figure on the other side of the lawn, sitting with a group of guys. She tensed, a look of alarm crossing her face. From this distance his features were fuzzy, but in her mind flashed the image of the Being from her dream, surrounded by light, emerging from the mist.

Like the rainy day on the lawn, she could discern a slight glow about him.

She realized that the path they were on was heading directly for him. She slowed to a stop.

"What's wrong, Tay?" Sam asked.

"Umm, nothing. You know that guy I was talking about?"

"Yeah."

"That's him."

"Who?" Sam asked.

"That one in the middle of the group." Taylor tried to gesture discreetly.

Just as Sam, Marla and Jennings turned to look at who Taylor was referring to, Gabriel turned his head slightly, his gaze falling directly on her. Taylor wanted to look away, but she found herself incapacitated, unable to pull her eyes from his face, from his eyes, as he locked on her stare. Despite having been saved by him in her dream, she found herself fearful upon seeing him again. *Stop being irrational,* she told herself.

"Oh, I met him one night. He's Gabriel Knight," Sam said matter-of-factly. "I didn't know you knew him too, Tay."

Taylor pulled her stare away from Gabriel long enough to reply, "I don't really. We just talked once on the lawn."

"I've talked to him a few times. He's gorgeous, but there's something strange about him. He's nice enough, I guess. He seems interested in you though, Tay. I think he's coming over."

Gabriel left his friends behind, sauntering over towards Taylor, his eyes never leaving hers.

"Hi, Gabriel," Sam said. "This is Marla and Jennings." She motioned to each of them in turn. "And I think you already know Taylor."

Ignoring Marla and Jennings, he said, "Oh yeah, the one from the lawn. Do you still have the four-leaf clover?" Gabriel's voice was seductive with a soft musical tone to it.

"I think I lost it," Taylor lied. She felt uneasy in his presence, as if she was in some kind of danger.

"Would you like to go for a walk?" He spoke only to Taylor, taking her hand.

When his hand touched hers, the images from the first nightmare rushed back into her mind. The burning in her throat, the cold grey fog, and the two Beings—one of whom was a dead ringer for Gabriel—became vivid pictures in her head, as if they were memories from real life. Taylor wanted to scream, but instead she shook his hand from hers and said, "Slow down, cowboy, we were just heading to dinner."

Gabriel's face fell, his confidence dissipating. He looked a bit stunned, like he'd never been rejected before. As quickly as his smile had disappeared, he was grinning again. "Last one there's a freshman geek!" he yelled as he took off.

Naturally, Sam was the first one after him, although Marla and Jennings weren't far behind. Taylor recovered from her brief shock and jogged towards the Commons. Given her late start, she was the last one into the building and the rest of the group were already there laughing, as if they were old friends.

"I guess you're the geek. Sorry, Taylor," Gabriel teased.

"It isn't the first time," Taylor joked back. She tried not to look at him, but couldn't help herself. Even out of the sunlight, in the artificial lighting, he had a glow about him, just like the Being from her dream. She was surprised that no one else seemed to notice. The glow appeared to intensify around his head, almost like some of the paintings she'd seen of the archangel Gabriel in her high school art history class. Funny that he should wear the same name. Gabriel.

As Taylor looked closer at the bright face before her, his perfect features suggested he was a model for a men's fashion magazine. Again, she noticed his unusually dark eyes. While it was obvious that they were blue, the ring of color was extremely thin relative to the size of his black pupils. This gave his eyes a very dark appearance, like a rock star who wore too much black eye makeup.

The Commons were well-lit and so, she expected his pupils to contract, to regulate the amount of light entering his eyes. She glanced at her other friends' eyes and could see that their pupils had contracted to tiny specks, while his remained fully dilated. *Odd*, she thought to herself. As she mulled over her observations, she realized that the other four were looking at her, laughing.

"Earth to Tay…," Sam droned, waving her hand in front of Taylor's face.

"Sorry, I think I spaced. Let's get some food. See you later, Gabriel," she said, eliminating any chance that Gabriel would think that he'd been invited. Taylor felt out of control—this was not the way she'd planned her next meeting with him. Needing to think, she turned and walked towards the entrance to the dining hall.

Gabriel chased after her. "Hold up, Taylor!" He looked a little sheepish, like he was unsure of himself, a far cry from the confident guy she'd seen earlier. "Would you…would you like to hang out some time?" he asked.

Taylor was a bit surprised by his request, and by the adolescent quality to it. *Hang out? He was potentially some kind of radioactive, dream-invading alien and he wanted to hang out?* She also wasn't used to this kind of attention, which was typically reserved for Samantha. "Um, let me think about it, Gabriel," she said.

"No problem, can I have your cell number so I know how to get in touch with you?"

"Why don't you give me *your* number and I can call you when I've thought about it?" She thought it sounded a bit harsh as she was saying it, but Gabriel seemed unfazed by the line that was normally the kiss of death for a guy.

"Sure, sounds great," he said. While he read out the digits, she typed his number into her iPhone under "Gabriel Glow-worm".

"See ya, Gabe," she said, waving goodbye.

"Only my grandmother calls me that," he retorted.

As soon as they entered the dining hall, Sam started the interrogation. "Why didn't you invite him to dinner?"

"I don't know. I just didn't feel up to it."

"Are you going to call him?" Sam asked, clearly excited that Taylor had attracted the attention of a good-looking guy. Sam was always trying to play matchmaker for her and had grand dreams of them getting married in the same year to guys who were best friends, too.

"I really do have to think about it," Taylor said.

"What's to think about? He's gorgeous and he's clearly interested in you! And you were the one who said you wanted me to help you find him."

"I know, Sam, but there's something weird about him. Did you see the way his skin almost radiated light, even when we went inside? And his eyes were dilated, like he was on drugs or something."

"I didn't notice the 'light' thing, but if you mean he radiated hotness, then yes, I noticed that! I know what you mean about his eyes, but they make him look kind of serious and mysterious. Maybe he just had an appointment with the eye doctor and they put drops in his eyes to dilate them. C'mon, Tay, don't be such a buzz kill. You *are* allowed to have fun. This is college, remember?"

44

"I'm sure you're right, Sam. I'll text him later," Taylor promised in a lame attempt to appease her well-intentioned friend.

"That's the spirit!" Sam exclaimed.

They were soon distracted by their rumbling stomachs and the various buffet-style food stations around the cafeteria; large, colorful signs identified each type of food: pizza, stir fry, pasta, salad, dessert, drinks, and so forth.

Over dinner, Taylor learned more about Marla and Jennings. They'd been dating for three years and had known each other for about ten. Their entire families, dating back a few generations, had graduated from UT and mostly still lived in the area. Marla's mother and Jennings' father were both professors at the university. Their families had season tickets for the football games; they never missed a Beaver's game unless an act of God prevented them.

"You'll be going to all of the football games this year," Marla said. It was more of a statement than a question. "All freshman get free season tickets to the games."

"Of course we'll go, won't we, Tay?" Sam said.

"Sure," Taylor replied simply.

In addition to learning a bit about their new friends, Sam continued to gush about how excited she was for Taylor. But Taylor barely heard a word she said. She couldn't stop thinking about Gabriel: his face, his eyes, and her screams in the middle of the night.

As the conversation continued, none of them noticed the pair of dark eyes that watched them from across the crowded cafeteria.

Nine

Gabriel watched Taylor from across the room while pretending to be interested in the conversation of the normal freshman guys he was sitting with. She would not be able to see him from this distance, although he kept her in his sight at all times. He was able to see her as if he was looking through binoculars—perfectly clear, like he was sitting next to her. The bright lights in the dining hall were devoured by his nearly fully-black eyes, and then streamed across the room with the focused power of a magnifying glass. *Of all my abilities, this one is underrated,* Gabriel thought.

He gazed thoughtfully at her as she sat with her friends. Earlier, he had been impressed with her ability to resist his charms, but wasn't worried. He was versatile, which was one of the many reasons he'd been selected by the Council for this job.

Not interested in food tonight, he excused himself from the table and strode purposefully out of the hall. Rounding a corner into a dark alleyway, he checked in front and behind himself, and seeing no one, leapt forcefully into the night sky. Reaching an altitude of a thousand feet in just over two seconds, he arched his back, extended his arms, and with a sharp *pop!* magnificent, white-feathered wings protracted from his neck, just below the hairline. The impossible, five-foot wings extended two feet past his fingertips, giving him mobility without limiting the use of his arms.

With a burst of speed, Gabriel soared towards the largest structure on UT's campus: the football stadium. He'd arrived at school three months earlier than Taylor in order to prepare for the task at hand. While participating in the monotonous weeks of the summer session, he made a few friends, earned straight A's in his courses, and found the time to prepare for her arrival. The rafters high above the stadium had become one of his favorite spots to think while he waited.

He was perched there now, having made a trip that would normally take twenty minutes on foot, in less than a minute. Like his ability to see long distances, flight was powered by light. If the moon and stars shone brightly, Gabriel never had difficulty harnessing their light to fly any distance he chose. On a particularly cloudy night, he could usually still muster enough light-power from street lamps or houses. In a worst-case scenario, he could utilize his powerful, battery-operated mini-Maglite, which he typically kept in his pocket, like all of his kind did. He preferred flying to walking.

Now, as he sat, Gabriel remembered back to when he was just a child being taught by the adults. He must have come so far that they would trust him with such an important mission. Growing up, he was never convinced that the legends were true, but now that he'd seen the girl for himself, he was fast becoming a believer. Her *aura* was more brilliant than he thought possible. Licking his lips eagerly, Gabriel looked forward to testing it in battle. He was starting to hope she would survive.

The Great War had raged for decades, with neither side ever really gaining an advantage. Now the War was on the verge of being won, with the pitiful existence of humans resting in the hands of Taylor Kingston, and she didn't have a clue. If only he could get her alone.

Just then his cell phone vibrated, indicating that a text message had been received.

It was from her.

Ten

Despite her strange dreams and thoughts about Gabriel, Taylor felt alive when she arrived back in her dorm room. She also felt free, for the first time in her life. Sure, she had a responsibility to attend her classes, study, and perform all of the other rather dull activities that go along with college, but she didn't have her dad looking over her shoulder, and she could make most decisions by herself. *No wonder so many kids go crazy when they get to college*, she thought. There was so much freedom! Maybe there should be some kind of transition phase, where freedoms are slowly given to students to reduce the shock of total freedom. *Nah*, she thought, *it's better to get it all at once.*

It wasn't that she didn't have a good relationship with her dad. She loved him and liked spending time with him. But she was ready to give life a shot on her own. Taylor's father, Edward Kingston, was a 55-year-old widower, who owned a small ice-cream franchise called the Ice Cold Creamery. Eddie was your typical overprotective father, who liked to continue to think of Taylor as daddy's little girl, despite the fact that she'd moved out-of-town to attend college. When he moved Taylor into her small dorm room, he'd become quite emotional when it came time to leave.

While she was still thinking about her father, the images from her dreams suddenly flashed through her mind, like an alarm clock set to go off just then. As usual, she was losing control of her thoughts, as more and more they shifted subconsciously to Gabriel, his easy-on-the-eyes smile, and how "he genuinely seems interested in you," as Sam had said during dinner. Enough was enough. She couldn't wait any longer. Taylor unlocked her iPhone and pulled up his number. She thought, *what the hell, I'm at college, meeting boys is part of the deal,* and then typed a simple text message:

hi gabe, it's taylor. now u have my #. would like 2 hang out sometime if u still want 2.

She reread the message, happy with herself. It didn't sound desperate, showed a bit of her personality by calling him Gabe again, and left the ball in his court. She pressed SEND. To her surprise, he replied in less than a minute:

hi taylor, so glad u txtd me. i'm just sitting around right now if u aren't busy?

Taylor was surprised to feel butterflies dancing through her stomach. At first she thought it might be a sort of uneasiness, like she had experienced before, but then she realized that they were excited butterflies, like she was some damn boy-crazy flirt. *Get a grip*, she thought, *he's just a cocky guy.* Even so, she needed to talk to him, if only to determine who he really was. She replied to his text:

sounds good. where should we meet?

He replied:

north side of commons

They agreed to meet in ten minutes. Not one to primp, Taylor pulled on a pair of mismatched socks—one gray, one red—and a pair of old sneakers. She didn't bother to put on any makeup or change her clothes, opting to remain dressed in her sweatpants and tee. She was about to leave when Sam walked in with a towel wrapped around her body.

Sam said, "I love that the showers are always nice and hot, although the pressure leaves something to be desired. Where are you off to?"

"I'm just catching up with Gabriel for a few minutes." She tried to sound casual.

"What!? When did this happen?"

"Just now. I sent him a text and he asked if I wanted to hang out."

"You little flirt! I think this college thing is going to be good for you."

Reaching for the door, Taylor said, "It's not like that, I just want to ask him some questions. I'll be back soon."

"But not too soon, hon, enjoy yourself," Sam replied with a smile.

"I'll try," Taylor said.

Taylor walked swiftly to the Commons. She was trying to time it perfectly, so that she arrived right on-time. She didn't want to appear desperate by being early, but she was also not the type to be rude by making someone wait. To her relief, the area was deserted when she arrived. A lone bench was waiting, unused at the moment. She sat down to wait. Within seconds, she heard a melodious voice from behind.

"Hello, Taylor," he said.

She jumped a little and turned, startled at how easily he'd snuck up on her. "Son of a—can you not sneak up on me like that? Where'd you come from?"

"Oh, nowhere in particular, I kind of just swooped in!"
He laughed, a beautiful smile spreading across his face.
"Thanks for texting me, I was really happy when you did."

She didn't hear a word he said as she stared at him,
completely awestruck. His tight t-shirt clung to his well-
toned muscles like a second skin. It looked natural, like he
was born that way. His glow was as strong as ever and
even more noticeable under the night sky.

"Earth to Tay…," Gabriel said, imitating Sam's tone
from earlier in the day.

"What?" Taylor said, pretending like she'd been paying
attention.

"Am I boring you, Tay? That's the second time you've
spaced out while in my presence."

"Sam's the only one who calls me Tay," she retorted.

"And as I said earlier, my grandmother's the only one
who calls me Gabe. So I guess that makes us even," he
said, the perfect grin returning.

Deciding to go on the offensive, Taylor asked, "Did
you go to the eye doctor today?"

"No, why do you ask?" Gabriel said innocently.

Taylor ignored his question and asked another. "Hmm,
interesting. Then did you get hit by a radioactive meteor
today?"

"No, not today, but the day's not over yet." He
continued smiling, but behind the smile she could tell that
he was thinking hard, like he was trying to work something
out in his head.

Gabriel tried to keep a stone face, as if her questions were just normal get-to-know-you type questions, but in his mind he was stunned. He'd never met a human that could so easily see his *inner light*. In one very rare case, a human with a particularly strong aura told him that he had very strange-colored skin and asked him what nationality he was. Gabriel was able to easily lie his way through that one. He was a smooth liar.

In this case, however, Gabriel wouldn't lie about these simple questions. He would need to lie to Taylor many times before his mission was over, and so, he figured he would start with some truth.

"Look, Taylor, I want to answer all of your questions, but not here," Gabriel said honestly. "Can we go for that walk I asked you for earlier?"

Taylor looked at him intently, trying to read between the lines. Why should she trust someone she just met and barely knew, especially before he'd answered any of her questions? He could be a rapist or a murderer for all she knew. But something said he wouldn't open up to her unless she gave a little. "Sure. Let's go," she said.

They walked together in the direction of Center Avenue, an appropriately named street that ran directly through the center of campus. However, when they reached the road, Gabriel grabbed her hand and pulled her left, away from the heart of campus. "I want to show you something," he said.

"Where the hell are we going?" she asked, trying not to sound afraid, although her heart was hammering.

"The football stadium. I was here for the summer session and I found a great spot there to think, or in our case, to talk."

Taylor's heart slowed back to normal as the answer sounded reasonable and she didn't detect a trace of a lie. After all, someone as beautiful as Gabriel couldn't possibly be a rapist or a murderer, could he? But still, her gut was sending all kinds of alarms to her brain. Something felt off. She looked at him as they walked and he looked back, grinning again, like he could read her thoughts and found her internal conversations to be hilarious.

She realized that he was still holding her hand as they walked along, but she didn't try to shake it off this time. It felt wonderfully warm and seemed to give her a strange energy. She barely even noticed the silence as they walked, unspeaking. The quiet would normally bother her, causing her to babble on with meaningless small talk. For once, she didn't.

After several minutes, when the silence was finally broken, it was Gabriel who said, "Why do you believe that you're not special?"

Surprised by the question, Taylor replied defensively, "How do you know that I...I mean, I don't think I'm not...why do you ask that?" She knew there was a bit of an edge to her voice but didn't care.

"Don't be offended, Tay...Taylor. I promise, I didn't mean anything by it. It just seems that you worship the ground that Samantha walks on, when it should be the other way around."

"I don't worship...wait, are you saying that *you* think I'm special? How could you even know that? We just met. And what do you mean by special? That I ride the short bus to school?"

Gabriel laughed. "Not *that* kind of special. I just have a good sense about people." They'd almost reached the stadium. "Plus, you noticed certain *things* about me that other people generally don't, or can't, notice."

Taylor thought about this for a minute before asking, "So are you going to answer my questions about those *things* now?"

§

Gabriel liked the way she noticed his word choice and turned it back on him. She was feisty. He thought this was a good sign; maybe she was *the one* who would change everything. He realized she'd stopped walking and released his hand; her hands now rested firmly on her hips, as she waited for a response to her question. Gabriel stopped as well, pausing before speaking, choosing every word carefully.

"Taylor, I think it might be best if I *show* you the answers."

ฦ

She stared at him, trying to decipher his last statement, but with nothing making sense, she shrugged and waited patiently.

He took a few steps back from her and closed his eyes. She watched intently, but with an amused grin on her face, wondering how long he would laugh at her after his prank was over. She'd become used to the dull glow and the dilated eyes to the point where she'd been unaware of these oddities for the last ten minutes, except maybe subconsciously. Now that she was watching him though, the luminosity of his skin was the only thing she was aware of.

As if on cue, the outline of light around his body and head began to brighten. The light increased slowly at first, and then faster and faster until it was like she was looking into the sun. Temporarily blinded, she closed her eyes and put her hands in front of her face to shield them. Even with her eyelids and hands to protect her, she could still see the light, as it seemed to penetrate both skin and bones.

Just when she was considering turning away from him, the light dimmed and Gabriel's body was returned to "normal", with only the dim glow surrounding his six-foot frame. "What the hell was that?" she demanded, taking a step back.

Gabriel raised his eyebrows; he seemed to be surprised by the ferocity of her tone. "That was me. That's my body."

"You expect me to believe that? Because I don't. I think that either my first guess was close to the mark or you have some kind of crazy light source hidden in your pocket. Which is it?"

Gabriel continued to look puzzled as he asked, "What do you mean *your first guess?*"

"Are you a bit slow? Earlier I mentioned a radioactive meteor, remember?" She didn't try to hide her sarcasm.

♫

Gabriel couldn't help but laugh now. He'd never shown his full inner light to a human before, but he always expected something more like terror or amazement or even wonder, but not this. Maybe Taylor *was* special. He'd told her that just to flatter her, but perhaps there was more truth to his words than he realized.

"Are you laughing at me?" She glared at him.

"No, no," was all Gabriel managed to get out before he started laughing again. He realized that he'd forgotten why he was even with this entertaining girl. Something about her distracted him from his mission. She continued to scowl at him. "I was just laughing because I didn't expect your reaction. I thought you might be scared of me, but this gives me hope that you may not run away screaming when I show you my next trick."

"Oh great, there's more. Look, I'll only watch the next one if you promise to show me how you did it."

"Fair enough, I'll show you all of my tricks afterwards," he said.

"Okay, let's see it then." She stood, waiting, her hands returning to her hips.

He arched his back like he had earlier that night, but this time he didn't extend his arms to the side. With the same sharp *pop!* massive wings burst from his neck and rose above his head gracefully. He allowed them to hang in the air for a moment before folding them neatly behind his back.

He waited for the fear to register in her eyes, but she surprised him again by clapping. "Now that was actually impressive, how much did you spend on those retractable wings? They look like something from a Vegas show! Can I touch them? You should really do the light-thing and the wings-thing at the same time, now that'd be cool!"

Gabriel was happy she wasn't afraid of him in his natural state, but knew that things might change when she realized exactly how *natural* it was for him. He started with, "I actually got them for free," which was mostly the truth although technically he didn't get them, he was born with them. Then he added, "Yes, you may touch them."

Taylor walked over to and then behind him. He felt her hands gently stroke his fifth and sixth limbs. She exclaimed, "They're so soft. I've never seen anything like them." At least that much was true.

Then she pushed a single finger through the feathery surface and Gabriel had to pull away, laughing hard. "Stop it, that tickles!"

"Did I touch your back?" she asked.

"No, you tickled my wing."

"C'mon, Gabe, we talked about this already. You promised to come clean with me on your little tricks."

"I'm trying to, but you're making it rather difficult. Let's try this a different way. Feel the top part of my wings, where they protrude from my skin."

❧

Taylor ignored his ridiculous use of the phrases *my wings* and *protrude from my skin*, as she obeyed his request. When she felt closer to his skin, it really did feel like the wings were somehow attached to his neck. It seemed impossible, because she'd have noticed them while they were walking over. Come to think of it, the wings were bulky enough on his back that it was beyond explanation as to how he'd been able to hide them under his clothing until now.

"Now stand back, Taylor." She did as she was told, continuing to puzzle over the mystery. With a soft *whoop!* the wings appeared to rush up and into the back of his neck. She stepped forward again to examine him, her astonishment growing.

There was a gash on his neck that looked like a scar that had been reopened. She rubbed her hands along the back of his shirt, feeling only his spine, his muscles, his skin. With a jerk, she backed away from him, her hands trembling. "What...what are you?"

Gabriel turned slowly, a beautiful smile forming on his face, the glow around him radiating light once more. His wings reopened in an impossible display of beauty and grace. "Isn't it obvious?" he said. "I'm an angel, of course."

Eleven

Dionysus paced across the wide space. The walls of the room were filled with light from top to bottom. The light came from within the walls, rather than from some fixture attached to them. The floors and ceilings were the same; a different material maybe, but similarly filled with a brightness that would be blinding to a human who gazed directly upon them for too long. But Dionysus wasn't a human.

"Why hasn't he checked in yet?" Dionysus asked.

Even in his stressed tone it was clear that he commanded authority and expected his question to be answered by any who heard it. In this case, there was only one there to listen.

"I'm sure he will soon," assured Michael, the other angel in the room.

Michael was the second most experienced member of the Archangel Council of the Twelve, of which Dionysus was the Head. Despite his age, Dionysus had the body of a thirty-year-old Italian stallion and a full head of white-blond hair. Both men were stunningly handsome and could charm just about anyone with a smile and a wink. They also happened to control the most powerful army on the planet.

"I'll give Gabriel one more day and then I'm going out there," Dionysus threatened.

"Give him time," Michael said.

"Time…," Dionysus mused. "Yes, time I can give. But he must keep us updated, even if his report is that progress is slow. He may be a rising star, but he WILL respect us!" His last statement came with a roar, which caused Michael to lean back, away from his friend.

"He does, Dionysus. He is still young and wants to impress us. He probably doesn't want to report until he's made some real progress." Michael paused. His face was tense, as if he expected another explosion of rage from his leader. But Dionysus was calm again, like his fit had been an anomaly, a rare subsidence of control.

His next words were spoken evenly, controlled. "One more day," he said simply.

Twelve

Stunned, frightened, dazzled. Those were just a few of the litany of feelings that coursed through Taylor's body as she gawked at the creature in front of her. She considered running, but was fairly certain her legs would be no match for his wings. Birds, planes, insects: anything with wings could move fast.

Gabriel looked every bit like the angel that he claimed to be, except even more beautiful than Taylor could have imagined an angel to look like in her wildest dreams. Despite the brightness of his being, she was able to look upon him; apparently he had toned it down a bit this time, likely for her benefit.

His biceps and chest seemed to have strengthened and tightened, like he'd just finished a long day of hard labor. His face was majestic, almost regal, as if he was descended from a long line of kings.

But still, as dazzled as she was, her strongest emotion was fear, rising up from her gut like a bad case of indigestion. She had to get away from him. "I'm going to walk away now," Taylor said.

"Taylor, wait," Gabriel said, putting out a hand and taking a step forward.

"Stay away from me."

"I'm not going to hurt you."

Said the freakishly winged, glowing creature. "Don't follow me," Taylor said, trying to keep her voice steady when she was shaking inside.

"Please. Don't." Gabriel's voice was pleading, almost weak, a mismatch to how he looked.

Ignoring him, Taylor turned, started walking away, slow at first and then quicker, opening up her strides, expecting to be grabbed any moment. When she got ten steps away she realized he wasn't coming after her.

She ran.

ƒʒ

It could have gone worse. It also could have gone better. By allowing the girl to leave without further explanation, without swearing her to secrecy, he'd put everything at risk. But he knew chasing after her, using force and his powers to stop her, could've been disastrous. He needed to give her space, time to think about things, get them straight in her head. Then he'd try again. And again. As many times as necessary until she trusted him.

He stared at his phone, wondering if he should call his lord to give an update. Bad idea. If he told Dionysus what'd happened, he wouldn't react well. Better to hold off until he had some good news.

♄

Standing outside her doom room door, Taylor pressed her head to the wood, her mind whirling. She was sweating from the run back, her heart pounding. Having to take the stairs because the elevator was broken didn't help either. *What the hell had just happened?* She pinched herself once. Nothing. Not trusting even her tried and true method of separating dreams from reality, she pinched herself again, harder. *Ow!* Her skin turned red where she clamped it with her fingers. She had pinched so hard it had the potential to bruise. She was definitely awake. The Gabriel she's just seen was no dream. But an angel? C'mon—it had to be a trick.

She took a deep breath, readying to face the barrage of questions from her roommate. She pushed through the door. "Hi, Sam," she said, as cheerily as she could manage.

"That was quick," Sam said, looking up from a textbook she was reading. "How was it?" Although Sam's question was casual, Taylor could see twenty other more pointed questions bursting from behind her smile.

"Eh, okay, I guess."

"Just okay?" I dunno, how do you classify watching a guy flare up like a light bulb and pop wings from his back? Okay's probably not exactly the right word, but…

"Yep. Just okay."

Sam frowned. "Will you see him again?"

"We live in the same area, so I'm sure I'll see him." Taylor busied herself getting her backpack ready for her next day of class, trying to act disinterested in the whole conversation.

"Tay, you know that's not what I meant. Will you *see* see him again?" No hiding from that question. Two "sees" was more than Taylor wanted to think about, but she knew her friend wouldn't leave her alone until she answered.

"Maybe. I haven't decided yet."

"What's holding you back?" Argh, please, for the love of God just let it go, Taylor thought. Please, please, please!

"He's just a little weird," she said. A *little* weird? Talk about the understatement of the year.

"Yes, but in a hot, you-should-have-ten-babies-with-him kind of way, right?"

Taylorfound herself laughing, glad for something to snap me out of the nutso experience I'd just had. "We'll see," I say. "Not about the babies, but about the hanging out with him again. That's the best I can do."

Sam rolled her eyes, but left it at that, for which Taylor was thankful.

♫

When Taylor awoke the next day she'd made a decision. She couldn't just leave things the way they'd ended with Gabriel, him standing there pleading with her, glowing like a lightning bug's butt, his cupid-wings looking like a strikingly good Halloween costume. It's not that she felt bad about the way she left, but more curious about everything. There's no way she could continue walking around campus doing normal college things when there was potentially a real, live angel doing the same thing.

So the first thing she did was sent him a text: I want to meet.

His reply came almost the moment she sent it: Tonight. Same place. Same time. Are you OK?

His question took her by surprise and she felt the butterflies dancing again. He cared how she felt? He barely knew her.

She didn't respond to the text, although she kept looking at it the rest of the day, unable to concentrate in her classes. The day crawled by without her seeing him.

Sam was ecstatic that Taylor was going to see Gabriel again, but Taylor could tell she didn't want to make a big deal out of it, just in case things didn't work out. "Hope it goes better tonight," was all Sam said before Taylor left.

"Me, too," Taylor responded, unsure of what *better* really meant.

Gabriel was the early one this time, sitting on the bench, waiting. "You came," he said.

Surprise, surprise. He was glowing. "You're glowing," Taylor said, sitting down next to him, leaving a healthy gap.

"You can see it," Gabriel said, raising an eyebrow. "No one ever sees it."

"Sees what?"

"Me," he said, sliding closer. "The real me."

"An angel?" Taylor said, sliding further away, to the very edge of the bench.

Gabriel chewed on his lip, looking more uncertain than she'd ever seen him. "Maybe this was a mistake," he said, starting to stand up.

"No," Taylor said, grabbing his arm, surprising even herself. A burst of electricity ran down her forearm, sending tingles through her chest. Gabriel sat back down and she removed her hand sharply, like she'd touched something hot. According to Sam, she had. "I'm willing to be open minded," Taylor continued, not sure if she actually meant it. "Last night I was just scared. I mean, you sort of took me by surprise."

Gabriel laughed at that. "I guess I should've expected your reaction."

"You think?" Taylor said, laughing and feeling slightly more at ease, although behind their lighthearted conversation, she still felt something that made her uneasy.

"Do you want to try again?" Ugh. Despite Gabriel's glow, and here on campus, talking with him seemed so surprisingly and refreshingly normal, that Taylor hated to ruin it by *trying again*, as he put it. But still...this is why she showed up.

"Okay," she said, between clenched teeth, unable to open her mouth any wider.

"Okay?" Gabriel said, confirming.

"Yeah. I'd like to see *you* again. The real you, I mean."

Gabriel grinned. "Okay. Do you mind if we walk over to the stadium again?"

"Sure."

The walk was different this time, much longer, and yet shorter at the same time. Every step felt achingly difficult, like her feet were stuck in cement. And yet they reached the stadium as if they'd flown there. *Flown*," Taylor thought. *Could Gabriel have flown there if he wanted?*

Gabriel glanced all around, checking that no one was nearby. "Are you ready?"

No. "Yes," Taylor lied. Let's get it over with. C'mon, angel boy, do your angel thing.

He did it.

Night turned to day as he lit up, as if pulling the electricity of the campus security lights into him and then radiating it back outwards. On this cloudless night, even the moon and stars seemed to push their light into him, until he was shining so brightly Taylor had to shield her eyes with her hands. She could barely make out a burst of feathers as his wings extended, rising over his head like a cape billowing in the wind.

Fear struck her heart and she wanted to run, to get the hell away from him, this freak of nature. What he was doing wasn't normal. But she didn't, because her curiosity and wonder wouldn't let her. The light lessened and she was able to look directly at him again. He was smiling, more beautifully than anyone had ever smiled before, like an angel. *No, not* like *an angel. An angel.*

Her initial fear began to ebb from her, as he made no attempt to harm her or even approach her. Logical thoughts of everything she knew, or thought she knew, about angels started to enter her mind.

They were the good guys right? Her family didn't make religion a habit, but she'd been to enough sermons to know that angels helped people. The term guardian angel was a comfort in itself. Lost in her thoughts as usual, she didn't notice that Gabriel had returned to his version of normal, showing just a subtle glow, with his massive wings tucked, almost magically, into the skin and muscle in his back.

He approached her cautiously. "Do you believe me now?" he asked.

"Yes," she breathed.

"Do you fear me?"

"No…well, I did at first, but not now. Can I ask you some more questions?" She was whispering.

Gabriel smiled. "Of course you can. But first I want to take you somewhere special to me. Would that be okay?"

Hesitating just slightly before answering, she said, "Okay."

"Are you afraid of heights?"

"Not at all," she replied. "The taller the roller coaster the more I like it."

His smile widened as he said, "Trust me, this will be *nothing* like any rollercoaster you have ever been on."

Without another word, Gabriel's wings flashed out and he scooped her up in his powerful arms, simultaneously leaping upwards in one swift motion. She gasped and closed her eyes, feeling the rush of air through her clothes and hair.

When she reopened her eyes, the campus lights seemed miles away, twinkling like stars. She could only see Gabriel's hands, but not his face, as he held her from behind, his arms firmly around her torso. His muscles felt strong against her body. Despite the height, she felt safe. *Safe*, she thought. Like in her dream! Gabriel must've been the one who gave her the water. But even thinking such a logical and calming thought, her gut wouldn't relent, sending shivers of dread through her. Why did she feel like this? Maybe she was too uptight, as Sam was always suggesting. Perhaps she just needed to let loose a little.

She realized that they were circling the UT football stadium, losing altitude with each pass, the warm night air whooshing past her. "Hang on!" Gabriel yelled.

Her arms dangling helplessly in front of her, she didn't have time to ponder what he meant before they suddenly dropped from the sky, falling faster than gravity would've caused. When she thought a collision with the steel stadium rafters was inevitable, she shut her eyes and prepared to die.

All was silent. No rush of wind. No pain. She was glad to have died painlessly. Or was this another dream? *It has to be*, she thought. She began to laugh at herself, amused that she'd believed the whole experience was real. *On a positive note*, she thought, *at least that means I'm not dead and can wake up now.* You always wake up when you die in your dreams. Going back to her go-to move, she pinched herself hard.

"Ouch!" she yelped, her eyes fluttering open.

"What are you doing?" Gabriel asked.

"Oh my gosh...you mean...that was real?" She paused before continuing. "That was awesome! Where can I buy tickets for the next ride?"

Gabriel looked pleased with her reaction. "Well, we're going to have to get down from here the same way we got up, so I guess it's a package deal."

"Can we go again now?" The thought of flying sent exhilarating bubbles through Taylor's gut.

"What happened to all those questions you wanted to ask me?"

"Oh yeah, I totally forgot. I guess we could talk about those first." Her heart was still racing in excitement from the greatest thrill ride of her life.

Gabriel said, "Why don't I just start from the beginning and tell you the whole story, and you can ask questions as we go along?"

"Assuming you're an angel..." Taylor said.

"I *am* an angel. You saw me fly."

"Good point. But you could be something far more sinister, disguised as an angel."

"Is that what you think?" Gabriel said, eyebrows raised.

"Jury's out. But I'm willing to listen to what you have to say."

"Thanks, I think," Gabriel said, smiling.

Taylor looked around, taking in her surroundings. They were situated in a wide, steel nook at the top of one of the ends of the football field. The spot was partially hidden by a series of large poles displaying the American, the College Football Association, and the UT flags.

Taylor also noticed that Gabriel's arms were still around her, protectively. Although the warmth from them felt like heaven, she peeled his glowing arms off and slid across from him, tucking her feet underneath her butt. She wanted the fewest distractions possible for this. Satisfied, she prompted him to begin, their knees almost touching as he leaned in closer. That's when he began telling the most remarkable tale that she'd ever heard.

Thirteen

His story began a mere 150 years earlier, in 1846. That's when the first demon evolved. A young man in his mid-twenties, Clifford Dempsey, was hiking deep in the Amazon Basin of Brazil. He was hoping to identify and catalogue at least one new species of insect. As a budding entomologist this was his dream, his passion. Still today, the Amazon is a dangerous place for even the most experienced guides. Deadly snakes, spiders, and poisonous plants patrol the rainforest while lethal piranhas and crocodiles swim hidden beneath the surface of the many rivers and streams. It was Clifford's first trip to the Amazon.

While scouting for food one day, Clifford was bitten on the back of his hand by a long, ink-black snake. Clifford tried to rip the snake from his hand, but its jaws were locked like a vice on his skin, its fangs imbedded in a large, blue vein. Eventually he was forced to chop the serpent's head off with a knife he carried in his belt. Black blood poured from the serpent's writhing body as his hand was finally released.

A sudden bolt of pain surged through him, from his feet to his head. Then, abruptly, it stopped. Clifford waited a minute, and feeling like himself again, inspected the snake. He was hopeful that it was not of the poisonous variety.

He opened his snake book and scanned through the pictures of black snakes. None of them resembled what lay before him. Its body was pitch black and as smooth as silk. Not an etch or a marking marred the surface of its skin. The decapitated head looked identical to the body, except for a spot of color on either side of its nostrils— blood-red eyes stared out from the dark skin. Its mouth hung open and Clifford saw that the fangs and gums were as dark as black onyx.

He bagged both pieces of the snake and brought them back to his camp for further inspection. Upon arrival at his fire pit, he opened the bag to find that the snake had been reduced to black ash. Sifting through the ash, his fingers took on a dirty look, like he'd just been reading a newspaper.

Confused and tired, Clifford drank two swallows of water and lay down to sleep.

Later, he awoke screaming as he watched fire spread up his legs to his torso. The flames licked the sides of his makeshift pup-tent, setting them ablaze as well.

He managed to roll out of the inferno and into the dead of night where he writhed on the rainforest floor. His eyes closed and Clifford saw images of burning flesh—*his* burning flesh—but at the same time felt that something was missing. He lay burning for what seemed like hours, but was really only a minute, before he figured it out.

He felt no pain.

Death by burning had always been sold as an excruciatingly painful way to die, but Clifford felt nothing at all, as if he was numb with shock. He slowly opened his eyes to see that he remained engulfed in flames, which had now covered the whole of his body. But still, no pain. He waved his arm in front of his face, and through the flames he could see the pink of his arm, rather than the charred flesh he'd expected.

As his breathing slowed and his heart rate returned to normal, the fire seemed to diminish until the last flame had expired. His clothes were gone, having been reduced to ash by the heat of the fire. His tent had created a small fire nearby, but its heat was waning as well. He inspected his naked body, but found no evidence of what had transpired; not even his hair had been burned away.

He remembered the snake and wondered if the venom had entered his brain, causing hallucinations. He checked his hand, looking for the telltale holes from the bite. The skin on his hand was smooth and unmarked.

The next few months were exciting for Clifford as he quickly learned that he was not hallucinating and that he was not only *not* dead, not even injured, but had been *improved*. He gradually gained mastery of his new abilities: he could now cause his entire body to be engulfed in fire one moment and then appear to be a normal human the next. Advancing in his skills, he learned to direct the firepower away from his body, setting trees and bushes on fire.

He could also heal exceptionally fast, which he enjoyed testing by using his knife on his own body and watching his blood evaporate into thin air as the wound sealed itself. The previously crimson blood that had once pumped from his heart had been replaced with the black blood of the snake. His movements were exceptionally fast and he became a deadly predator in the forest, killing animals to survive while he trained his new body.

Gazing at his reflection in a quiet freshwater pool one day, he noticed that his appearance had changed drastically as well. The color of his hair had darkened from nearly blond to deep black. The effect was not limited to his head; the hair on his arms, chest, and even eyebrows had all adopted the dark hue. His eyes had also changed from their previous brown to an inky black.

The changes were positive. Clifford was never considered to be a good looking man and rarely received any interest from women, but now when he saw himself in the pool, he was in awe of his rugged handsomeness and muscular physique.

The final major change that Clifford became aware of continued to intrigue and baffle him. Even on a cloudless sunny day, a smothering darkness seemed to surround him. He wasn't sure, but his new instincts told him that somewhere within this darkness lay an even greater power than what he'd discovered so far.

Months, or maybe even years later, Clifford emerged from the Amazon, bored of the monotonous days in the forest. He was ready to repatriate into society, in spite of his changed being.

His first human contact was with a tan-skinned woman who was drawing water from a well. She didn't hear him approach and when he spoke he startled her.

The woman jumped back, her eyes wide with terror as she gawked at the man in front of her. The darkness that surrounded him seemed to confound her vision and, while much of his face was hidden, her fear increased as she focused on the two black eyes that pierced through the shadows.

Trying to calm her, Clifford raised his arms above his head to show he meant her no harm, but she viewed it as a threat and ran towards her village. He could only make out one word that escaped her lips. "Daemon, Daemon!" she yelled.

Clifford stood shell-shocked, wondering what to do next, the word *daemon* ringing in his ears. From the nearby village he heard yells, and saw a group of men carrying sharp sticks and bows sprinting down the path in his direction.

Angry at their response to his presence, he considered fighting them, but knew he'd easily kill them. He didn't want to hurt anyone, so he used his newfound speed to rush back to the safety of the forest and easily outran them, their cries fading away as day turned into night.

Through the sleepless night he considered the woman's description of him. *Daemon.* Maybe that's what he was, an evil demon from the depths of Hell. Surely his condition was not natural and therefore, maybe he didn't belong in this world. But why not? He was entitled to life just like any other creature on the planet.

A darkness grew within him and he began to embrace the title of demon. It's what he was. He made the decision to further develop his abilities and then put them to use against any who would not accept him back into human society. He was not ready for a major battle yet, but he would be soon.

Training began immediately, as he focused on those abilities that he didn't fully understand. Meditation helped him harness the power of his mind and sync it with his enhanced body. A breakthrough occurred when he was able to reduce the darkness that surrounded him to a gray shadow by intently thinking about it. It took some concentration, but with time he was able to maintain this reduction of his darkness. He could never remove the shadow completely—it had become a part of him—but he could lessen it to such a degree that he could escape detection.

Just as he was able to minimize the darkness around him, Clifford found that he could expand it. On a sunny day, he could cover the forest in a shroud of darkness and cause the wind to whip through the trees, ripping off branches along the way. Once he even caused a dark cloud to appear and lightning to strike amidst heavy rain. He was ready.

Fourteen

Now fully in control of his powers, Clifford made his way through South America and back into the United States. He used his speed to avoid all human contact until he had crossed the border into southern Texas, eventually stopping in Dallas.

His first contacts with humans were wonderful. Most people assumed he was an outlaw, his dark, mysterious look fitting in with many of the rough-edged villains that roamed the desert. Liking the way people regarded him with fear and respect, he adopted the outlaw lifestyle.

He joined a small gang of bandits and quickly took over leadership, as his abilities served him well in his new life.

He gained their respect by drinking hard, winning fistfights, knocking off banks, and eventually by single-handedly winning shootouts with cowboys and lawmen.

With the territory came the adoration of women, and his good looks made him the center of attention in this respect. Clifford had a different girl every night, many of whom became pregnant and bore his many children. He witnessed the birth of his first child, a boy. The first thing he noticed about the child: his deep, dark eyes.

When he used a small knife to cut the boy, to his astonishment his skin healed within seconds. Clifford was joyous. He could pass on his powers to his offspring! From that day forward he kept the births of his children a secret and took them away to be raised in a hidden camp in the mountains.

Once his children were of age, he killed the other men in his gang and taught his children the story of the snake and their responsibilities as demons. He counseled them to keep their powers secret and expand their numbers.

Clifford's family's criminal activities allowed them to continue to prosper, but they remained on the move and did not flaunt their power. Most of their activities resulted in unsolved crimes and murders.

Eventually Clifford died at an average age, but his children followed his teachings and continued to build up their numbers and secretly infiltrate all aspects of human society.

Four generations and about a hundred years later, two of Clifford's great, great grandchildren from opposite branches of the family tree began a torrid love affair that resulted in the birth of a child. It was the first time that two demons had produced offspring together.

The result was a creature with a deformed face and batlike wings that sprouted from its upper back. While the creature was hideous in appearance, it was relatively intelligent in mind. Although it lacked the power of speech, its demon parents were able to teach it their history and ways. The creature grew to full-size in mere months.

Full-size was a behemoth twelve feet tall with massive hind legs, short arms, and razor sharp claws. While not as powerful as its parents, it used fire as its primary weapon, breathing flames from its mouth in explosions of force. Once the demon clan had seen what the "child" could do, they *produced* dozens of similar creatures, although each looked as different from each other as a cat from a dog.

Fifteen

Gabriel had been talking for a long time, with Taylor captivated by every word. She had many questions, but held them in, assuming they'd be answered over the course of the story. Eventually she could no longer contain her biggest question.

"Why do I see the red-eyed black snakes in my dreams?" she interrupted.

Gabriel stopped his monologue, a look of surprise crossing his face. He shook his head, like he'd almost forgotten that he had an audience for his story.

"What do you mean?" Gabriel said.

Taylor realized there was no way that Gabriel could know about the snakes. She opened up to him. "Since I was a little girl I've had nightmares about the snakes from your story. I used to fear them, but have learned to live with their constant presence. I no longer fear them, but I still hate them." Taylor didn't mention that her most recent snake dreams had included Gabriel in them, it was too embarrassing.

Gabriel said, "I've wanted to ask you about your tattoo."

"It's just my way of coping with the nightmares," Taylor said.

Gabriel nodded. "It suits you."

"Thanks," Taylor said, smiling slightly.

"To be honest, I have no idea why you see the snakes in your dreams. It might've just been fate's sadistic sense of humor preparing you for what I'm telling you."

Taylor nodded; she was unsatisfied by the response, but it was as good a guess as any.

"Shall I continue?" Gabriel asked.

"Yeah, but first I have one more question. You've talked a lot about demons, but you're an angel. What does all of this have to do with you?"

"A fair question, I was actually just getting to that," he said. He continued carefully, pausing to think before almost every word, as if he was afraid of misrepresenting some key fact or anecdote. He said, "While most of the demons were of similar mind and wanted to realize the ultimate goal of destroying humankind and inheriting the earth as the superior race, there was one who disagreed. His name was Dionysus."

"That's a strange name for the 1950s," Taylor said.

"Nevertheless, that was the name he'd been given when he was born into demonhood," Gabriel replied. "You see, Dionysus thought that demons and humans could co-exist on the earth and help each other. He constantly argued with the leaders of the demon clan and tried to convince them to change their ways.

"Dionysus was appalled at the appearance of the strange demon lovechildren. He referred to the creatures as *gargoyles* and believed them to be an abomination.

"One day an argument erupted into violence. Dionysus fought fiercely against three other demons, but was eventually backed into a corner and subdued. He was brought before the clan leaders and banished from his home. They told him never to come back.

"Dionysus was full of rage at his family's evil plans. As he passed from the shadow of the mountain, he emerged into the sunlight. Despite being under the sun, he saw that the area immediately around his body remained cloaked in shadow.

"He dropped to his knees, tortured by his inability to fully experience the warmth and light of the sun. He summoned all of his strength as he focused on driving the darkness from his body. To his surprise, some of the darkness receded and a single beam of light touched his chest. This small token of relief from the darkness strengthened Dionysus further and he attempted to thrust the remaining darkness away. He roared in agony as the darkness was ripped from his frame. His bones splintered and tore through his skin, leaving countless gashes on his arms and legs.

"Black blood poured from each wound and evaporated into the air. A mere human would've surely perished from the injuries, but Dionysus's body quickly repaired itself.

"Dionysus looked at his arms, his legs. He saw that the shadow had been lifted. Bathed in its life-giving rays, Dionysus closed his eyes and absorbed the power of the sun into his being. He lay there for hours until he was aware that the sun had set beneath the horizon.

"When he opened his eyes it was dark, but he perceived a source of light nearby. Afraid that someone might discover him, he looked around anxiously, but saw only darkness. It was then that he looked closely at his new body. It glowed softly despite the dark that had fallen on the earth."

"He was the first angel," Taylor whispered.

"Yes, he was. And Dionysus soon realized that he was changed in many ways. His body could still heal itself, but he now drew his power from light rather than darkness. He was inherently good rather than evil. It was the beginning of the angel evolution."

"So his powers were stronger than the demons' and he kicked their asses?" Taylor asked.

"Not exactly. The demons' powers were still a major force to be reckoned with. For the last sixty years Dionysus has built an army that has protected humans against constant attacks by the demons. The fight is referred to as the Great War by both sides. Given each side's equal and opposite powers, no advantage has really been gained at any point."

"Come on, that would mean the demons are still out there. It sounds a little farfetched to me."

"Unfortunately, they are. Many of the unsolved crimes you hear about on the news are the handiwork of the demons. But the angels are out there every day keeping the demons at bay and protecting the humans. We feel that the tide in the War is finally turning in our favor."

Still skeptical, Taylor asked, "Do you fight too?"

"We all do, Taylor. As they say, with great power comes great responsibility."

"Are you screwin' with me, man?" Taylor asked bluntly.

Gabriel looked amused. "I wish I was, but it's all true."

Taylor's head was spinning. Her thoughts once more turned to the snake, and to Gabriel's courageous victory over it. "I think there's something else I should tell you about my dreams," she said.

Sixteen

"I've had a few snake nightmares lately...," Taylor started, "...and I think you were in two of them."

To her surprise, Gabriel replied, "I know."

"What the hell—" Taylor started, but was interrupted by Gabriel.

"One of my abilities is to alter the dreams of any human I choose," he explained. "In your case, I wanted you to know that I was a friend. I saw the snakes, but I didn't realize that they'd plagued your sleep your entire life."

"Yeah, and your plan kind of backfired when you poured the sand down my throat!" Taylor tried to sound angry, but a hint of a smile gave her away.

Gabriel didn't get the joke. "That wasn't supposed to happen and it wasn't me that choked you. I gave you the water." He sounded a bit defensive.

"I was just joking, tough guy." Her face became serious again as she asked, "Then who was the other Being in my dream? The dark one. Was that a demon?"

"I'm so sorry, Taylor. As I mentioned earlier, while angels and demons have many different powers, some are the same. Demons are able to control dreams too, and in this case, a demon hijacked the dream that I'd created for you, and turned it into a complete nightmare."

As Taylor pondered his last statement, she became aware that it was getting light out. She yawned. "What time is it?" she wondered aloud.

Gabriel checked his watch. "Just after six."

They'd been talking all night.

"Dammit! I have to get to class!" Taylor started to get to her feet and then swayed as she looked down from the rafters.

Gabriel grabbed her arm to steady her and said, "It's Sunday, no school."

"Oh."

"Regardless, I should get you home so you can get some rest."

"Screw that. I still have too many questions, like who was the demon from my dream and what does he want with me? And why did you invade my dream in the first place? Why have you told me all of this?" She yawned again.

"I promise, I *will* explain everything, but only after you've slept. You have nothing to worry about; you are in no immediate danger from that demon or anything else."

He put his arm around her. She felt relaxed and very, very tired. "I guess I could sleep for a few hours first," she said.

A moment later she was asleep. Gabriel picked her up, spread his wings, and soared back towards the dorms.

Seventeen

As Gabriel headed to his dorm after delivering Taylor to her room, he was smiling to himself. *Damn, I'm good*, he thought. Not only was she in awe of the story he'd told her, she was in awe of him, too. He could tell. Having her fall for him was all part of the plan and would ensure her cooperation with the plans of the Council.

Crap, he realized he'd forgotten about the Council. He was supposed to call to update them once his second contact with Taylor had been made. He flipped open his cell phone and pressed the speed dial for Dionysus. He smiled again as he thought of how many other angels would be jealous of his direct contact with the Head of the Archangel Council.

Dionysus picked up on the first ring and Gabriel's smile faded quickly when he heard the harsh tone on the other end of the line. "Where the hell have you been?" Dionysus snapped. "You were expected to check in hours ago!"

"I...uh..." As good a liar as Gabriel was, he couldn't think of a single one at the moment and it was better that he didn't try; Dionysus would see right through the lie and would be even more furious. "I forgot. I am very sorry, my lord." Gabriel hurried on before Dionysus could reprimand him again. "But I have very good news for you that I think you'll be interested to hear." He paused for a reaction.

"Go on," Dionysus commanded.

"I have made second contact with the girl and I believe she may be exactly what we think she is. I told her the story that we agreed on and she took it quite well. I'll be meeting her again tonight."

"Have you experimented on her yet?" There was a dark edge to his voice that him sound like a mad scientist who was attempting to create a monster from a human, like Frankenstein.

"Not yet, I thought it was too soon, but I'll start with a simple test tonight to verify that she's the one." Gabriel spoke confidently, but inside he wasn't sure how he'd convince her to do anything this early on in their relationship.

"You do that. And if she resists, do what you need to force her." His voice was as sharp as a knife; to Gabriel it almost sounded as if he hoped she *would* resist.

"I will, my lord," Gabriel said, secretly hoping it wouldn't come to that.

Without another word, the line went dead. Gabriel shook his head, confused for the first time since he began the mission. He needed to get his priorities straight, make sure that he was prepared to do what had to be done. While he could have fun with her, he had to ensure he didn't grow attached to the girl. In the end, she was just a tool, a means to an end. Things were only going to get harder, especially with that demon hanging around, messing with Taylor's dreams.

Eighteen

Taylor's eyes opened when she heard the door open. She sat up, scanning the room and trying to figure out where she was. The room was empty. It was light in the room, despite the blinds being drawn. She rubbed her eyes and a myriad of visions suddenly spiraled through her mind: Gabriel with wings, Gabriel flying her through the air, Gabriel telling her an impossible story about angels and demons and gargoyles.

Clearly, none of it had happened. More likely, she'd fallen asleep and missed her meeting with him. Her mind was always creating crazy stuff, like when she was taking a test and trying to concentrate, and green leprechauns began dancing through her head, playing harmonicas or accordions. Another time it was leaping clowns strumming on banjos and harpsichords. Bottom line, she'd lost control of her imagination.

The door opened again and Sam walked in. Upon seeing Taylor sitting up, she smiled. "Good morning, sleepy head," she said cheerily. She had a smirk on her face, clearly amused by something.

"What time is it?" Taylor asked groggily. She did'nt see the humor in the situation.

"Nearly two in the afternoon. But after your late night I'd say that's not too bad." She was laughing now.

"What late night?" Taylor said, unable to stop a hint of alarm from creeping into her voice. She rubbed her eyes again and tried to remember. Forcefully, it all came flooding back into her mind again. It still felt like a dream. It couldn't be true. She felt dizzy.

"You don't look so good, Tay." Sam's amused look vanished and changed to one of concern for her friend.

"I'll be fine," Taylor said, lying back down on her soft pillow. "How exactly did I get home?"

The amused look was back. "Geez, Taylor. Even though Gabriel claims you didn't have anything to drink, I'm not sure I believe him."

"You saw Gabriel?" Taylor asked, ignoring the jab. "How did he....look?" Visions of a winged and glowing Gabriel knocking on the seventh floor window and passing Taylor through to Sam popped into her head.

"Beautiful, as usual," Sam replied. "You're a lucky girl."

Apparently, Gabriel hadn't been stupid enough to show up at their room with his wings extended and his built in light-bulb on its highest setting.

Taylor said, "Look, Sam, nothing happened, I swear. I definitely wasn't drinking. We just went for a walk, found a quiet place, and talked all night long. I got really tired and fell asleep, I guess. How did he get me home?"

"Oh my gosh, Tay, it was so romantic. I heard a knock on the door this morning and there he was, holding you in his gorgeous arms. He said he carried you all the way home and found your security pass in your pocket and used it to get into the dorm."

She really did make it sound romantic, but Taylor didn't want her to get the wrong idea. Or was the wrong idea really the right idea? Now that she knew the truth, she wasn't exactly scared of him anymore. And she did like him and he was *very* easy on the eyes. He was an angel, after all. One of the good guys. *What am I talking about!?* He couldn't possibly, actually, realistically be a real live angel. *Could he?*

"All we did was hold hands, Sam," Taylor said, trying to think. *Oh, and flew around campus powered by the moonlight*, she added internally.

"Hey, I'm not judging, Tay. But even holding hands with *him* is quite an accomplishment." A flash of

100

skepticism crossed her face. "Are you sure you didn't kiss him? Not even a little peck?"

"I'm sure."

"Hmmm. I'm not sure I believe you, but even if it didn't happen on the first date, I'm sure it will happen tonight, on the second date."

Taylor started to object, but then realized what Samantha said. "What do you mean the *second* date?"

"Oh, did I forget to tell you? Gabriel wanted me to give you a message when he dropped you off. He said, 'Same place at eight o'clock tonight.' He also said that he promised to have you home much earlier so you can get plenty of sleep for class tomorrow." Sam's face rose into a devilish grin. "Do you think you'll kiss him tonight?"

"No...I mean, I don't know. He's cool, I guess. It's just nice talking to him. He's interesting, different than other guys our age. I thought he was just a testosterone-filled pretty-boy, but now I've realized he's more than that." *Yeah, a whole lot more.*

Taylor was forced to spend another half hour answering Sam's probing questions about what they did, what they talked about, how beautiful Gabriel looked from different angles, and on and on. Taylor lied easily, giving her the usual crap about family, friends, college majors, and favorite movies. For the first time in her life, Taylor had a secret that not even Sam knew about. She felt bad about it.

Eventually Taylor ended the potentially endless interrogation by begging for a hot shower and some food. Sam grudgingly let her go, and after she was clean and full, Taylor opened her laptop and connected to the internet.

First, she did a simple Google search for *angels*. At the top of the search results page, she clicked a link. A new page appeared:

"Angels are messengers of God in the Hebrew Bible, the New Testament and the Quran. The term 'angel' has also been expanded to various notions of 'spiritual beings' found in many other religious traditions. Other roles of angels include protecting and guiding human beings, and carrying out God's tasks."

The description was consistent with the little that she'd learned about angels at church, although now she wished she'd listened more. She read it again. *"...protecting and guiding human beings..."* She thought about this particular line. From what Gabriel told her, he was trying to protect her. And she was a human being. He'd not mentioned God even once though, and his story about the creation of angels and demons didn't really have any spiritual aspect.

Also, the fact that these strange Beings were, according to Gabriel, created rather recently, within the last two centuries, made her fairly certain that they had nothing to do with the ancient stories of angels and demons, God and Satan, or saints and sinners.

Taylor did another search, this time for *demons*, and pulled up another page:

"In religion and mythology, occultism and folklore, a demon is a supernatural being that is generally described as an evil spirit; however, the original neutral connotation of the Greek word daimon does not carry the negative one that was later projected onto it. A demon is considered a spiritual entity that may be conjured and controlled. Many of the demons in literature were once fallen angels, however there are many that say that they are born from Hell itself."

The last sentence made Taylor shudder, as if a cold breeze had passed through the room. *Born from Hell itself.* That didn't sound good. But the middle part said that the word demon wasn't always necessarily negative.

She thought back again to her dream and the demon that had poured sand down her throat. She shuddered again. Gabriel had said she "was in no *immediate* danger." While this statement comforted her at the time, upon reflection, he was really just confirming the fact that she *was* in danger. She needed to speak to him as soon as possible. Eight o'clock couldn't come soon enough.

Nineteen

Christopher Lyon was a demon. He'd been born a demon and he'd die a demon. Since he was little, he'd been ahead of his peers in both natural talent and God-given brains. Because of this, he'd been able to climb through the ranks in the demon army in record time. Just having turned nineteen, he was the youngest mission leader since the creation of the army more than fifty years earlier.

Given his track record and age, Christopher was the obvious choice for his current mission. The Elders had come to him six months ago when they'd first discovered the girl. The plan was simple: once she left home for college, make contact and tell her the truth. Of course, that was all contingent on reaching her before the angels did.

He and the Elders had been blindsided by the speed with which the angels moved on her, almost without caution. He was not surprised, however, that the Archangel Council had chosen Gabriel Knight. Like Christopher, he was an obvious choice. As charming as he was determined, Gabriel would be able to lie his way straight through her defenses.

Christopher's task was now more urgent than ever. He'd planned to try to gain her friendship slowly over the course of the year and then break the news to her. But there was no possibility of using that tactic now. He'd been watching from the shadows when Gabriel revealed himself to her and carried her away. God only knew what lies he'd told her about the demons and about Christopher, in particular.

He'd tried to warn her about the angels when he entered her dream, but Gabriel made a genius move when he poured the sand down her throat. Christopher knew that Gabriel would've told her it was the demon that tried to kill her in her dream.

Christopher had reported all of this to the Elders, but they had little to offer in the form of advice. Instead, they told him they trusted his judgment and would support whatever decisions he made. While it felt good that they had so much faith in him, Christopher had no clue what to do and wished they'd just given him the answer.

He sat on a roof wondering what to do, while he watched Taylor through her window. She was working on her laptop.

Twenty

Taylor had just finished reading through the results of another internet search, for *gargoyles*, when Sam came back from the gym. Taylor's last piece of research didn't ease her mind:

> *"A French legend that sprang up around the time of St. Romanus ("Romain") (AD 631–641), the former chancellor of the Merovingian king Clotaire II who was made bishop of Rouen, relates how he delivered the country around Rouen from a monster called Gargouille or Goji. La Gargouille is said to have been the typical dragon with batlike wings, a long neck, and the ability to breathe fire from its mouth. There are multiple versions of the story, either that*

St. Romanus subdued the creature with a crucifix, or he captured the creature with the help of the only volunteer, a condemned man. In each, the monster is led back to Rouen and burned, but its head and neck would not, due to being tempered by its own fire breath. The head was then mounted on the walls of the newly built church to scare off evil spirits, and used for protection. In commemoration of St. Romain the Archbishops of Rouen were granted the right to set a prisoner free on the day that the reliquary of the saint was carried in procession."

The passage was consistent with what Gabriel had told her about gargoyles. If the demons really did want her dead, she truly hoped that they wouldn't use a gargoyle to do it.

She was brought back to reality when Sam said, "The fitness center is awesome, Tay! You should come with me next time."

Taylor cringed. "Sure, you know how I *love* those places," she replied, not hiding her sarcasm.

"C'mon, Tay, it's a great place to meet boys."

"That is exactly why I hate it. It's nothing more than a meat market. Everyone gets dressed up in their cute little gym outfits and tries to get noticed. I'd much rather exercise on my own in my comfy sweatpants and t-shirt."

Sam pretended to look crushed. "I guess you don't need as much help as I do to attract the boys here at college. You've already got the hottest one chasing you!"

"Quite a change from our high school days, huh? I can give you some tips if you want," Taylor joked.

Sam laughed. "That would be great. Seriously though, do you think you'll meet up with him again tonight?"

"I'm not sure yet." Taylor tried to be non-committal so that Sam didn't make too big of a deal of it, but in her mind she knew she'd see Gabriel. Her questions demanded it.

"Well I think you should. This could turn out to be a really good thing for you."

"I'll think about it." Changing the subject, she said, "Are you ready for dinner?"

After a quick shower, Sam was ready. Marla and Jennings joined them on the way out. The group headed to the Commons. Upon arrival, Taylor heaped food onto her plate. Not having breakfast made her hungry for the rest of the day. She ate hurriedly, forgetting that a shorter dinner meant more time to kill before her rendezvous with Gabriel. When they left the dining hall it was seven o'clock; she wished it was eight.

Sam, Marla and Jennings decided to go to the pool hall, but Taylor begged off. She needed some time to clear her head. After a few minutes of walking, she found herself sitting on the bench at the north end of the Commons, where she'd meet Gabriel later on.

Her thoughts were muddled as she tried to make sense of everything that had happened in the last two days. She had so many questions and she struggled to put them in a logical order. She liked feeling organized to the point where she thought she might be a little bit OCD, but every answer seemed to lead to ten other questions, leaving her feeling like the situation was in disarray, completely out of her control.

While Taylor waited, the sun went down and the campus security lamps were illuminated. The north end of the Commons was deserted, as it seemed to always be. The entrance faced away from the dorms towards empty fields, and therefore, no one really had any reason to use this side. Perhaps that was why the angel liked to meet her here.

Taylor peered to the right, where a path angled in the direction of the lonely grasslands. Suddenly, she was acutely aware of a presence approaching from the path. Her intuition was proven true when a shadowy figure appeared, ambling towards her. She couldn't quite make out any of its features, as the presence seemed to create its own darkness, despite walking on the lighted pathway.

Right away she knew: it was the demon.

Not just any demon, but the one from her dream. She also knew that her life was over. She was defenseless, a sitting duck waiting to be picked off. Her eyes darted to the entrance to the Commons. It was too far to run, especially given what Gabriel had told her about the lightning-quick speed that demons possessed.

The demon was close now and, although it was partially veiled in darkness, she could see its handsome face, which was wearing of all things, a huge smile. If she wasn't so damn scared she wouldn't have been able to help but to smile too.

The creature spoke enthusiastically. "Hi there!"

Taylor was stunned momentarily; she'd forgotten that demons could speak just like humans. She was more expecting it to snarl and snap at her and then eat her for dinner, but instead its voice was low and pleasant and even soothing. She didn't answer.

"Are you a freshman at UT, too?" the demon asked.

Now that it was speaking to her, Taylor realized there was a tiny ray of hope that she could survive this encounter. If she could just keep it talking until eight, Gabriel would arrive to rescue her.

"Uh, yeah," Taylor said, trying to keep her voice from trembling.

"That's great, me too," it said. "My name's Christopher Lyon." It extended its hand and she looked at the fingers like they were the hairy legs of a dead tarantula. However, when she saw that it didn't have scaly skin, sharp claws, missing fingers, warts, or any other undesirable features, she took its hand and shook it. As it turned out, he had quite nice hands—they were tanned, soft and smooth. Looking over the rest of him again, she saw that his entire body was evenly tanned, and the tank top he wore showed off a lean, hard body. He had short, dark facial hair that projected a rugged handsomeness usually reserved for tough heroes or cunning villains in the movies. She already knew which category he fell into.

Taylor realized that she was no longer thinking about *it* as an *it*, and had transitioned to using *he* and *his* in her mind. *That's dangerous*, she thought. *Don't trust him….it.*

"I'm Taylor. It's nice to meet you, Christopher." She was feeling bolder and decided to try leading the conversation. If nothing else, she'd feel more in control. "What are you majoring in?" she asked. "I'm doing Psych."

"Pre-Med, but I don't know if I'll stay in it. I've heard that Bio 4 is a killer," he said with a slight groan.

"Wow, so you want to be a doctor?" she asked. Taylor noticed she wasn't feeling particularly scared anymore. The handsome, soft-spoken demon had actually managed to put her at ease. Probably one of his abilities.

"An emergency room surgeon, to be precise," he said. "You know, like the ones on *ER* and *Grey's Anatomy.*"

Taylor didn't know what to think. He seemed so genuine, with an honest face and honest eyes, but Gabriel had warned her that demons were fantastic liars. If he was telling the truth, then she was baffled. Why would a demon want to become a surgeon and save human lives when, according to Gabriel, their ultimate goal was to wipe out the human existence entirely?

"Awesome," she said genuinely. "It sounds like it'd be really hard though."

His beautiful lips parted into a smile as he said, "Yeah, about fifty percent of the students drop out in less than a semester. I think I'll be okay though, my best classes were all math and science ones in high school."

Taylor smiled back almost flirtatiously. *What am I doing?* she thought. She never acted this way around anyone, and yet, she was feeling a strange connection with this boy…demon…whatever he was. Not an attraction, but a good feeling. She felt happy and at ease with him. If he weren't trying to kill her, she might actually want to be friends with him.

He continued: "Anyway, I have to get going, but we should hang out sometime, if you're interested?"

Two guys asking me out in two days, now that's a record, Taylor thought. *But neither of them human,* she laughed to herself. Just her luck. "Sure, that'd be great, what's your number?" She saved his cell number in her phone, didn't offer her own, and watched as he turned and walked away.

What'd just happened? Wasn't *he* the one that was supposed to kill her? You know, the sand down the throat causing a painful death by suffocation? She glanced at her watch; she had ten minutes to go before Gabriel arrived. She hoped he'd come early.

Twenty-One

Christopher was surprised at how well his first contact with Taylor had gone. She seemed tentative at first, but he *was* a mysterious, dark-looking guy, so that wasn't really surprising. Maybe Gabriel hadn't yet told her as many lies as he thought. Maybe there was still a chance. Christopher was glad he'd trusted his instincts and approached her. He'd continue to be patient and wait for her to contact him on his cell phone.

Lost in his thoughts, he didn't notice the streak of light overhead. As he continued to puzzle over his conversation with the strange girl, the light came closer and closer, eventually blinding him as it smashed into him.

Damn angels, he thought, as he was thrown backwards. Christopher was angry with himself for getting so distracted by the girl.

He managed to rip the strong, bright arms off his shoulders, recovering neatly into a somersault. His demon instincts made this part of his life easy. Fighting angels came naturally to him and he truly enjoyed it. In less than a second, he recognized that it was an overcast night with no trace of the moon's light and very few stars. That was good for him. The angel's strength and power must be coming from the lighted pathway and nearby buildings.

With a quick flick of his hand, the campus lamps were covered with webs of darkness, their bright lights extinguished. When he raised his arms above his head for his next maneuver, he was hit from behind by what felt like a freight train. *It was just the angel*, he thought. He could tell that the attack wasn't nearly as powerful as the initial one, so his trick with the lamps must be working.

Suddenly he was airborne, the angel's powerful wings propelling them both skyward. He didn't struggle, knowing that his iron body could easily sustain a fall from this height. At about a hundred feet, the angel released him and let him fall like a rock towards the earth. Christopher contorted his body during the free fall, like a skydiver with a disabled parachute, trying to find the best angle to land. Just before hitting the ground, he felt a massive weight on top of him, accelerating him into the earth. He hit head first with a heavy thump that sent mind-numbing shockwaves through every part of his body.

Dazed for a moment, Christopher looked up to find he was in a crater, several feet beneath the surface. *What a clever angel*, he thought to himself. This one was born to be a fighter, it had to be Gabriel. Above him, a bright figure stepped into view, silhouetted against the dark sky.

"Stay away from the girl," Gabriel said.

"Ahh, Gabriel, it has been too long since our paths last crossed," Christopher said. "We should really do this more often."

"Stay away from the girl," Gabriel repeated, more forcefully this time.

"Now, you know I can't do that. Not with you spinning all sorts of ridiculous lies in her ear." Christopher opened his mouth to speak again, another sarcastic comment planned. Instead, all he got was a mouthful of dirt as Gabriel buried him alive.

Despite his super strength, it took a few minutes for the demon to dig his way out of the deep grave that Gabriel had prepared for him. While holding his breath for that long wasn't difficult for him, it wasn't very fun with clumps of dirt in his mouth; he nearly gagged two or three times. When he finally escaped the earthy prison, the angel was long gone.

As he spat the remaining filth from his lips, his teeth, and under his tongue, he vowed to get revenge.

Twenty-Two

Shortly after Christopher left, Taylor noticed a bright light in the distance, shining from the direction that the demon had left. She thought it might be the angel approaching, but when he didn't appear after a few minutes, she assumed the light had come from a passing plane or falling star. When her digital watch read ten minutes past eight, she became concerned that Gabriel had stood her up.

Two minutes later, a friendly, "Hey, Taylor, I'm glad you got the message," startled her from behind.

As she turned and saw the angel she said, "Could you please stop doing that? Arriving from the direction I'm facing will be fine. Anyway, you're late. I almost left."

He smiled, flashing his brilliant teeth. "Sorry, Taylor, I'll try not to let it happen again. I was delayed when I ran into an old friend." He laughed as if it was an inside joke and he was the only one on the inside.

Quickly getting over her initial spat of anger, Taylor tried to lighten things up. "Thanks for the ride home last night." She smirked. "I'm shocked that I didn't wake up. And it's a bit disappointing that I didn't get to experience another trip on the greatest amusement park ride around."

"Oh you liked that, did you? You're my first passenger, so it's nice to hear such positive reviews," he said. "Would you like another ride tonight?"

"Hmm, tempting," she said, "but I think I'll pass. After everything that happened last night, I wouldn't mind keeping tonight as normal as possible so I know for sure it's not just some weird dream caused by the meatloaf I ate for dinner last night."

"Fine by me. Why don't we just find a quiet corner in the Commons to chat for a while?"

Taylor agreed and a minute later they found a spot in the empty study hall; students wouldn't start using this space much until later in the semester when mid-year exams were scheduled.

Taylor said, "I have more questions." She wanted to control the conversation this time as she didn't want to be sitting in class the next day, unable to concentrate because of unanswered questions from her conversations with the angel.

"Fair enough. I also want to thank you for not overreacting when you saw me yesterday," Gabriel said.

If he only knew what I was thinking when I first saw him, he might not be thanking me, Taylor thought to herself. In any case, she was glad she was able to appear relatively unfazed upon seeing a real living, breathing angel. "No problem," she said casually. "That leads to my first question: Why the hell did you show me what you are? You told me a couple of times that I was the first person…I mean, the first human, to see you as an angel. So…why me?"

"You are special," he replied. "As I alluded to yesterday, you observe certain details about me that most people don't, or can't, see. For example, the glow you noticed is something I have to control. Around most humans I can keep it sufficiently dim that they can't even see it. However, to your eyes, I'm never able to decrease the brightness enough; it seems you'll always be aware of it….which makes you special." He paused to let her take it in.

"So you showed your *angelness* to me because you knew I could tell there was something different about you? That sounds ridiculous, you could've just stayed away from me or transferred to a different school and I'd have never known a thing about angels and demons."

Gabriel's face lit up with excitement. "Now you're getting to the heart of my reasoning. It's not *because* you can see my light, but *why* you can see it. That's what makes you special."

Taylor cocked her head to the side. "You know why?"

Gabriel nodded rapidly. "We, as angels, refer to it as your aura. Each human has an aura, and as far as we know, it's always been that way. An aura is a light that comes from within you. In humans, that light is generally very dim, as opposed to angels, who have extremely bright auras. Because there's such a contrast, we refer to humans as having an aura and angels as having an inner light.

He continued, "Your aura is much stronger than *all* other humans."

Taylor's eyes widened. "Why?" she asked.

"We have no idea," Gabriel said.

"Okay, so I have this big aura which allows me to see who you really are. Big freakin' deal. That still doesn't explain why you revealed yourself to me." Taylor's eyebrows were tensed into a scowl; she was getting frustrated upon hearing so much new information, but still not getting an answer to her basic question: *Why me?*

"Sorry," Gabriel said. "I'm still getting to that. Because angels have the ability to harness the power of light, we're also able to harness the aura of humans. With most humans, however, the aura is so small that the incremental power gained from them is of no real use to us. Even if we were to try to harness the power of a hundred humans, or a thousand, for some reason the power gained isn't cumulative. In other words, we can only use the power of the strongest aura amongst the group."

"Are you saying that I'm some kind of an angel weapon?"

Gabriel's eyebrows arched in surprise. "Very perceptive, but I wouldn't exactly phrase it that way. You aren't the weapon; more precisely, you're a potential power source for our angel fighters."

"Yeah, but how many could I power? Two or three angels?"

Gabriel laughed. "Taylor, when I say you're special, I mean you're *really* special. You could power the entire angel army."

Now it was Taylor's turn to laugh. This was getting absurd. She was just a rather average girl that'd never done anything particularly amazing in her whole life and now she was supposed to believe she was the secret weapon for a clandestine army of angels fighting a secret war against a vicious band of demons? She laughed again.

"What's so funny?" Gabriel asked curiously.

"Oh, nothing. I just didn't realize that whenever I stumbled over my words or said something stupid or tripped over my own feet it was really just my incredible aura doing it all." Taylor smirked.

"Very funny. Your aura doesn't affect your daily life and as far as we know, angels are the only beings that have any use for it. If you don't believe me, we could do a simple test?"

"What sort of test?"

"I can harness your power and verify its strength."

Taylor tried to look nonchalant. "Will it hurt?"

§

Gabriel said, "Nah, it may actually make you feel good, almost like a drug." Gabriel knew from the human testing that occurred in the '60s that the short-term effects on a human were, in fact, kind of like a buzz and that eventually the human subjects would crave the angels' use of their auras to the point of addiction. He certainly wasn't going to mention the known effects of prolonged use of her aura; namely, deterioration of her vital organs, decreased lung capacity, various forms of cancer, and ultimately, death.

"Okay fine, but only one test and just for a short amount of time."

Trying to hide his excitement, he said, "Let's go."

§

So much for tonight being normal, Taylor thought as they left the Commons.

Twenty minutes later, they were deep in the grassy field past the north end of the Commons. Along the way, Gabriel answered her many questions about what other kinds of powers angels had and what effect her aura would have on them.

He described the many abilities that he had at his disposal, including complete control of the power of light, extraordinary senses, and super strength. Not to mention the ability to fly at impressive speeds and with perfect precision. He also compared his standard angel powers to a Volkswagen Bug. He said that by using her aura, he should become more like a red Ferrari.

In her mind she thought how funny it was that someone as perfect as he was thought they needed improvement. It made her feel even more average than usual.

"Okay," he said. "I'm going to start with one of my simple powers with no help from you."

"Go for it," she said, thinking she'd have no idea how to "help" when the time came.

Gabriel backed away a few paces and aimed his arm in the direction of one of the many hay bales dotting the field. Without warning, an orb of light was discharged from his hand. The ball of energy collided with the target less than a second later, creating a circle of blinding light.

Taylor looked away, shielding her eyes. When she turned back, the hay was gone and in its place was a single, thin wisp of smoke and a fist-sized hole in the ground. She looked up at the dark sky, seeing only a handful of stars between the large clouds. Then she did a full three hundred and sixty degree turn. She could barely make out the lights from the campus in one direction. Looking back at Gabriel she could see that he was, by far, the brightest object in their near vicinity.

"Pretty impressive," she said, "but it was only hay." Inside, she was thinking *Holy freaking cow!*

"I can show you later, but the impact would've been nearly the same had it been a brick wall. However, on a demon's flesh, a weak attack like that would be easily repelled," he explained.

"I thought you said you needed light to use your powers? It's a dark night and we aren't even near artificial lighting," Taylor said.

"My sensitivity to light is so high that I can draw enough power from the few stars in the sky to do what you just saw."

That only impressed her more, although she wouldn't admit it. The stars were millions or even billions of miles away, but somehow this angel was able to tap into their energy.

Ready for more, she asked, "What's next?"

"Ahh, now for the real fun. Let's see what we can do between the two of us." He rubbed his hands together.

"What do I need to do anyway?"

"That's the cool part," Gabriel explained, "you don't actually have to do anything. You just stand there looking pretty the way that you do."

Taylor's heart skipped a beat upon hearing the beautiful angel refer to her as pretty, but she hid it by snapping, "Well on with it then!"

Gabriel seemed immune to her abruptness. "As you wish, my queen," he said.

He looked at her intently, as if he was studying a piece of modern art at a trendy gallery, and then forcefully extended one arm towards her and the other towards a large rock outcropping on the edge of the field.

Before Taylor saw the light, she felt her stomach drop, like she was in a free fall. She felt a warm tingling throughout her body; the feeling extended to her outermost extremities, from her fingernails to her toes to the tip of her nose, and everywhere in between. The sensation wasn't unpleasant like a foot falling asleep or hitting a funny bone; rather, it was like the bubbles from a sauna, kneading and massaging sore parts of her body. She noticed she was now glowing similarly to Gabriel, her aura manifesting itself visibly. At that moment, for the first time in her life, she experienced complete, unchained, irresponsible, beautiful, pure happiness.

All of these feelings and emotions poured through Taylor's body in less than five seconds, and then a massive beam of light streamed from Gabriel's outstretched arm. Gabriel roared; it didn't sound like a cry of pain or fear, but a bellow of sheer physical effort. The beam charged through the large rocks as if they were made of recycled paper, and continued on a destructive course, tearing a wide path through the night-cloaked forest.

Along its trail, trees collapsed or were disintegrated like toothpicks in a fire. At varying points, large explosions erupted high into the night sky. With a violent shudder, Gabriel finished his battle cry and collapsed in a heap.

The incredible feeling encompassing the whole of Taylor's body subsided and she was left laughing on the soft ground, as if she was being tickled by a thousand feathers. Her laughter morphed into concern upon seeing Gabriel's exhausted body. His pants and shirt were torn and singed, like he was the sole survivor of a violent house fire.

Taylor's worry disappeared when she saw that Gabriel was grinning, in-between taking huge breaths of air. Upon catching his breath, he yelled, "That…was…AWESOME! The Council is never going to believe…" He trailed off. Springing to his feet, he put his arm around her shoulders. "You really are special, Taylor."

Taylor, still feeling the effects of the event, beamed proudly; a rare time when she was willing to accept a compliment. She did feel special, invincible even. As he looked seriously into her deep, brown eyes, she felt drawn to him. She tried to resist, but like metal to a magnet, she leaned in and kissed him deeply on the lips.

When she pulled away, every nerve ending in her body felt at peace. She swooned and would've collapsed if not for Gabriel's strong, protective arm curling behind her back to support her. She'd never felt anything like this before. It was ecstasy. Abruptly, her life had meaning. She knew that this boy—this angel!—had something to do with her purpose in life. She wasn't sure exactly what yet, only that she was getting closer to it.

PART II

128

Twenty-Three

Gabriel was still in awe of the power he'd wielded through his *use* of the girl. After dropping her back at her dorm—via walking this time rather than flying—he returned to where he'd conducted the experiment. In his mind he replayed the instant destruction that he'd caused. He'd never created a full beam of light before; it was always some form of an orb or a ball. Never a beam.

Not to mention the distance reached by the weapon. He ran at angel speed along the course his test had taken, mentally calculating the distance in his head. Thankfully, he had the foresight to perform the trial at the edge of a large forest; the beam caused damage for more than two miles! With a standard light orb attack, he could only reach distances of a mere five hundred feet.

The scope of the damage was also impressive. Anything in the direct path of the light had been instantly vaporized, including rocks, trees, and other vegetation. Any wildlife would've been wiped out, too. There were large craters at various points, evidence of the combustion that they'd witnessed during the fireworks display.

The one. She was actually *the one.*

Growing up, he and his friends had often debated whether the legends they'd heard were true. Their debates started when a small angel in their group had come to them one day with a story that his father had told him. His father was a member of the Archangel Council of the Twelve, which made him a very credible source.

The tale went something like this: When the very first modern angel, Dionysus, began creating his army to fight against the demons, he had a dream. In his dream, he witnessed many battles in the Great War. The battles continued to result in a stalemate, with neither side making much progress. The angels and demons were both so strong and so powerful that they could thwart any attack from their enemy.

Dionysus also saw a vision of a meeting of the demon Elders. They talked about preventing the angels from obtaining a weapon; the one weapon that would allow the angels to defeat the demons. They spoke of the weapon being held within a human girl. *The one,* they called her.

Dionysus knew they were telling the truth, as he could see the fear in their eyes and the determination on their faces.

When he awoke he was overjoyed. All he needed was to find the girl and force her to show him the weapon. He scouted the earth looking for the girl, and along the way learned much about the human race. Dionysus discovered that all humans had a light within them, similar to the angels, but different somehow. He named this their aura. The sizes of the auras varied widely, but most were rather weak, which was expected—they were only humans after all. He did, however, come into contact with a handful of humans with larger auras. These were extremely rare, but when he found them, he befriended the subject and was able to practice enhancing his powers through the use of their auras.

He burned the spent bodies when he was finished.

The effects of human aura use were impressive, with his strength doubling or tripling in some cases, but not to such a degree that victory against the demons would be guaranteed. It was at this time that he had another dream where he became privy to top secret information within the innermost demon leadership. He learned that the demons had, like him, scoured the earth in search of the girl and had also come up empty handed. They believed the girl had not yet appeared on the earth. They formed a special operations force to watch for her appearance to ensure she could be neutralized before falling into the hands of the angels.

Dionysus's hope was rekindled and he looked to a time when the girl would appear. He passed his story on to the Council, where it was expected to be kept secret, until a time when its truth could be proven.

As a young boy, Gabriel had been on the side that didn't believe the story. He believed that his friend's father had used the story as a trick to get him to go to sleep. For one thing, Dionysus wouldn't have hurt humans, even in the name of science. Also, humans were weak; he didn't see how they could be useful in the War.

Now he knew that he'd been wrong.

Gabriel couldn't wait to tell the Council how he'd charmed the girl and been able to test their theories without any measure of resistance from her. What would they say? They'd probably want him to bring her in for further testing. He wasn't sure he was ready to do that just yet. There was something about Taylor that intrigued him. Clearly she was falling for him. But it wasn't completely one-sided. He'd felt a certain chemistry during their kiss, as well as when he connected with her aura.

The Council would likely want to make use of her immediately without any regard for her life. He would normally agree with them. After all, their pursuit was a noble goal that warranted certain....*losses*. Like the girl, for example. Gabriel was surprised by his feelings for Taylor and wasn't sure yet what to make of them. Was there a way to spare her life while still utilizing her power? The Council didn't think so, but he wasn't so sure. If he could just buy some time, then maybe he could formulate a foolproof plan.

An idea began to form in his head as he pulled out his phone and hit the speed dial.

Twenty-Four

Christopher's heart was still racing as he watched the angel making the phone call. He'd nearly been obliterated by the powerful force demonstrated by Gabriel a few minutes earlier. Luckily, he'd been paying very close attention and leapt high into the air while the light raged beneath him. The tree branch he'd grabbed onto came crashing to the ground when the tree it was attached to had its trunk disintegrated by the power of the blast. Thankfully, he was high enough that his landing had occurred well out of the destructive path.

All his optimism from his successful meeting with the girl had given way to fear after his battle with Gabriel and the raw power he'd just witnessed. When she kissed the angel, he knew that the opportunity for patience was gone. He'd need to act quickly if he had any hope of stopping Gabriel. *Damn angel*, he thought.

Twenty-Five

Taylor was going to have trouble sleeping tonight, her thoughts occupied by an angel. Her mind went over his eyes, his face, his voice. And oh those wonderful lips! The kiss had been truly special and she could tell that he felt something, too. He'd even seemed a bit awkward afterwards, like any average, teenage college boy. Except that he wasn't. He was a gorgeous, awe-inspiring, winged, glowing angel.

When she arrived home, Sam had demanded all of the details. Taylor told her about how they'd found a quiet nook just to talk, how sweet he was, how it just felt right to move in for the first kiss. *At least the kiss part was true,*

Taylor thought, even if it hadn't exactly happened that way. Of course, Samantha had gushed on and on about how happy she was for Taylor and whether Gabriel had any cute friends, and on and on.

But Taylor really didn't care about any of that right now. Lying in bed, all she really cared about was seeing him again. Her last thought was of his face as she fell into a restless sleep.

Twenty-Six

"Now is not the time to be patient," Dionysus said. He was locked in a heated discussion with Gabriel about what to do next. Because he was extremely pleased with the news regarding Gabriel's progress, he was willing to listen to his opinion on how to proceed going forward, even if he didn't agree with it.

Gabriel replied adamantly, "I just think that the situation is very sensitive and if we act too quickly it'll attract more attention than is necessary. We've been patient for the last fifty years, another six months won't make any difference to our overall plan." Gabriel spoke confidently. Dionysus liked that.

"I appreciate your opinion," Dionysus said. And he did. Dionysus was sick and tired of the many yes-men, or more appropriately, yes-*angels*, in his life that'd do anything he said, but never added any real value. Of course, he had many uses for them as well. "We have a Council meeting scheduled for tomorrow and I'd like you to be there to express your point of view. After that, we can let the majority rule as this is a major decision that affects everyone."

"Thank you, my lord, I appreciate your consideration," Gabriel said.

Dionysus hung up and smiled. He'd given the young angel a glimmer of hope that his mission could be extended. In reality, he'd crush his idea and do what he wanted. That's why he was the Head of the Council.

Twenty-Seven

Taylor awoke more than an hour before her alarm went off. Sam's eyes were already open, staring at her from across the room. They both knew that before too long they'd dread waking up for their eight-thirty in the morning class, but it was still new to them so they didn't mind yet.

Taylor also had something to look forward to. Before he'd left the previous night, Gabriel had promised to walk her to class before heading to his own lecture.

Sam took her typical hour and a half to get ready and looked like the prom queen that she was by the time she finished. Taylor was ready in a half hour after a quick and refreshing shower, a bowl of cereal, and throwing on a comfy pair of jeans and a t-shirt. As she waited for her roommate to blow dry her hair and apply makeup, she powered up her laptop and pulled up the local news and weather. The leading story was about the mysterious destruction of a narrow strip of forest to the north of campus. The police and wildlife rangers were unsure of the cause at this point—whether it was a natural phenomenon or an intentional act by an unknown perpetrator.

Taylor was shocked. Although she knew they'd done some damage, she didn't realize the extent in the dark. Not good. She'd have to talk to Gabriel about that.

After checking herself about ten times in the mirror, Sam was ready and they bounded out the door, spotting Marla already waiting at the elevator.

"Wow, Marla, this is the first time I've ever seen you without Jennings," Sam joked.

Marla smiled, her cheeks turning red. "He had to go back to his dorm sometime, I suppose." She didn't sound very convincing.

"He really is sweet," Sam said seriously. "If only I could find a guy like the both of you."

Marla looked at Taylor. Then Sam looked at Taylor. When Taylor remained silent, Sam urged, "C'mon, Tay, out with it."

Grudgingly, Taylor replied, "I kind of...well, I did...I mean...I kissed Gabriel last night."

"Aww, Taylor, that's wonderful, I'm so happy for you," Marla replied earnestly.

"Thanks," Taylor replied weakly. She changed the subject. "Did you finally meet your roommate, Marla?"

Marla's face fell. "Yes, Kiren arrived late last night. She seems really weird," she replied glumly.

"She can't be that bad," Sam said encouragingly. "Once she starts hanging out with all of us I'm sure you two will become good friends."

"Thanks, Sam, but I really don't think so. When she walked in she basically told me that she wasn't here to make friends and that she wouldn't cause any trouble for me if I didn't cause any trouble for her. Then she told me she likes it dark and turned off all the lights and installed black lights around her side of the room. Her hair is colored neon-yellow and looks freaky under the lights. To be honest, she scares me a little. If you guys don't mind, I may be spending a lot of time in your room when I'm not with Jennings."

"I'm so sorry, Marla, of course you can spend as much time in our room as you want," Sam said. Taylor nodded in agreement. "And my previous offer still stands. We can look into getting a triple room for next year—it'll be just the three of us!"

Marla's smile was back at the prospect of having Taylor and Sam as roommates.

As the girls headed towards the boys' dorms, they saw that Jennings and Gabriel were waiting together. Taylor frowned as they approached, anticipating the awkwardness that was sure to come.

To her surprise, it didn't.

Gabriel strode forward confidently and wrapped his arms around her, giving her a warm hug. Any embarrassment vanished as quickly as the trees had the night before. His embrace felt incredibly warm, as one would expect from an angel. She was in heaven. Touching one hand to her face he kissed her deeply, letting his lips linger on hers for a second before pulling away.

"Good morning, beautiful," he said.

"Good morning," Taylor managed to squeak out. She was completely unaware of the many eyes that were watching them. Contradicting feelings assaulted her. Things felt like they were moving way too fast, but at the same time, everything with Gabriel felt so natural. But still…she just needed to slow down.

He tried to grab her hand, but she shook him off. *What was she doing?* A guy wanting to hold her hand was a good thing, right?

Gabriel gave her a strange look, but then, before an awkward silence could set in, he said, "Let's go!" His enthusiasm was contagious and he energized the entire group.

Along the way, the group chatted about which classes they were looking forward to, which ones they were dreading, and where to go for lunch. Everyone ignored the elephant in the figurative room, which was the fact that Gabriel and Taylor appeared to be dating already, only a short time after arriving at school.

Two minutes into the walk, Taylor couldn't resist it any longer and grabbed Gabriel's hand, feeling more like a hormone-affected girl than ever before. He smiled at her but didn't comment.

Taylor was disappointed when the short five minute walk to her and Sam's classroom came to a close and she had to say goodbye to Gabriel. Her hand still felt warm from his touch, and, much to her disgust, butterflies were fluttering out of control in her stomach. She kissed him lightly on the cheek and said she would see him later, which earned her another warm smile in return.

Their first class was easy, with a lecture on art history and no homework assignment. Both girls were in a good mood when they exited the building, and glad they had a one hour break before their next class, which was also together.

They turned left towards the Center Square, a large outdoor mall-like area in the dead center of campus. They were hoping to find a coffee shop to recharge before round two. Sam was chattering on about something— Taylor wasn't really paying attention—when she stopped abruptly. Taylor looked at her friend, who was staring towards the entrance to one of the buildings they were approaching. She followed her friend's gaze until she saw what, or more appropriately, *who* had caught Sam's attention.

Standing there was a familiar dark and handsome figure. Resting casually against a concrete pillar, he was looking back at them with a casual smile on his face. It was Christopher Lyon.

Amidst her blossoming romance with Gabriel, she'd forgotten all about the strange demon she'd met the previous day. She hadn't even told Gabriel about it, which was probably stupid and dangerous. *No*, she thought, *there was no reason to.* Christopher didn't threaten her in any way and was even quite friendly to her. Seeing him a second time, she was still not scared of him, although, based on everything Gabriel had told her, perhaps she should be.

"Who…is…that?" Sam asked seductively, almost licking her lips. She said it more to herself, but Taylor felt inclined to answer.

"That's Christopher Lyon. I met him last night when I was waiting for Gabriel. He gave me his number." She said it so matter-of-factly that Sam turned and stared at her.

"You what?" she asked. "Are there any others you haven't told me about? You're becoming a serious hot-guy magnet!"

"It's not like that, Sam. He just happened to be passing by and introduced himself."

"And he happened to force his phone number on you as well? You don't get off that easy, Tay. Apparently I could learn a few things from you."

Taylor didn't know what to say so she just stood there. Sam headed for the shadowy figure. "Wait, where're you going?" Taylor asked, grabbing her arm.

"To talk to him, of course. I can't let you go on having all the fun. And I'll need your help since you already know him."

"I'm not sure that's such a good idea."

"Why not, is he a jerk? You know me, Tay, I've dated all kinds. There is really just one criteria for me: they have to be easy on the eyes."

"No, he actually seems nice. There's just something strange about him," Taylor explained poorly.

Sam laughed as she replied, "He'd probably say the same thing about you! And that's also what you said about Gabriel at first, remember." Her hands were on her hips. "Now stop with the excuses, let's go." Sam turned and walked towards the demon before Taylor could respond. Jogging after her, Taylor caught up just as she arrived at the building entrance.

Sam didn't waste any time. "Hi, I'm Samantha," she said, "but you can call me Sam. And I believe you've already met my friend, Taylor."

The demon looked pleased that the duo had approached him. "It's nice to meet you, Sam, and yes, I've had the pleasure of meeting Taylor," he replied.

"Mmm, a gentleman, that's a rare thing to find on a college campus these days," Sam said flirtatiously. "What are you doing for lunch today? Do you want to grab a slice at Perfect Pizza in Center Square?" Taylor's stomach lurched. Gabriel was going to be there, too! *An angel and a demon having lunch together—how nice*, she thought.

"Sure, thanks for the invite. What time should I meet you?" he asked. Christopher either hadn't noticed or was ignoring the green color that'd clouded Taylor's face.

"Noon. Although we'll probably be there for at least an hour and a half if you can't come that early," Sam said.

"Awesome, it's a date," Christopher said with a sly grin. Taylor couldn't be sure, but it seemed as if he knew exactly what he was getting himself into with this lunch.

After they'd walked out of earshot, Sam said, "You were right, he *is* really nice and even cuter up close. We're both doing well for ourselves so far, although I'm not sure I'll be kissing Christopher in only two days. You move a little faster than me," she joked.

Taylor didn't even object to Sam's comment because she was far too busy figuring out what to do about lunch.

Twenty-Eight

Taylor's last class before lunch seemed to drag on and on, and eventually she and Sam distracted themselves by writing notes to each other, just like they used to do in high school. Naturally, Sam started the chain:

Sam: what r u thinking about?
Tay: lunch, u?
Sam: me 2!! can't wait 4 pizzas.
Tay: not what i meant.
Sam: ??
Tay: not sure i can go.
Sam: why not?

Tay: i have this thing…

Sam: u have 2 go, need u 2 b my wingwoman.

Tay: u will b fine.

Sam: no really u need 2 come, M & J can't come so it will b me, my hot guy and ur hot guy…2 weird!!

Tay: not sure G can come either.

Sam: why not?

Tay: not sure, just said he might not come.

Sam: I'll drag u if i have 2!

Taylor couldn't come up with a good excuse not to go to lunch so she resigned herself to the coming storm. If Sam really did like Chris, which she seemed to, then he and Gabriel would cross paths sooner or later anyway. It might as well happen sooner to get it over with. She wasn't stupid enough to just let it happen though; a little warning to all parties might go a long way. Despite the professor's rules against use of cell phones in the lecture hall, Taylor eased her phone to the top of her backpack, just far enough so she could see the screen while leaving it half hidden. She typed a brief text message to Chris first:

this is taylor, what the hell r u doing? i know WHAT u r and coming 2 lunch is a bad idea.

She waited in anticipation for a response. She was rewarded a few minutes later with a soft buzzing as a text message was received:

Chris: hi taylor, so nice 2 hear from u. what am i exactly? why such a bad idea?

Tay: stop being a child! u r a demon and my bf is an angel. bad idea!

Chris: i appreciate ur concern, but we r both big boys and can handle ourselves.

Tay: so stubborn…whatever, don't say i didn't warn u.

Chris: i won't, see u at lunch.

Next, Taylor texted Gabriel:

Tay: hi G, wanted 2 give u a head's up that sam is bringing a "friend" 2 lunch

Gabe: the more the merrier, why did u think i needed 2 know?

Tay: he is NOT human

Gabe: ahh, i c

Tay: r u sure u should go?

Gabe: wouldn't miss it

Tay: why r boys so frustrating?

Gabe: DNA

Let them work it out, Taylor thought. They'd be in a public place so nothing really bad could happen, right?

Twenty-Nine

When their professor finally dismissed the class, both girls were starving and more than ready for lunch. They arrived at the pizza shop almost ten minutes early and grabbed a table before the lunch crowd arrived in full. Sam ordered three large pizzas for the four of them despite Taylor's objections that it was way too much food. Sam countered with the fact that there'd be two large boys that'd likely eat a pie each so they could just split the third.

In their childhood, Taylor and Samantha had been to many birthday parties together, many of which had included pizza as part of the festivities. As long as she could remember, they'd had the same affinity for mushroom pizza, so Sam ordered one of those and, assuming the boys would want meat, ordered a pepperoni and a meatlovers for them to share.

Taylor saw Gabriel approaching across the courtyard. He was hard to miss given how he seemed to soak up every ray of sun and shine it back out. Sam didn't seem to notice. He walked confidently towards the shop, but every now and then his eyes darted warily from side to side, as if he was expecting a sneak attack from the demon.

Entering the shop, he spotted them in their corner booth and a big smile crossed his celebrity-like face.

"How was class?" he asked, sliding into the booth beside Taylor. He put his arm around her, but she reached back and pried if off, which drew a frown from Gabriel.

Sam said, "Not bad, but it got a bit slow there at the end. By the time it was twelve, all I was thinking about was cheese, crust, and mushrooms. I actually started gnawing on Taylor's arm."

"At first it kind of hurt, but then it felt kind of good, like a massage," Taylor replied, ignoring Gabriel's frown.

Upon hearing Taylor's comment, his frown turned to laughter and soon it became contagious, with all of them laughing so hard they had to hold their stomachs. Sam had made the mistake of taking a sip of her Diet Coke after she spoke and now she looked like she might spew it out. That only made them laugh harder until she was finally able to swallow the brown liquid with a loud gulp.

Shortly thereafter, the first pizza was served and Taylor started to wonder whether Christopher would chicken out. She kept it to herself, but Sam—never the quiet one— voiced what they were both thinking.

"Do you think I got stood up?" she asked.

Taylor feigned concern for a second, and then said, "Only if all of the planets are in alignment and a giant meteor is about to collide with the earth." Taylor changed from joking to serious in an instant as she touched her friend's arm and said, "I wouldn't worry about it, Sam, no one has ever stood you up and they'd have to be crazy or inhuman to do so." In her mind she hoped that maybe Christopher Lyon *was* crazy enough.

"You got the inhuman part right,' Gabriel said, smirking, and earning a smack from Taylor.

Sam didn't seem to notice the exchange. "Aww, thanks, Tay. And you were right, he's heading across the Square right now."

Gabriel and Taylor turned to look through the glass window, and sure enough, there was a dark figure moving towards the restaurant.

"Game on," Gabriel said under his breath. Taylor kicked him under the table, but he just grinned. It'd felt like she'd kicked a telephone pole.

Christopher walked in with his usual easy smile. Locating the group in the corner, he slid into the booth next to Sam. Taylor noticed how strange it was to see Gabriel and Christopher together—one sucking the light out of the room and the other contributing to the light. Demon and Angel. Dark and Light. Evil and Good. Beautiful and Beautiful. Taylor nearly laughed out loud at her thoughts. At least they had something in common: they were both uncommonly handsome.

Settling in to her role, Sam started the conversation. "Chris, meet Gabriel. Gabriel...this is Christopher."

"I think I've seen you around, it's very nice to meet you," Chris said.

"Yeah, I think we've *bumped* into each other before," Gabriel replied. He added, "It's nice to meet you, too."

Both of their eyebrows were lowered into scowls that were bordering on glares. Their faces certainly didn't match the cordiality of their words. This was one of those numerous times when having Sam around was invaluable. She'd almost certainly keep the conversation light and moving.

On cue, Sam said, "So, Chris...Taylor said she met you near the freshman dorms, so I assume this is your first year, too?"

Taylor glanced at Gabriel to see if he reacted to the fact that she'd already met Christopher but failed to tell him. And she couldn't plead ignorance as to his nature, because she'd already warned him about Chris coming to lunch, so Gabriel would know that she knew he was a demon. Gabriel glanced at her, but maintained his poker face. He was either unsurprised or hiding it well.

"That's right. I haven't decided on my major yet, so I may be here awhile." He chuckled. "Although that's not necessarily a bad thing as college is pretty cool so far."

Taylor said, "I thought you were Pre-Med?" Gabriel winced, as if by speaking to the demon she'd caused him physical pain.

"That's what I'm planning, but it's supposed to be pretty tough," Chris said.

"You want to be a doctor?" Sam exclaimed. Gabriel's frown deepened and Taylor kicked his tree-trunk-like leg again, cursing under her breath when pain shot through her foot.

Ignoring Taylor, Gabriel said, "I hear that 75% of first year Pre-Med students switch majors."

"I think I can handle it," Chris said.

Sam seemed to sense the change in mood and tried to steer the conversation in a different direction. "Tay and I were just saying how awesome it is to finally have some freedom. It's not bad having a meal plan either. Did you know we can use our meal cards to eat anywhere on campus?" Sam said.

"Yeah, that's awesome," Chris said. "I'm going to try to limit myself to pizza only once per week. The campus Creamery's a different story though, I may be hitting that up on a daily basis," he laughed.

"Tay and I have already been there about ten times so we may be joining you!" Sam said.

Gabriel remained silent, intently watching the exchange between Sam and Chris. Taylor hoped he'd stay quiet for the rest of lunch; in his current mood he'd only cause problems by speaking. Chris and Sam were clearly hitting it off, and it was better to just let nature take its course. *Her best friend and the demon—how weird*, she thought. *But not any stranger than her dating an angel.*

The other two pizzas arrived and the conversation slowed as everyone dove in. Sighs of "mmm, this is good," and "that hits the spot," was the extent of the speaking for a few minutes. After two or three slices the girls were nearly full and it became an eating contest between the two boys. Each pizza had ten slices and because Taylor and Sam only finished off half of their pizza there was plenty to split between Gabriel and Chris. When the count was even and the pizzas demolished, both guys stared at the last piece, contemplating their next move.

"You can have it, Chris," Gabriel offered. There was a twinge of forced politeness in his voice.

"Oh no, it's all yours, my *friend*," Chris replied coolly.

"No, that's okay, I'm full," Gabriel countered, clearly trying to show he was the better man.

"Oh cool," Chris said, grabbing the pizza and devouring it in three massive bites.

The girls giggled as Gabriel rolled his eyes and mumbled, "That's mature," under his breath. Chris grinned widely and rubbed his belly, causing the girls to crack up even more.

With the pizza gone and afternoon classes beginning shortly, each eater swiped their meal cards for a fourth of the cost of the pizza and then exited into the Square.

"Chris, can I speak to you for a minute?" Gabriel asked. Taylor warned Gabriel off with her eyes, but he ignored her and said, "See you ladies later." He tried to kiss Taylor on the cheek, but she dodged it.

Chris waited patiently.

Feeling like she had no control over anything, Taylor stalked off with Sam, who was smiling after her first "date" with Chris.

⟡

After the girls were far enough away, Gabriel said in a hushed tone, "What the hell do you think you're doing?"

"I've got no clue what you're talking about, considering we just met," Chris said playfully.

Gabriel wasn't amused. "I thought I made it clear when I was cleaning the dirt with your face that you should stay away from Taylor. Do you need me to make it clearer?"

Chris continued to look amused. "First of all, if I remember correctly and I think I do, you said to stay away from 'the girl', which could've meant a lot of different girls so I wasn't sure exactly who you meant. Second, I was there to hang out with Sam anyway and Taylor just happened to be there, too. And third, I can hang out with whomever I choose; it *is* college, our chance to be free."

Gabriel glared at him, looking like he was ready to pounce.

Chris continued: "If you're planning on spending much time with Taylor, you'd better get used to me being around, because I like Sam and I hope to spend a lot of time with her. Plus, I need to keep an eye on you. I wouldn't want you to do anything with 'the girl' that you'd regret later."

Unexpectedly, Gabriel's face softened, his eyes relaxed, and he said, "Look, Chris, I think we got off on the wrong foot. We both know that we're born as natural enemies, but now that we're at the same college just trying to have a good time, let's just forget about all of this and start over."

The demon's amusement gave way to annoyance. He said, "Coming from the one that brutally attacked me when I wasn't ready for it, I think I'll assume that was a lie. I know exactly what you're doing and why you're doing it. You have no interest in Taylor. You're trying to use her and I'm trying to stop you. And I will."

Chris expected an explosion of rage from Gabriel and maybe even a challenge to go settle things with something other than words, but instead he got a completely different reaction.

Gabriel's face remained passive. "Look, man. I didn't expect to, but I actually do care about Taylor. I didn't want to, but I do. Things with her feel right somehow. I swear that's the truth." Gabriel's face projected the innocence of a child.

"I'd like to believe you," Chris said. "I really would. I'd like to believe that there's even the tiniest bit of good within the angel race, but it's going to take more than just words for you to prove it."

"I will prove it," Gabriel said. He turned and walked away.

Thirty

As soon as Gabriel was out of view of any humans, he launched himself into the air and flew off at full speed. He had a three hour trip to the location of the Council meeting scheduled for that night.

Reaching a nice cruising altitude, like an airplane, Gabriel let his body's instincts kick in and carry him in the right direction. He turned his thoughts towards the meeting and how he'd have to convince a majority to vote his way. He'd need seven out of the twelve votes, because if it was deadlocked six-six, then Dionysus, as Head of the Council, would decide the outcome. Dionysus would likely vote in favor of a swift abduction of the girl, with no regard for her life.

Gabriel knew that he'd to convince them that his plan would lead to a better chance of achieving their ultimate plan. *The Plan*, Gabriel thought. How strange it was to think that while he was growing up, he'd never known what it was really all about.

As children, angels were taught the basics: demons are evil, angels fight demons, and angels have powers. Other than basic instruction on how to use their powers, there was very little else taught. Only the innermost circle of senior angels actually knew The Plan. And, of course, a highly exceptional junior angel, like himself, who was selected for a top-secret mission.

When he first heard The Plan, he wasn't sure what to think. It made sense in sort of a twisted way, but it'd made Gabriel a bit uneasy, too. However, his desire to gain the admiration of the Council eventually outweighed any *minor* moral concerns that he had.

The Plan was simple. Angels were clearly a superior race to humans. However, angels also agreed that demons were superior to humans as well. The first demon had been created from an evolved human and therefore, was naturally more advanced. The earth was theirs to inherit. But the demons didn't want to accept what was rightfully theirs. They wanted to co-exist with humans, as equals. They were defying nature.

On the other hand, the first angel was then created from an evolved demon, thus making angels the most superior race, leaving the earth as their rightful inheritance. In all honesty, the angels would likely have been willing to share the earth with the demons, but there were two issues: One, the demons, for some strange reason, wanted to protect the humans and co-exist with them, and two, Dionysus had discovered the path to immortality.

The second reason was the most important one, because angels aged at the same rate as humans, as did demons. However, while performing his worldwide studies of the human aura, Dionysus had learned that he was able to extract the aura from any human and replace it with his own inner light. His old body would die, but he'd be able to take over the human's body, with no change to his angel abilities. The new body would continue to age, but could then be replaced again and again with younger bodies to prevent him from ever dying of old age. It was like replacing an old pair of shoes, or the tires on a car. The feet live on, as does the car. Just the parts are replaced.

Under The Plan, the angels would do the following: One, end the existence of demons by winning the Great War; two, enslave the human race; and three, build a modern day Utopia where angels ruled the earth, and humans were used to provide eternal life.

At this point, ending the existence of demons was fully dependent on using Taylor's aura to wield a weapon so powerful it could obliterate the entire demon army. Once the demons were out of the picture, the angels could easily take control of the humans.

Once in control, the angels would set up camps where the most desirable humans would be harvested for future angel bodies. A human breeding program would be implemented to ensure there were always healthy and beautiful human bodies available to provide immortality for all worthy angels.

A lot about The Plan bothered Gabriel. Although he believed that angels shouldn't have to hide their true selves, he also believed that the humans had a right to live, too. While this was contrary to his mission and to The Plan, he figured it wasn't his decision to make and he couldn't do much except follow the orders given to him. But that was before he met Taylor. Now, he was confused. More confused than he'd ever been.

Before Taylor, life had been simple: learn about his angel heritage, join the army, follow orders, nothing more and nothing less. He never expected to feel such a powerful connection to the object of his mission. His instincts told him to be her advocate and help develop a new plan where immortality could be gained for angels while still allowing humans their freedom.

But Gabriel was smart enough to know the Council wouldn't agree with him and that he'd be put to death if he promoted such traitorous ideas. Instead, he was going to try to buy some time to come up with a solution. He mustered as much courage as he could before he began to descend towards the white fortress in the hills.

The compound, known as *Mount Olympus*, had been built by the angels twenty years ago under the guise of a research facility for emerging technology. A top Swedish architect was hired and no expense was spared in making it a marvel of modern architecture. The white sheen that coated the creatively angled roofs led some architects to describe it as "the Sydney Opera House on steroids".

The institution was highly secretive and no one except its "employees" knew what type of work went on inside. The directors of the facility, who were conveniently the same as the members of the Archangel Council of the Twelve, turned down thousands of resumes each year from highly ranked engineers, doctors, and scientists. Only angels were "hired".

The facilities were expansive, with six large structures surrounding an even larger building, and dozens of smaller buildings on the outside rings of the circular complex.

Security was tight, with a high steel wall encircling its boundaries. There were cameras and sensors every twenty yards that were monitored twenty-four hours a day, three-hundred-sixty-five days a year by security angels. The infrared sensors easily tracked all employees in the complex, based on the intensity of the inner light resonating from each angel, like a visual fingerprint.

If someone unexpected managed to enter the complex, they'd be immediately detected. If a demon entered, they'd set off the motion sensors without triggering the infrared sensors due to their low body temperature, which instantly created an anomaly in the system. An alarm would sound and all available personnel would be dispatched to the area. The alarm had never sounded in its twenty-year history and there'd never been a true security breach.

Gabriel knew his flight was being tracked as he landed gently in the designated angel landing area. Promptly, two security angels were at his side to escort him into the Dome of Light, the largest building in the facility, rising directly in the center. The first angel was big. The second was even bigger.

"Welcome back, Mr. Knight," the bigger one said.

"Thank you," Gabriel replied, "although it'll likely be a short visit."

"You're just in time, the Council is gathering in the Master's Room." Gabriel followed them through the archway that led to the Dome. Entering the magnificent building for only the second time in his life, Gabriel couldn't help but marvel at the beautiful carvings on the outside of the shimmering white dome.

Once inside, the perfection continued, although the décor was simple, even a bit scant at times. Everything, including the floors, walls, ceilings, and objects were lit from within by a mysterious power source. To an angel, it was pure beauty and pure power simultaneously, as art and utility were married in the flawless design. Various ornamental lights were attached to the walls and ceilings. These appeared in many forms, from something as small as a tiny glass orb, to lavish multi-tiered chandeliers that reflected millions of light particles from their crystalline entrails.

As an angel, Gabriel was expected to like this kind of atmosphere, but although he was in awe of it, he was also turned off by the almost mental-hospital sterilization feeling that the place gave off.

They arrived at the Master's Room, which was the only room Gabriel had ever seen within these walls. The security guard pressed a nearly invisible white intercom button on the wall and said, "Mr. Knight has arrived."

Without a verbal response or even a creak, the large pale doors swung open from the middle, allowing Gabriel a full view down the length of a long, glowing table. Eleven heads were already turned and looking at him, while the twelfth, sitting at the head of the table, could see him by simply staring straight ahead.

Gabriel entered the room, trying to appear confident when inside he was quaking with fear. During his first appearance in this grand hall he'd not been scared, but that was a different situation. At that time, Gabriel had known that he'd do exactly what they told him to. This time he'd provide an opinion that'd likely be in direct contradiction to many of the Council members' views. Essentially, he'd attempt to cause dissension within their ranks. He might make some very bad enemies today and that scared him.

Dionysus arose and extended a greeting. "Ahh, welcome, Gabriel. I've already filled the Council in on your remarkable achievements so early in your mission. We're quite impressed, but at the same time we didn't expect anything less from such a talented angel." Gabriel saw most of the heads nodding in agreement. There was no doubt in his mind that this was all part of their plan to make him feel important so he'd continue to bend to their will.

"Thank you, my lord," Gabriel replied. "It is such a great honor to be a useful warrior in this great cause."

"Yes, I appreciate your choice of words—'this great cause'—for that is truly what it is. And as part of this great cause, we're here to make an important decision for your mission. I've taken the liberty of explaining our differing views to the Council and you have a few early advocates." Dionysus smiled reassuringly. Gabriel couldn't tell if it was a smile of confidence that he'd already won the vote or merely to make him feel at ease, like a child.

Gabriel didn't expect the Council to already be aware of the two different views. This concerned him as he'd planned to build up his reasoning slowly, in a logical manner. On the other hand, Dionysus had implied that some of the Twelve might already agree with Gabriel's position, which at least gave him a fighting chance. Always the skeptic, Gabriel also thought Dionysus might be trying to trick him into a sense of false hope by implying someone might agree with him, when in fact he was alone on his side.

Gabriel just nodded, because he wasn't sure how to respond.

"Let's begin with a brief rationale for each of our opinions and then the Council can express their opinions and ask questions as needed. Once everyone is happy that we've considered all the necessary facts, we'll put it to a vote by the Council. Unfortunately, you're unable to vote, Gabriel." Which meant he was already losing one vote to nothing—Dionysus's vote against his uncast vote.

Dionysus continued. "So that means I only need to obtain five of the remaining eleven votes to obtain a deadlocked jury, which will fall in my favor as I have the right as Head of the Council to make a final decision. Good luck, Gabriel, you may begin."

Gabriel had made another incorrect assumption, as he thought that Dionysus, being the Head of the Council, would start with his argument. In hindsight it made sense for Dionysus to go last as he could then counter any of Gabriel's key points.

Gabriel cleared his throat to buy time as he desperately tried to translate into words one of the many thoughts that were chaotically swirling through his head. All eyes were on him now; if he stuttered or misspoke, the few advocates he might already have would quickly move back to Dionysus's side.

"Thank you for agreeing to hear my reasoning," Gabriel began, his voice surprisingly firm and clear. He tried to draw confidence from his unwavering voice. "As you all now know, I've made contact with the girl and verified that she's *the one*. I've been able to gain her trust in mere days and she seems to be somewhat infatuated with me, which was a major goal of my mission." He didn't mention that he was also *somewhat infatuated* with her.

One of the angels sitting closest to where he was standing said, "Well done, lad." He nodded to Gabriel to continue.

Gabriel proceeded. "Thank you. Despite Tay's, I mean, the girl's crush on me, I think it's unlikely I could convince her to fully cooperate with our cause at this time given the short duration I've known her. If we want to use her immediately, we'd need to force her cooperation, which could possibly lead to her death during combat.

"I know that our first instinct is to argue that one human death is of no concern if it leads to the success of The Plan, but she's not just another human. She's the one that Dionysus himself foretold would be the key to victory in the Great War. I've personally witnessed the absolute power we can wield with her on our side, and I think it'd be foolish to allow that power to be lost forever just to destroy the demons.

"Given the titanic success I've had in just a matter of days, I firmly believe I can fully convert her to our cause. If I can convince her to forsake her human world for a new and better world, in which she'll be treated as an equal, then we can continue to use the strength of her aura for years to come. We've been patient for so long and now that victory is within our grasp, we mustn't act irrationally in the eleventh hour.

"I ask for a mere three months, until the end of the school semester, to convince her to join our cause. Thank you again for your consideration." Gabriel finished with a flourish of energy and was pleased to see at least a few nodding heads and smiling faces.

Dionysus reclaimed center stage. "Well, I never expected such a strong performance from my counterpart, and after that speech I'm half-tempted to switch sides myself!" Most of the members laughed heartily at his joke, although Gabriel couldn't help but feel proud of the accolades poured out upon him by the Head of the Council.

"While I think there's definite merit to Gabriel's opinion and I admire his confidence in his ability to carry out this plan, I wholeheartedly disagree with his proposed approach. I have a number of concerns, the first of which is that I think it's hard to believe that a human being would forsake her own race, no matter how much of a charmer Gabriel is." Dionysus winked at Gabriel, and he felt his face turn red.

"Secondly, I fear that with a weapon of this magnitude nearly in our hands, we'd be foolish if we didn't grab it and take advantage of our good luck. The demons are as cunning as they are deadly and I don't believe they'll wait on the sidelines while Gabriel slowly brainwashes the girl.

"Lastly, I agree with Gabriel that the girl could prove to be of use to us even after the demons are eradicated, but as foretold, her main purpose is to help us win the War. While possible, there is no guarantee that she will die in that cause, regardless of whether she joins us willingly. Please consider these points as you vote." He ended succinctly, looking each member in the eyes as he formulated the words.

Gabriel felt a drop of sweat squirm down his back. The members began looking around, some of them whispering to each other. There was a brief span of silence, which allowed them to think about what they'd just heard and frame any questions.

Gabriel was bothered by the silence and tried to distract himself by looking at each of the Council members in turn. Each of them was beyond four decades in age and, although their bodies were beginning to show some wear, each was stunningly beautiful by human standards. From what they told him, none of them had used the power of immortality to take on a new body. Not yet. To Gabriel's knowledge, Dionysus was the only angel that'd ever moved to a new body.

There were seven males, including Dionysus, and five females on the Council. Since the creation of the Council, only three members had ever been replaced, all of them killed by demons in battle.

Generally the members wouldn't participate in actual fighting and were instead responsible for the overall strategy. However, during one particularly pivotal battle, half of the Council had elected to join the army ranks as they always had the option to do. The battle was fierce and many angels and demons were destroyed, leaving less protection for the six Council members who were fighting. According to the stories that Gabriel had heard, they fought valiantly, killing many demons before all six were struck down, three dead and three seriously wounded. The three that'd died were replaced and the three that were wounded remained on the Council to this day, although they'd never elected to return to battle.

When it seemed that Gabriel could endure the silence no longer, Michael, who was Dionysus's second in command, said, "I'm not sure what else there is to think about, we're so close to finishing this war, let's bring the girl in and end it now."

Gabriel's heart sank. With both Dionysus and Michael recommending the aggressive course of action, it would likely be ratified unanimously by the remaining members. Gabriel's shoulders slumped and his head dropped, ready for the defeat that was sure to come.

"I disagree. I don't think it's that simple." Gabriel heard the words, but couldn't comprehend them. Who had spoken? He raised his head and saw that it was the angel who'd complimented him on the success of his mission. His name was Andrew. Gabriel's eyebrows lifted in surprise and he looked around, curious to see if any of the other angels would agree with Andrew.

"I, for one, would vote with Gabriel at this juncture," said another angel. Gabriel remembered that her name was Johanna. He held his breath. Did he have a chance?

Michael said, "Fine. If it won't be unanimous, let's take a preliminary vote to determine whether we need to discuss the details of the situation further. All those in favor of Dionysus's plan…" Five hands went up, including Michael's and Dionysus's. Gabriel's heart skipped a beat. They only needed one more vote to win, but they didn't have it yet.

"All those in favor of Gabriel's plan…" To Gabriel's shock, five hands went up in his favor, completely based on the magnitude of his short speech. Gabriel had to do everything in his power to control the urge to raise his own arm in support of his proposal.

Michael continued. "So we have two undecided at this point, Thomas and Sarah, if my memory serves me correctly." The two undecided angels nodded once to confirm.

"As always, the angels that have chosen one side or the other in the preliminary vote have the right to change their vote at any time before the final vote. As Dionysus explained earlier, Gabriel will need both of the undecided votes in his favor in order to have his plan win. Now, Thomas and Sarah, what questions do you have to help you make your decision?" Throughout the voting and

Michael's speaking, there was no reaction from Dionysus, his face as blank as a Texas Hold'em champ.

Thomas began with, "Gabriel, my biggest concern is one that Dionysus stated. I'm worried the demons will be able to disarm the girl before we're able to use her. How big of a risk do you think that is?"

Gabriel was ready for the question. "Based on what I've seen on the ground thus far, I believe it to be a very low risk. Currently, the demons only have one resource in place at the university, Christopher Lyon—who's merely a fly on the wall—to watch what I'm doing. He's had multiple opportunities to abduct the girl, but has made no attempt thus far. I had one minor clash with him and I easily defeated him. I could've probably killed him had I wanted to, but I didn't want to stir things up with the demons before I had a chance to fulfill my mission in its entirety.

"I'd also like to add that if you select my plan, I'll certainly continue to report to the Council regularly regarding my progress as well as any demon activity in the area, and if anything changes we can always reconvene and decide to modify the plan."

"Thank you, Gabriel, that satisfies my question," Thomas replied. "You now have my vote as well."

Gabriel tried to look calm and collected, but inside he was jumping for joy. The vote was even now with just Sarah to convince. She took the floor.

She said, "My concern is more about your ability to turn the girl. If you're unable to do this in the next few months, it will have been a complete waste of time and may jeopardize the entire operation. How confident are you that you can do what you say you can?"

Gabriel also expected Sarah's question and answered it boldly. "While it's impossible to be certain of anything these days, I'm highly confident that I'll be successful. From our research we know this is a girl who's never been in a serious relationship before, and we all know the power of human emotions. In a matter of a few days, I've already stolen her heart, and while at this time I'm not in a position to bend her to our every will, I know that by cultivating her feelings for me I'll soon be able to attract her to our cause. With her as a willing partner, we'll reap much more value from her, thus guaranteeing our future success."

Sarah smiled. She was clearly impressed with his ability to move an audience with words, an ability he never really knew he had. She also seemed to admire his confidence. "I, too, am satisfied and will vote in your favor. I call for a final vote if no one has any other questions?" Gabriel felt like he was out of his body and floating through the room as he realized that, just like that, he'd won.

No one had any additional questions and Michael asked whether anyone had changed their vote from their preliminary position. No one had. Michael concluded. "In that case, there's no need for a final vote as the two votes needed by Gabriel have been pledged and his plan has been approved by the Council. Good luck to you and we look forward to hearing continued reports of your success with the girl."

Dionysus added, "Congratulations, son, you are a worthy adversary. I think we have all seen great leadership potential in you today."

Gabriel tried to act cool as he said, "Thank you, my lord, I won't let the Council down." Not wanting to show them how truly happy he was, Gabriel turned and walked through the twin doors, which were already opening, as if by magic.

Once outside the building, he took a deep breath and yelled, "Woohoo!" He sprinted for the angel take-off circle and then sprang into the air, wings already extended as he sped off into the dark night sky.

Thirty-One

Taylor had looked for Gabriel at dinner, but didn't see him anywhere. She'd wrongly assumed that they'd go together. She wondered where he could be. Christopher had met Sam, Taylor, Marla and Jennings at the Commons and they'd all gone to one of the cafés. This time, Taylor was the odd one out.

Taylor had planned to give Gabriel an earful: about how childish he'd acted at lunch; about how Sam was her best friend and she'd support her in anything, even dating a demon; about how maybe Christopher was an exception to the rule that all demons are evil. But now, Taylor was worried that something had happened to him. She hadn't seen him since...well, since he'd confronted the demon.

Christopher had asked her whether Gabriel was coming and she honestly didn't know so that's what she said. As she answered Chris, Taylor tried to read his face to see if he was hiding anything with his question; however, he seemed to have no idea where Gabriel might be. Taylor was somewhat surprised by the strength of her disappointment when dinner was over, and Gabriel hadn't made an appearance.

As they were walking out of the Commons, her phone vibrated. It was a text from Gabriel. She couldn't have been happier with what it said:

Hey beautiful, so sorry i missed dinner. I went 2 my guidance counselor 2 change 1 of my classes and then i wanted 2 start reading the assignment 4 my new class. lost track of time at the library. still here, prob have another hr of reading. I really want 2 see u tonight tho, do u have time?

Taylor was giddy at the thought of seeing him, but played it cool when she replied:

No probs, had dinner with the usual gang. Have a couple of things planned, but could prob catch up with u at 9ish?

He answered straight away:

Perfect, see u at 9 at our spot.

Despite her relief at hearing from him, she had to swallow a bite of anger. Not only had he acted like an idiot during lunch, but he'd also completely forgotten about her all day. His excuse was just an excuse—it wouldn't have taken more than thirty seconds to send a text message to her earlier, letting her know he'd miss dinner. She took a deep breath, intent on controlling her anger.

Only two hours to kill, Taylor thought. The time would crawl by as those "things" she said she had to do amounted to walking back to her room and laying on her bed. That'd take up about five minutes.

"Who are you texting?" Christopher asked.

She'd forgotten the demon was walking with them. She'd actually forgotten that she was walking with anyone. "Gabriel. He's in the library and forgot about dinner."

"He forgot about *youuuu,* you mean," Christopher joked.

Taylor didn't find it funny. "No, Sherlock, he was being responsible and studying and lost track of time. For your information, I *am* meeting up with him soon."

Sam grinned. "That's great, Tay, I was getting worried about you. I thought you were going to kill someone at dinner, you looked so miserable."

Taylor's face showed genuine surprise. "I...I did? Sorry, I didn't even realize it. I guess I wasn't very good company."

"That's okay, *Tay*. We had fun anyway," Christopher said, continuing to joke with her.

Not in a bad mood anymore, Taylor smiled and went on the offensive. "I saw that you were way too busy stuffing your face to have said much either. After the thirteen pieces of pizza at lunch today, I thought you wouldn't need to eat for the next few days. Be honest, Chris, are you eating for two?"

Laughing at their own stupidity, they filed into Taylor and Sam's dorm.

The two hours flew by. Marla and Jennings left after an hour to do homework, but Chris stayed the entire time. He and Sam were really hitting it off and Taylor grudgingly had to admit that he was fun to be around. Demon or no demon, he had a good sense of humor and seemed to be a genuinely nice guy. *I'd better not tell Gabriel that though*, she thought.

When it was five minutes before nine o'clock, she told Sam and Chris that she had to go meet Gabriel.

"I'd better get going, too," Chris said.

"Oh c'mon, it's still early, stay for a little while," Sam said. There was a gleam in her eyes. Taylor had seen that look before.

Anxious to avoid walking out of the building with Chris, Taylor said, "Yeah, you guys stay and have fun, I'll be back soon."

Chris agreed to stay for a while, although Taylor could tell he wanted to follow her. She wondered what he'd have done. Would he have picked a fight with Gabriel? Would he have tried to hurt her? She couldn't really imagine him being violent; he just seemed to be so good-natured.

She left the room, closing the door on the way out.

Thirty-Two

As Taylor approached "our spot", she was happy to see that he was already there waiting.

"Have fun studying?" she asked.

"No, it was awful being apart from you for that long," he replied.

"Yeah, it only took you about five hours to think of me." Her temper fell in between a crack and was lost. She bit her lip, trying to gain control. Realizing her comment made her sound needy—or even pathetic—she said, "Look, I'm not like that. I don't need you to check in with me every five minutes or something, but after what happened at lunch…"

"You thought the demon might've done something," Gabriel finished for her.

"Yeah, it's just you were acting so immature..." Gabriel's expression turned defensive, his mouth poised to contradict her, his eyes flashing with anger, but Taylor rushed on. "I know, I know, Christopher was being stupid too, but you were worse, Gabe."

Gabriel's face fell, all fight leaving it, as his arched eyebrows caved and his fiery eyes softened. "I'm sorry," he said. "You're right."

Taylor was surprised by his response. She'd expected a fight, if only a half-hearted one. Not a complete surrender. "Thanks for admitting you were wrong," she said, suddenly longing to feel his touch.

He didn't disappoint. He took two giant steps forward, grabbing her in his arms in a bear hug. He easily lifted her off of the ground and spun her around in a surprising show of affection. Her heart smashed around in her chest, and she felt the same warm sensation she'd felt earlier when he'd kissed her. *Earlier.* It felt like it'd been a lifetime ago that she'd last seen him, touched him. Minutes away from him were like hours. Hours were like days. Days were like...well, she didn't exactly know what days away from Gabriel would be like, but she hoped she wouldn't have to find out.

Gabriel released her and said, "Want to go for a ride?" She nodded, her eyes giving away her excitement, as they gleamed with anticipation.

Clutching her in his arms he ran at angel speed. They were out of sight from the campus in mere seconds and then they were airborne. The thrill of flying hadn't diminished from the first time around. He yelled, "Hang on!" as he flipped her up onto his back. She wrapped her arms around his neck and locked her hands together.

It felt like she was lying on a down blanket; it was incredibly soft and warm nestled in between his two wings. On either side of her she could feel the gentle undulations of his extra appendages rolling up and down, overcoming the pull of gravity. She now knew what it was like to be a bird. And it was wonderful.

She wasn't surprised when he began circling over the football stadium. It was a great spot where they could be alone and he could be his true self.

Gabriel landed high above the football field, twisting his body so he could pull her back out in front of him. Like a groom carrying his new bride across the threshold, he walked her over to where they'd sat the last time they were there, out of the wind and out of sight.

As he set her down softly, Taylor felt a remarkably strong urge to be close to him, to feel his body against hers. She always knew that she was heterosexual, but Taylor had never felt an attraction like this for any of the boys in her high school. Although she hoped he felt the same way, she worried that he didn't. This didn't stop her from curling up close to him, her hands touching his hard chest, his broad shoulders, and finally resting intertwined with his fingers.

He kissed her again and again that night and she let him.

Thirty-Three

"Level with me, man. What's going on here?" Christopher had been trying to get information from the angel for twenty minutes with no luck.

"Nothing. I just like her. I like the girl," Gabriel replied.

"That's a load of crap. It's no accident that we're both at the same school watching the same girl. And she has a name."

"I know she has a freakin' name, man. She's my girlfriend."

"Yeah, right. She's your target, nothing more."

"Oh, yeah? If you're so smart, then what're you doing with Samantha?" Gabriel asked.

"Look, I didn't expect to get serious with any girls here. It just sort of happened and I like it, but that has nothing to do with Taylor. I'm not the one pretending to date *the one*."

"I'm not pretending! It just sort of happened for me too!"

"Oh, so if she broke up with you tomorrow, you'd just leave her alone?"

"No, I'd try to get her back....because I like her," Gabriel replied.

"Look, man, I'm taking a big chance just talking to you like this. I'm trying to give you the benefit of the doubt, but if you're not being honest with me…"

"Then what? What're you gonna do about it?" Gabriel pushed him.

Christopher glared at him. "I'll have to kill you."

"Is that right?" Gabriel said, pushing him again.

"Don't do this, Gabe."

"You're not gonna do a damn thing about it," Gabriel said. When he attempted to push him again, Christopher grabbed his arm with his left hand, while simultaneously jabbing with his right fist. He was quick, but Gabriel was quicker, blocking the attack and sweeping his leg in a karate-style kick. Chris went down hard, grunting in pain. Gabriel locked his fingers into a two-fisted club and slammed them into Chris's chest. He followed it up with four jabs to Chris's face.

Gabriel stood up. "I should kill you now," he said.

Chris was hurting, but his demon body was already repairing itself; the air came back into his lungs, his sore muscles strengthened, and his bloody nose dried up. "Go ahead, at least you will show who you really are. Instead of the filthy lie you've been living." He stood up. "What are you waiting for? Do it!"

Gabriel stared at him, his muscles tensed. His breathing was heavy and his face red with rage. After ten seconds, his body relaxed and the color left his cheeks. "Consider this proof that I really care about Taylor. If I didn't, I would have no problem hurting her best friend's boyfriend...Tearing you limb from limb." Gabriel stalked off, leaving Chris to puzzle over the truth of the angel's words.

Thirty-Four

The desk flipped over and tumbled to the floor with a crash, having been wrenched from the floor and the wall, where it'd been attached for safety and security. His tirade had lasted for ten minutes and there wasn't much left in his room to destroy. Besides, if he kept it up, one of his neighbors was bound to complain about the noise.

When had life become so damn difficult? He sat on the floor—having flipped his bed and mattress over during his tantrum—and put his head in his hands. The answer to his question was easy, and he knew it. But for some reason, he thought that speaking the answer out loud, or even in his mind, would somehow give power to it, allowing it to destroy him. Even so, denial was unhealthy.

He gritted his teeth and growled, "Since I met *her.*"

Life used to be easy. Work hard, seek power, seek fame, and if you're lucky, kill a few demons along the way. But ever since he'd heard Dionysus's plan, something had been eating him from the inside, a relentless cancer, hellbound on recreating him. At least that's how he'd thought of it until now. But that was just another example of his denial.

Gabriel's parents were good people—his mom an angel, his dad a human. They taught him to seek to help people, to protect humans—and to fight demons. So that's what he'd done all his life; that is, until the Council had sent him on this mission to abduct the girl, Taylor. All for the sake of a plan that centered on the destruction of the human race.

"ARGHHHH!" he roared.

Why couldn't he make sense of it? And now he had the dark one asking him questions. Questions he didn't know the answer to, or was afraid to think about. All he knew was that he felt a connection with Taylor. That his life felt inexplicably tied to hers, in a way.

He had time. His powerful speech to the Council had bought him some time. To think. To analyze. To come to his senses, maybe. All he could do was explore his feelings for Taylor and see where they took him. And when it came time to make a decision, he would, even if it was a hard one.

Gabriel realized that he'd continued to grit his teeth as he thought about things and now they ached from the friction. His cell phone rang. It was Taylor. He smiled for the first time in hours.

Thirty-Five

She was sitting on the grass, like before. Except today was sunny, not rainy. The lawn was packed with other students enjoying the weather. Next to her, Sam was lying on her back, reading a large textbook. Something about Renaissance artists for one of the classes they had together. Taylor would read it later. Now, she poked and prodded at the recently cut blades of grass. She still wanted to find that elusive clover, the one with four flippers.

Surely the one that Gabriel had found for her didn't count—couldn't count—not really. She needed to find it on her own. Plus, she'd destroyed Gabriel's clover.

Unease had grown within her, bigger than before, like a genetically modified pumpkin, bulging and round. But she had Gabriel, so why was she feeling this way? The only answer she could come up with was the missing clover, and so, she searched.

An hour later she still hadn't found it. Samantha was asleep, the book resting on her chest.

"Mom?" Taylor whispered. "Are you there?"

Dread filled her. Not the answer she was looking for. A single tear dripped from her eye. What was wrong with her? She had the best boyfriend ever—a freaking angel, literally!—and yet she was feeling horrible! It was not the way that all the sappy romantic movies that she hated so much made it out to be. A good relationship was supposed to make everything better.

Coincidentally, she gritted her teeth at the same time that Gabriel was gritting his own. *Suck it up*, she commanded herself. Stop feeling sorry for yourself! And stop depending on some stupid clover for happiness.

She retrieved her phone from her backpack and dialed his number.

Thirty-Six

After another two weeks of dating Taylor, Gabriel was more confused than ever. Things with her were so...so easy. When they kissed he felt it. Not like in the literal sense, when his lips touched hers. Yeah, he felt that, too, in tingles and waves rolling through every last nerve ending; but deeper than that, in his very being. Deep down in his soul something was rolling through him, changing him.

Could he get the best of both worlds—loyalty to his people *and* her affections—by convincing her to join the angels? Or more pointedly, *should* he even try to convince her? He hated to admit it, but the demon had grown on him. If it wasn't for the darkness that constantly surrounded Christopher, he'd almost call him his friend. As if that was possible! Friends with a demon, ha! Dionysus would punch a hole through one of his light-filled walls if he knew.

It was a dangerous game Gabriel was playing, walking down the middle of the road, unwilling or too scared to pick a side. That he knew, and yet, day after day he continued to do just that. Hopefully an eighteen-wheeler wasn't about to flatten him into angel goo.

Thirty-Seven

Time plodded on, and with it, the semester. Day by day, week by week, Taylor forced herself to be happy, to ignore the strange, dark sense of foreboding she felt in the deepest pits of her soul. The semester was more than halfway finished and her life seemed to be perfect. She spent most days going to class, having lunch with her friends, walking hand in hand with Gabriel around campus, and lying in the grass studying with him. Her grades were looking good, things with Gabriel had been unbelievable, and her relationship with Sam was better than ever.

Then why did she feel like this?

For the most part, she was able to ignore the negative feelings and focus on the good things that were happening in her life, and over time, the negativity had waned, giving her a sense of peace, but never completely, never like before.

She was lying in the grass, her head resting on Gabriel's chest. Enjoying the benefits of living in a warm weather climate, she was wearing her favorite pair of well-worn jean shorts, a lime green tank top, and bare feet, her flip-flops kicked aside haphazardly. Her defeated tattoo was facing up, her skin well-tanned around the dark edges of the serpent. More than sixty days had passed since her last snake nightmare, the one in which Gabriel slew the hideous monster, and Taylor had stopped counting. After a month she'd started wearing clothing that showcased the tattoo again. After two months she added a second tattoo, this one around her ankle: another inky snake, but this one's red eyes were closed—not sleeping, but lifeless—revealing only its dark black eyelids. The newly etched serpent was strung up on a sword, pierced in four places, like an exceptionally long piece of meat on a kabob. Her dad was not going to be happy when he found out.

Her thoughts turned to one of her happiest memories: that night with Gabriel high above the football stadium. Their bodies had remained together, like perfect puzzle pieces, for hours that night.

Since that night, they'd had so many wonderful days together, sometimes doing fun things with their group of friends, like seeing movies, playing games, or just hanging out. Other days, they just spent time with each other, talking and laughing. Sometimes there was less talking. She didn't mind those days at all either.

Gabriel was very interested in her childhood and her family. She told him everything, opening up to him like she'd never done with anyone before, even Sam. She told him embarrassing things, like the time she laughed so hard in the third grade that she peed her pants. Or the time that she got three days of detention for slapping a boy on the playground because he'd gotten fresh with her. To avoid getting in trouble, she'd told her parents that she was selected to be part of an after school learning group for gifted children and that she'd be home late from school. She got away with it until her brother ratted on her, which led to her being grounded for a month and her hating James for twice that long.

James, she thought. *Why did she have to go to the same school as him?* Annoyingly, he had found out that she had a college boyfriend and he notified Eddie immediately, like she was committing a crime. This led to painful phone calls where her father tried to get her to tell him about Gabriel without him showing that he knew she was seeing someone. She refused to tell him, answering his questions as vaguely as possible.

Finally he gave up and was honest with her, informing her that he knew about her boyfriend from James. Taylor gave him a hard time about it, telling him she didn't appreciate him enlisting her brother to spy on her. Eddie turned it around though and made her feel bad by using the dad card: how she was so important to him and that he just wanted to make sure that she was okay. Making a big mistake, Taylor forgave him, and then, thinking he'd been granted access to her personal life, Eddie began to ask her embarrassing questions like, "You and Gabriel are being safe, right, Taylor?"

She'd tried to sound angry at the insinuation by saying, "God, Dad, we haven't even done anything yet!" This seemed to placate him as he went on to commend himself on what a good job he'd done raising her.

Gabriel had also told her about his unique childhood. What it was like to grow up as an angel, how and why the existence of angels was kept secret, and more details about the animosity between angels and demons.

One thing he told her that she was the most surprised about was regarding the religious aspect, or more accurately, the lack of a religious aspect to it all. He'd told her that religion didn't come into play in his world. He said it was possible that at one time the biblical version of angels and demons appeared on the earth, but that the current version had no connection to Heaven and Hell, and were merely humans in a highly evolved state.

Taylor had also questioned him a lot about Christopher and why he seemed so friendly when he was descended from a race that Gabriel had told her was hell-bent on eradicating mankind. Gabriel explained that not all demons supported their mainstream cause and that Christopher was of the relatively good variety. Taylor was extremely relieved, as she was worried about Sam, who'd been dating Christopher since they met, which was an abnormally long period of time for her best friend to be with the same guy.

The four of them, Taylor and Gabriel, and Samantha and Christopher, had spent many hours together and had become a pretty tightknit group, almost inseparable. Even the angel and the demon seemed to have become good friends, although the relationship sometimes seemed strained and unnatural. Maybe that was the reason for Taylor's continued unease.

Today, however, Taylor forced away her negative thoughts and focused on the present. She and Gabriel didn't have any classes on this Friday afternoon and all of her friends were going to go hang out at the campus pool hall later that evening. The pool hall had become the group's go-to spot when no one came up with any other ideas.

The lazy day drifted by as the afternoon sun began to drown on the horizon. They'd barely said a word while lying on the lawn, but Taylor didn't care. She just needed to be close to him.

When the last wink of sunlight danced out of sight, Taylor sighed and sat up. She looked at Gabriel with admiration in her eyes and he looked back, equally fascinated. They kissed and then stood up, walking hand in hand back to the dorms to put their barely-used books away.

After returning home they met up with Sam and Christopher, who'd likely used the afternoon to make out, one of their favorite activities. Marla and Jennings met them soon after and they all walked to dinner together. They had a nice, long dinner. Other than her frustratingly persistent dark thoughts, Taylor didn't have a care in the world.

PART III

"Something's wrong, shut the light
Heavy thoughts tonight
And they aren't of Snow White

Dreams of war, dreams of liars
Dreams of dragon's fire
And of things that will bite, yeah

Sleep with one eye open
Gripping your pillow tight

Exit light
Enter night
Take my hand
We're off to never-never land"

Metallica- "Enter Sandman"
From the album *Metallica (Black Album) (1991)*

Thirty-Eight

They were in the pool hall, laughing at a ridiculously difficult shot that Gabriel had just sunk—he was by far the best player—when Christopher came back to the corner table they were using. Trying to get away from the noisy hall, he'd gone outside to take a call on his cell phone. When he returned, Taylor knew something was wrong by the look on his face. It was a shock to see, as Christopher was one of the most care-free, easygoing people that Taylor knew—she'd never seen him scared or upset—but now his face was tense, stressed.

Gabriel noticed as well. "What happened?" he hissed.

"I didn't invite them, I swear," was the extent of Chris's reply.

"Invite who?" Taylor asked.

"Them," Christopher said, motioning over his shoulder, back from where he came.

The door to the hall swung open and three dark guys entered the room, their eyes sweeping from side to side. Instantly, the already shadowy pool hall darkened even further. The demons were huge, wearing tank tops to show off their impressive biceps and chests. Taylor felt her breath catch as she thought, *This is it.* Soon sand would be down her throat and she'd choke to death, her dream becoming a reality. Or perhaps they'd use poisonous black snakes to do the job.

Gabriel pushed her behind him as the gargantuans sauntered over.

"Heya, Christopher," one of the meatheads said. "Funny meeting you here." He glared at Gabriel.

"What do you want, Jonas?" Christopher said harshly.

"Hey, no need to get snippy. We were just checking out the on-campus facilities provided by the university."

"Now why would you want to do that? You're not students here."

"Au contraire, my friend, we just transferred. We heard that UT was where all the action was." Jonas, who seemed to be the spokesman for the group, appeared pleased to be able to contradict Chris.

"Well then, I guess you have every right to be here. Why don't I give you a tour of the campus?" Chris suggested, clearly trying to get them away from the pool hall and his friends.

"Oh no, we wouldn't want to be an inconvenience, we'll just stay here and shoot some pool with you," Jonas said.

Gabriel, standing quietly until now, stepped forward within inches of Jonas's face and said, "That wasn't a suggestion. Chris and I *are* going to give you a tour of the campus. Let's go." Taylor was close enough to hear Gabriel whisper, "Don't make a scene. We'll answer all of your questions outside."

Jonas thought about it for a second and then nodded his head once in agreement. The four demons and Gabriel headed for the door. Gabriel yelled to Taylor that they'd be back soon. A pit the size of a watermelon ballooned in Taylor's stomach as she watched Gabriel leave, flanked by the muscly, dark figures.

When they left, Sam asked, "What was that all about?"

The other three shook their heads in bewilderment. They'd have to wait for them to return to find out.

§

Outside, Gabriel was surrounded by demons. Three were demanding answers from him and Chris was trying to mediate. "Let me explain," Chris said.

"This better be good," Jonas said. "The Elders were not happy with your last report. Or the one before that either. That's why we're here."

"Okay, it's simple really. Gabriel and I have reached an agreement," Chris explained. "He doesn't want any harm to come to the girl and neither do I. So we're staying in close proximity to her, as well as to each other, to ensure she's safe and that neither of us tries anything sneaky."

Jonas said, "You know, I'm really glad that you've become BFFs, it almost makes me want to shed a tear. But there's a major problem with your little agreement. You and your pretty little angel friend are on opposite sides of a bloody, half-century-old war, in which the girl has become a key weapon. Sooner or later someone is going to have to make a move in this little chess match and we're thinking it should be us."

"Dammit, Jonas!" Chris spat out, blood flooding to his face. "We've sworn to protect all humans and help ensure they're able to live normal lives. That includes Taylor. We can't just grab her and neutralize her when there's currently no threat to her!"

Gabriel listened intently to the verbal battle, glad that Taylor wasn't around to hear it. She would've been extremely confused after all of the lies he'd told her so far.

Jonas laughed at Chris. "You've got to be kidding me! *No* threat to her? She's got a freaking angel for a boyfriend and not just any angel, the angel that's charged with tricking her into helping the evil angel cause. Grow some stones and take care of business, man!"

Chris didn't flinch. "Gabriel's told me that was his original mission, but he now has reservations about it because of his feelings for the girl," Chris replied.

"Feelings!? And you actually believe this *pigeon*. You've been awfully quiet, pigeon, are you saying you care about the girl?"

"That's accurate," Gabriel admitted, ignoring the insult. "I was charged with convincing Taylor to join our cause. If she wouldn't agree, I was given license to use requisite force to kidnap her. However, I quickly developed feelings for her—strong feelings—and now place her safety above the requirements of my mission.

"I could be executed for telling you this, but it's necessary to gain your trust. The Council wanted to take the girl months ago, but I convinced them to give me until the end of the school semester to persuade her to join the angel cause of her free will. I was hoping that'd give me enough time to come up with another plan. So far, I have nothing."

"You have two weeks," Jonas replied.

Gabriel stared at him, not sure what to make of his time-based statement. "Two weeks for what?"

"Two weeks to come up with a plan to protect the girl and keep her out of the middle of this war."

Chris jumped in. "That's ridiculous, we've made an agreement and we have until the end of the semester, which is two months away, to come up with a plan that works for everyone. Two weeks is impossible."

"Nothing I can do. The deadline has been mandated by the Elders. Deal with it."

"And what exactly do you think you're going to do in two weeks if we don't have a sufficient plan?" Gabriel asked, a challenge in his tone.

"Take the girl and neutralize her," Jonas said coldly.

"What the hell is that supposed to mean?" Gabriel snapped back, his blood pressure rising. His body was glowing brighter now, in anticipation of a physical confrontation.

"It means whatever we want it to mean, pigeon," Jonas sneered.

"I'll kill you before I let you take her," Gabriel said.

"We'll see who dies," Jonas replied. "And I'm dead anyway if your pigeon Council gets their hands on the girl. So I've got nothing to lose."

Christopher stepped in front of Gabriel, apparently expecting him to strike at Jonas. Gabriel managed to keep his head though, realizing that even with his strength and training he was no match for three burly demons.

Instead, Gabriel just said, "You're right, we *will* see. Now, if you don't mind, I'm going back to see my girlfriend. Don't bother me for two weeks." With that, he turned on his heel and went back into the pool hall.

Before the door closed, Gabriel heard Chris say to Jonas, "This was a big mistake."

"You better figure out whose side you are on," Jonas scoffed, before the three goons stalked off into the night.

ᔥ

Back inside the pool hall, Sam led the questioning. Taylor kept quiet, knowing that Gabriel wouldn't give her the truth until they were alone. She pretended to listen interestedly while Gabriel explained how those guys were old friends of Christopher's who'd gotten into some trouble and Chris stopped hanging out with them. Now they were pissed that he'd ditched their little gang.

Chris came in during the tail end of the story and reassured Sam that they wouldn't bother them again.

The other humans soon forgot about the incident as Chris was back to his normal antics, telling a joke about a priest, an ex-convict, and a gorilla in a bar. Everyone was soon in stitches. The mini pool tournament continued, with Gabriel and Taylor holding the table most of the night. It was no thanks to Taylor as she only made two or three shots all night, but Gabriel was able to clean up the table whenever it was his turn.

Taylor wasn't really into the game as she watched Gabriel from the corner of her eye. She could tell something had disturbed him.

At around ten o'clock she forced herself to yawn and then let her eyes blink slowly a few times. Sam said, "You look exhausted, Tay."

"Yeah, I am. I think I'll head back to the dorms, but you guys stay and have fun. Gabriel, can you walk me back?"

"Sure, let's go. See you all tomorrow," he said.

Taylor waited until they were a few blocks from the pool hall before asking, "What *really* happened with Chris's so-called ex-friends?"

"It's nothing to be worried about, Taylor. I can handle it."

Heat rose in her head. She blurted out, "Screw you! Stop treating me like I'm some kind of a child, man! I can tell that you're worried about it, so I'm going to be worried about it, too."

Gabriel seemed taken aback by the sudden outburst. "Hold on, Taylor. I'm sorry, you're right. I need to be completely honest with you, even when I'm trying to protect you. Let's go to the Bird's Nest and we can talk." Taylor was momentarily pacified by the suggestion. The *Bird's Nest* was the name she'd given to the spot high above the football stadium where she'd first learned the truth about what he was.

"Okay," she said, trying to breathe evenly.

They walked a block further and darted into a dark alley that was well-hidden from the street. Gabriel grabbed her as if she were a paper doll and did what Taylor liked to refer to as, "his angel thing". Seconds later they were high in the air, speeding across campus.

Soon they were in the Bird's Nest. She looked down at the beautiful stadium. It'd been prepped for the following day when the football team had a very important game against their cross-state rivals, the Tigers. The UT Beavers were undefeated and on the verge of playing in the National Championship game. A win against LTU tomorrow would ensure their first ever appearance in the country's most coveted college football game.

Fresh lines had been painted on the field, the white paint shining under the night security lights. There was a large banner stretched across the home entrance to the field, which the players would charge through when they stormed onto the gridiron.

Remembering why they were there, Taylor looked at Gabriel expectantly.

§℞

Gabriel's mind was racing as he decided how much to tell her. He opted to continue to lie on the biggest issues, but be as truthful as possible everywhere else. The tactic had served him well thus far, but he was worried that it would catch up with him soon.

Gabriel said, "I've tried to tell you as much as I could from the very start, but for your protection I've left out certain details that I didn't think you'd ever need to know." Gabriel realized then that he hated having to lie to her. It used to come so easily for him. Now, it felt contrary to every instinct in his body. This unnerved him, as he'd always prided himself on being a smooth and cunning liar when the need arose. What the hell was happening to him? Was he becoming soft?

Taylor frowned. "Continue," she instructed.

"I've told you and shown you how powerful a weapon you are if used by my people…"

"Because of my strong aura," she interrupted.

"That's correct," Gabriel confirmed. "And then you asked what that meant."

"Yes," Taylor said, remembering back to the many conversations they had while in the Bird's Nest, or lounging out in the sun.

"I told you that all it meant was that if the need ever arose, that the angels—my people—might come to you to ask for your help."

"That wasn't true?" Taylor asked.

"Not exactly. At the time I told you that, the angels already wanted and needed your help."

"Then why didn't you just ask for it?"

Gabriel lied again, masterfully mixing deceit with a bit of the truth. It stung him like a bee. "Because I wanted you to be able to enjoy your first semester at college and not be burdened by the problems of my world. I was able to convince the Archangel Council to wait until the holiday break at the end of the semester to ask you."

Taylor took a deep breath.

"You should have told me," Taylor said, frowning. "I would've understood and we could've talked it through together. I don't want to keep secrets from each other." A burst of anger heated her forehead. She'd been so trusting, so believing of everything Gabriel had told her; in short, she'd been blinded by his angelness. Now she saw that he was capable of deceiving her like anyone else. And no matter how he justified it—he said it was for her own good—she still needed to be able to trust him one hundred percent. The dread she'd felt on so many occasions rushed back, momentarily paralyzing her.

Gabriel said, "I don't know. I guess I should have. I just didn't want you to be stressed out about what would happen at the end of the semester while you were trying to have fun and do well in school. But you're right I should've told you. I'm sorry."

She wasn't about to let him off the hook that easy. "So now I'm stressed about what will happen at the end of the semester anyway *and* I'm stressed about the fact that my boyfriend's been lying to me all along."

"I'm so sorry, Taylor. I'll do anything to make it up to you."

"You can start by never lying to me again."

"Deal," Gabriel said much too quickly. "No more lies."

Pretending not to notice the business-like manner in which Gabriel had conducted himself, Taylor said, "Back to the other problem: you needing my help. You told me about your lie, but what's changed? We're only halfway through the semester, so we still have time before you need my help, right? And what does all this have to do with those behemoth demons in the pool hall tonight?"

"It's all related," Gabriel explained. "We need your help in defeating the demons and, although the angels *are* willing to wait until the end of the semester, the demons are now fully aware of your presence here at UT; Chris has been holding them off until now, but there's nothing else he can do. The demon leadership sent those goons here to threaten me into leaving you alone. They said that if I was still hanging out with you in two weeks, they'd come to take you away. They've realized how powerful you are in the hands of the angel army and are worried we're going to use your powers to destroy them."

Taylor's head started throbbing. "Take me away? Who the hell do they think they are? They can't do that. I won't let them."

"And I damn well won't let it happen either, Taylor. If you agree to help the Archangel Council, you'll have the full protection of the angel army."

Taylor's eyes narrowed. "And if I don't agree to help the angels?"

"Then you'll only have my protection, but that'll be more than enough. I could whip those pathetic demons with two wings tied behind my back."

Taylor wasn't comforted. "What exactly is it that the angels' want me to do in exchange for their protection?"

Gabriel's face tightened. "Easy. All you have to do is appear on the battlefield with us in the next battle. We'll protect you behind the strength of the entire angel army and I'll personally connect with your aura to attack the demons. We'll finally wipe their evil from the face of this planet forever."

Taylor said, "Look, man, I don't know if I'm up for being used to hurt people."

"Not people," Gabriel corrected, "demons."

A look of sudden realization appeared on Taylor's face. "What about Christopher? How does he fit into all this? He's a demon, will I be responsible for destroying him, too?"

"I'm sorry, Taylor, but yes. I know you think he's nice and cool and that he's your friend, but who do you think told the demons that you were here?"

"Not Chris," Taylor refuted, "he'd never do anything like that to me."

"He could and he did," Gabriel said. "He admitted it to me when we went outside, although after he told the demons, he did try to keep them away from you. He may be a nice guy, but he is still a demon at heart, and loyal to his own kind."

Taylor's head was spinning. How could the best days of her life turn into such a mess so quickly? Her thoughts were scattered, but she managed to ask, "What do we do?"

Gabriel put his arm around her and said, "I'm willing to do whatever it takes to protect you, but I can't guarantee I can do it on my own. If the demons bring a small army here, I'll inevitably lose. If we try to hide, they'll eventually find us. You have a very special gift that we could use to win the most important war this world has ever seen. I'd ask you to consider helping us."

Taylor maneuvered out from under Gabriel's arm. "I need to think," she said. Closing her eyes, she tried to work through it logically. The demons were trying to get to her. Gabriel could protect her for a while on his own, but not forever. Demons are evil, although not that evil if Chris was one of them. Angels are good, but not good enough to prevent Gabriel from lying to her. She'd be helping a noble cause. The angel cause. On paper, it sounded like the right decision, but something about it didn't feel right. Anytime she thought about helping the angels, she felt like an army of fire ants had invaded her pants. Not good.

Taylor tried to avoid thinking about Christopher or Sam, as she knew these would be emotional, rather than logical thoughts. The more she tried to forget them, the more her memories about them flooded her mind. *Dammit!* They were her friends, she couldn't just exclude them from the picture. There had to be another solution.

"Damn you for putting me in this position, Gabe," Taylor said. "I can't help the angels. I can't hurt Chris and Sam, even if it gives me the best chance of survival. We have to come up with another plan."

Gabriel's face fell, but only for a moment. "What do you propose?" he said.

Thirty-Nine

Taylor and Gabriel had planned meticulously for a week. They'd done it in complete secrecy, usually from the Bird's Nest or deep in the library. They'd continued to act as normal as possible around their friends, being careful not to miss lunch or dinner. Changes to routines led to questions and they wanted as few questions as possible.

Of course, the demon was asking questions anyway. He knew that time was running out and that a solution had to be reached. Thankfully, he wasn't aware that Taylor knew about the situation, so he didn't interrogate her.

However, Chris pulled Gabriel aside on an almost daily basis to ask, "Have you come up with anything yet?"

Gabriel lied each time, saying, "No, not yet, but I think I'm close."

Finally, on this Friday night, exactly a week from when the deadline was mandated and a week before it expired, Gabriel was ready for the first phase of the plan: deceit.

Gabriel was ready for Chris when he said, "We've only got a week to go, man, we seriously need to come up with a plan now!"

Gabriel smiled and said, "I've figured it out."

Chris replied, "You have? That's great, tell me."

"Okay, it's simple really. We tell your little friends that we've got a plan that'll satisfy all parties, but that we just have to get it cleared by the Archangel Council before we give it to them to propose to the demon Elders. We set up a time on the last day of the deadline, Friday, to meet them.

"Except we're not going to meet them on Friday, we'll be long gone by that point. You and I will take Taylor away the day before, Thursday, to a secret place. I know for a fact that neither the angels nor the demons are aware of this place. We hide her there together until we can come up with a long-term solution."

Chris's face fell. "But that's only a quick fix and they'll surely find us at some point, and then we'll all be screwed."

"Look, I can't think with the clock ticking like a bomb that's about to blow up in my face. It'll buy us some time and then we can come up with a better plan *together.*" Gabriel continued to emphasize the word *together*, hoping Chris would buy the lie. "Unless you have a better plan?"

"Okay, okay, I guess it's the only choice we have, but how will we escape with her unnoticed? Those thugs have been watching you and Taylor everywhere you go."

"To be honest, I could probably just fly away with her under my arm; there's no way they could easily follow me from the ground. However, to play it safe, I think we should create a diversion. We'll get Samantha to dress up like Taylor and wear something that hides her face and then I'll walk out towards the stadium with her. They'll follow me as they always do. You then take Taylor to a predetermined location and drop her off. I'll come back with Sam, leave her at the dorms, and then go and get Taylor. Your little punk friends will think I'm leaving the dorms alone, without Taylor, and so they'll leave me alone. I pick up Taylor and fly her to a safe-house. Easy."

Chris thought for a minute and then asked two questions: "First, how do I know where you go, and second, why do you trust me with Taylor, I *am* a demon?"

"I've got the coordinates for the location we'll be at, give me your phone." Chris handed his cell over and Gabriel punched in a longitude and latitude. He had no intention of telling Christopher where they were going so he just made up the coordinates.

"There, now you can find us. Why do I trust you? Because you haven't done anything to betray my trust. You could've called in a small gang of demons to come and take her away at any time, but you didn't. So I know that you're looking out for her best interests like I am."

Chris seemed satisfied by the response. He said, "Thanks. If you'd have told me a few months ago that we'd be working together, I'd have checked them into a five-star padded room. Maybe you're not such a jerk after all."

"Uh, yeah. Ditto," Gabriel said, feeling terrible. A sick feeling chewed at his stomach, like he'd eaten rotten fruit. Ignoring it, he asked, "Any other questions on the plan?"

"No, I'll schedule a meet with Jonas today so we can set up a time to meet them on Friday. When we don't show up to the meeting they'll start hunting us, but by then we'll be long gone."

Gabriel forced a smile. "Exactly."

❧

"What the hell am I doing?" Gabriel whispered under his breath. His heart was racing and sweat bled from every pore. He really did feel sick, like he'd caught the flu while talking to Chris. But he knew it wasn't anything that natural.

It was like each lie he told to his friends, to his girlfriend, birthed another strain of a soul-eating cancer, tearing him apart from the inside. And eventually it'd kill him.

He ducked into an alley and slumped against a brick wall spray painted with sunken green eyes and lips turned up into a devilish grin. For a moment he wondered whether he was looking into a mirror.

He was backed into a corner by the damn demons, by the Archangel Council, by his own deceptions, and now he'd have to do something that Taylor might never forgive him for. It was the only way. He clenched his fists, hardened his jaw, and took to the air, relishing the cleansing rush of the air over his gently-glowing skin.

Forty

On Saturday, Christopher agreed a meeting with Jonas and his henchmen for the following Friday at noon.

A day passed without event.

On Monday, the angel, the demon, and Taylor were all going through their normal routines: wake up, shower, brush teeth, go to class, go to lunch, etc. Although they were all worried about how well the plan would work later in the week, they thought for the time being the demon spies would leave them alone. They were wrong.

Gabriel and Christopher were in afternoon classes when it happened.

Taylor had been dismissed from class early and was walking alone to her last class of the day when abruptly, Jonas appeared beside her and grabbed her hand. She felt a powerful twisting of her body—and maybe her mind, too—and then all went dark.

A few moments later her sight was restored and she was alone in a clearing in the woods. She turned 360-degrees to get her bearings, but all she saw was dense forest surrounding her. The forest was quiet.

Without warning, a piercing shriek erupted from somewhere within the woods. Taylor turned towards the sound, covering her ears with her hands. A loud splintering sound followed, and she saw several trees flap wildly from side to side before collapsing with a thundering crash.

Something dark was advancing towards the clearing.

Unsure of whether to run, scream, or hide, Taylor remained frozen in place, her eyes wide with terror. Another tree fell, then another. A dark form stepped into the clearing. It was like nothing she'd ever seen.

Huge, clawed hind legs gave it stability as it walked slowly on two feet towards her. The creature's body was massive, in direct proportion to its legs, but its front arms were relatively small, reminding her of a smaller version of T-Rex. The monster's head had characteristics that were both human and reptile with small, jet-black eyes and a set of knife-like teeth accentuated by two long fangs protruding beyond its lower lip. Its entire body was covered in scaly skin so black it could almost be defined as the absence of light.

Taylor knew at once what it was: *a gargoyle*.

Finally, she screamed, knowing it'd be fruitless, because surely there was no one near the secluded spot. Even so, she had to try. Turning, she ran onto an overgrown path that led through the woods, away from the clearing. Sharp branches scratched her face and foliage raked her legs, as she recklessly charged down the rarely used trail. She heard another ear-shattering shriek from the gargoyle as it pursued her. Trees snapped like toothpicks, branches broke, and leaves shook.

It was catching up.

Just as her lungs started burning from the sudden exertion, the noises behind her ceased. The silence was almost worse; she didn't know where the beast had gone. Afraid to stop, she ran a bit further, albeit at a slower pace, until she reached another clearing. She chomped at the air, trying to suck in much needed breaths. Still gulping down oxygen, she stumbled to the other side of the clearing. When she was almost halfway across, a solid thump startled her from behind.

Taylor whirled around to find the gargoyle towering over her. It was only a few yards away. She noticed something she'd missed the first time she'd looked at the alien creature: Two small wings protruded from its back, barely visible above its muscly shoulders.

Taylor had two quick thoughts before the gargoyle attacked: One, *I'm going to die*; and two, *those are awfully small wings for such a large guy*. The monster moved towards her. Not knowing what else to do, Taylor screamed again at the top of her lungs.

From the corner of her eye she saw a flash of light.

Forty-One

Jonas chuckled to himself from the shadows, as he watched the gargoyle advancing on the girl. It'd been so easy. Of all his powers, teleportation and the ability to teleport others were his favorites.

Back on campus, he'd teleported so that he was directly next to her and then, as soon as he touched her, he teleported her to the middle of the forest where his "little" friend was waiting.

Jonas wanted to scare both the angel and the girl before their meeting later that week, to ensure they didn't try anything sneaky. The girl was obviously scared already and the angel would be equally scared when the girl told him what'd happened.

He put a dog whistle to his mouth, ready to sound the stop command once Freddy, as he liked to call this particular gargoyle, had gotten close enough to her that she could smell his bad breath. The girl screamed again. That's when he saw the flash of light. *Damn*, he thought, *even a full-grown gargoyle is no match for a highly trained angel.*

Forty-Two

Gabriel was sitting in class, ignoring the professor's lecture, doing what he'd been doing for the last week: harnessing the power of the lights in the room to heighten his hearing ability. By this point, he could pretty much hear every word that Taylor said, whether she was right next to him, or a few miles away. He'd accomplished this by training his angel ears to pick out the exact frequency of her voice from the many others in the surrounding area.

Of course, he hadn't told her what he was doing.

On this occasion, he hadn't heard anything from her since she answered a question midway through her previous class, which likely meant that she was out of class and walking alone to her next lecture. The silence didn't concern him so much, as it probably meant she was safe. If she wasn't safe, sh'd be crying, yelling, or reasoning with her attacker or captor.

This was the logical reasoning that streamed through Gabriel's head as he listened for her next sound. The next thing he heard from Taylor froze him with fear. A high-pitched scream tore through his ear drums, causing him to wince in pain.

Instinctively, his mind coordinated the analysis of the information with his ears, and determined the direction and the approximate distance of the yell. *North. Nearly two miles. Must be the forest.*

Without a word, he darted from his seat in the back of the crowded lecture hall, slammed through the exit, and charged outside. Once in the open air, he ran at normal human speed until he was out of sight. As soon as he had an opportunity, he transformed into full angel form and raced off towards where Taylor's vocal signature had resonated.

Flying faster than he ever had before, he reached the target area in mere seconds. He was low to the ground, scouring the dense foliage for any sign of her. He passed one clearing and approached another. In the second clearing he saw something unexpected: a gargantuan black shape moving through the open space.

As he closed in to investigate, another earsplitting scream disrupted the calm quiet of his flight. It was coming from exactly where the dark shape stood.

He thought that the creature might be carrying Taylor, so he needed to be careful how he attacked it, fearing that he might injure her at the same time, but as he passed the gargoyle he could see that she was out in front of it. Barely. It was closing fast.

That was all the motivation he needed as he cut hard to the left and locked his flight path directly on the gargoyle, soaking up the bright sun to gain strength.

Harnessing the sun's life-giving rays, Gabriel's body emitted a blinding light more brilliant than any Fourth of July fireworks display.

He slammed into the beast, knocking it backwards several feet. He hung onto its arm as it sprawled on the earth, landing several hard, blazing punches to its head before it came to rest on its chest. Mustering all of his strength, he grabbed both its wings and pulled them like he was trying to uproot a pesky weed from a garden.

"Nooo, don't!" came a cry from his right, but he ignored it and kept straining at the wings until he heard a satisfying crunch and the wings ripped from the gargoyle's back. He tossed them aside and looked to see who'd tried to stop him.

Jonas approached slowly, his palms open at either side, as if trying to capture a cornered animal. "Calm down, Gabriel. I can explain."

Gabriel stepped down from the gargoyle's back and the creature groaned. "I'm going to kill you and then finish off the beast," Gabriel replied.

"No, please, I was just trying to scare her so you guys wouldn't try to trick us on Friday. I swear I was going to stop it before it hurt her."

He's scared, Gabriel thought, *fear creates weakness. This pathetic demon is nothing without his posse.*

As if in response to his thoughts, two fiery shapes blazed across the clearing, coming to a stop on either side of Jonas. The reinforcements had arrived. With a sneer, his confidence was regained, and Jonas cracked his knuckles. He said, "We'll see who kills who."

In his rage, Gabriel had nearly forgotten what he was doing there until he heard a voice yell, "Please, no! Leave him alone!"

All four turned and saw Taylor, tears streaming down her face, running towards Gabriel. When she got to him, she jumped into his arms, wrapping her legs tightly around his back. Her shoulders shook as she sobbed uncontrollably.

"I *am* scared," she wept. "Jonas, you accomplished what you wanted to. We're not going to try anything. Please just leave us alone until Friday."

Gabriel held her tightly and said, "You're safe now, it's going to be okay." He glared at the demons and commanded, "You heard her, get the hell out of here!"

Unsure of how to respond, Jonas shrugged and motioned for his thugs to follow him. "We'll cut you a break this time, pigeon, but next time we won't be so nice," Jonas said, clearly trying to sound tough in front of his buddies. They disappeared.

Gabriel ignored the parting comment and turned his full attention to Taylor, a look of concern etched on his face. "Are you okay?" he asked.

To his absolute surprise, the tears dried up and Taylor gave him a wicked smile. "Yeah, I'm fine, not a scratch on me."

Gabriel gawked as his girlfriend. "Weren't you scared?"

"Well, at first I was, of course, but once I saw you coming I knew you'd save me. And if you didn't, I had it all planned out. I was gonna kick it in the nuts and run like hell. I'm not hurt, so there's really nothing to be concerned about anymore. Plus, if what Jonas said is true, I was never really in any danger." She said all of this very matter-of-factly, like she was solving a math problem out loud.

Gabriel was completely mystified by where this kooky, fearless human girl had come from to turn his life so completely upside down. He said, "Well then, if you're fine I guess you don't need a ride home." He set her back on the ground and flew off.

§

"Hey, wait a minute!" Taylor yelled after him, laughing.

In less than the time it took her to blink, Gabriel was back by her side, laughing too.

"I *will* take a ride back," Taylor said. "I just didn't want you to make too big a deal out of the gargoyle thing. I was afraid you would change our plans."

"'The gargoyle thing,' as you put it, could've killed you. They're dangerous and hard to control, and any demon that thinks they can is a complete fool. Like our friend Jonas, for example."

Taylor looked around Gabriel to see the hulking black monster on the ground. "Okay, okay, point taken. Is it dead?"

"Not yet, I just removed its wings, which is pretty much the only way to easily stop one of those things. When you pull the wings out, they slip into a sort of coma until the buds of the wings start to grow back. It usually takes about twenty-four hours. I should really finish him off though, I'm afraid those idiots won't come back to secure him properly."

Taylor moved around him to get a closer look. The gargoyle appeared to be sleeping, its chest heaving up and down as it breathed deeply, rhythmically. She could see two large holes in its back, where the wings had been wrenched from its skin. There was a trickle of black liquid, presumably blood, coming from the wounds.

She walked to the other side of it, where Gabriel had tossed the damaged wings, only to find two piles of ash.

Following her, Gabriel said, "Demons and their offspring don't die in the classic sense. Their bodies turn to ash."

Taylor continued to look at the piles of soot. "What happens when an angel dies?" she asked.

Gabriel seemed taken aback by the question. "Why do you ask?"

"Just morbid curiosity, I guess. Do they turn into ash too?"

"No, but we also don't die like humans do. After a while, our bodies vanish into a bright, white beam of light. They say that each angel's beam returns to one of the stars in the sky, making that star shine brighter, so it can provide even more power to the remaining angels on earth."

Taylor looked reflectively at the sky. "I wonder how many angels are in the stars."

She was startled when Gabriel answered her rhetorical question with, "Exactly three hundred and sixty four." Her eyes searched his face for some meaning behind his words.

"How did they die?"

"All of them were killed by demons." Gabriel said bitterly.

"And how many demons have been killed by angels?"

Gabriel hesitated, and then said, "Five hundred and two, including gargoyles. We keep very accurate records of the angel and demon populations for purposes of our war strategy."

"Seems like such a waste," she mused.

§℞

Gabriel had never thought about it like that. He was always taught that the War was necessary and that sacrifices had to be made. Then he remembered that it was the angels who had the power to stop the killing, while the demons were just doing what they thought they had to do to save human lives. His loyalties to this girl were deadlocked with his loyalties to his race, to his people.

Gabriel suddenly felt a heavy strain on him, and for the first time in his life, all confidence in his ability to make decisions was sucked from him, like venom from a snake bite.

He had a strong desire to change the subject. "Why were you wandering out in the woods by yourself? I didn't hear anything out of the ordinary until you screamed."

"I wasn't, I have no idea how I got here. One minute I was walking on campus and then I saw Jonas, he grabbed my arm, and I was here running for my life."

"Ahhh, very clever," Gabriel said. "He teleported you. It's one of the demons' most powerful abilities. It's a skill that they didn't even learn to fully use for at least twenty years."

"It felt very strange, but it didn't hurt. Wait a minute, what do you mean you *heard* me scream?"

Gabriel shrugged. "I was worried about you so instead of listening in class, I trained my super hearing ability to recognize your voice so I'd know if you were ever in danger. It really paid off in this case."

"You were spying on me?" Taylor said, a small grin curling on the edges of her lips. "Did you find out anything interesting?"

Gabriel grinned back. "Eh, not really, just some things about how you think I'm gorgeous, that you can't get me out of your head and that you still get butterflies when you see me, nothing major."

"Oh, okay good. I'm glad you didn't hear the part where I said you're an arrogant little pretty boy who flies around like a butterfly trying to save the world."

Gabriel clutched both hands to the left side of his chest. "That hurts, Tay, it really hurts." He put his arm around her and squeezed hard. "You know, Tay, I really am scared to lose you." And he meant it. Which scared the hell out of him.

"Let's go home," Taylor said.

PART IV

"Too alarming now to talk about
Take your pictures down and shake it out
Truth or consequence, say it aloud
Use that evidence race it around

There goes my hero
Watch him as he goes
There goes my hero
He's ordinary"

Foo Fighters- "My Hero"
From the album *The Colour and the Shape (1997)*

Forty-Three

Gabriel was enjoying the verbal sparring. Given he was the only one who knew the full truth of what was about to happen, the conversation was pointless, but he wasn't going to stop it. Instead he just played along.

"We need to tell Sam what's going on," Taylor said.

"Trust me on this one, Tay, the fewer people that know, the better," Gabriel replied.

"Don't I get a say?" Chris asked.

"No!" Taylor and Gabriel said at the same time. They looked at each other and laughed.

The girl, the angel, and the demon were camped out in the library trying to make some team decisions while Sam was at the gym. Of course, Taylor and Gabriel were thinking about what to do based on their secret plan, while Christopher was basing his rationale on the plan that he thought they'd agreed on. Chris believed that he'd be part of a diversion set to occur on Thursday to allow Gabriel and Taylor to escape, and then he'd meet up with them later. Taylor knew that the real plan was for Gabriel and Taylor to fly off alone on Wednesday, leaving everyone else confused and unable to track them. However, she thought that she and Gabriel would hide together until they could come up with a permanent way to get both the angels and the demons off her back. That wasn't exactly true…like at all.

Gabriel tried not to think about it.

The discussion now was about whether to include Sam in any of the plans and whether to reveal to her the true nature of the guys that she and Taylor were dating. Taylor was voting yes, Gabriel said no, and they refused to let Christopher voice his opinion.

Taylor clearly wanted her best friend to know what was going on. She said, "I have an idea. I'll agree that we won't tell her now. We'll carry out the plan and find a safe place to hide. Then, after the semester is over, we're going to need Sam to keep up the ruse that I'm on an extended vacation with Gabriel. We'll need her to reassure my father or he's going to be freaking out and having the cops out looking for me."

"Fine. Deal," Gabriel said. He was the only one who knew the full truth. There'd be no need to maintain the lie about them being on vacation for very long. If his plan was successful, the mission would be accomplished in less than a week and she'd be back at school, finishing her classes and hanging out with her best friend, Sam, and her incredible angel-boyfriend—him.

♪♪

Taylor was surprised he'd agreed so easily, but wasn't about to question it. She grabbed Gabriel's hand and shook it before he could change his mind. Her mind wandered back to the plan they'd come up with. She'd lost track of the days and realized then that it was already Tuesday night, the eve of her escape from the demons. She shuddered.

She felt bad about not telling Christopher, but she knew that he couldn't be trusted after what he'd done. Although he did seem to be trying to make up for it now.

Taylor yawned and looked at her watch. It was only seven-thirty in the evening, but she wanted to get plenty of sleep because the real plan involved getting up ridiculously early.

"I'm going to head back and make it an early night, you guys want to walk back with me?" Taylor asked. After what happened earlier that week, she knew Gabriel wouldn't let her out of his sight. Chris decided to tag along, too.

With a sly smile, Taylor said, "Hey, Chris, a little birdie told me that demons have the ability to teleport and to teleport others, is that true?"

He smiled proudly; Chris was oblivious to what'd happened with the gargoyle, so he didn't realize that his ability to teleport had some bad memories for her. "Yep, absolutely, why do you ask?"

"Well, I was just thinking…my legs are tired and I'd rather get back to my room as quickly as possible so…do you think you could do anything about that?"

Christopher laughed, while Gabriel glared at Taylor. "That's a bad idea, Tay," Gabriel objected.

"It's fine by me," Chris agreed. "I can take you both."

"Or I could just fly us all there," Gabriel suggested, not wanting to give in.

"Nah, I'm too tired to hang on, let's just *port*," Taylor insisted.

Gabriel smirked. "Port?"

Taylor grinned. "Yeah, you know, teleport. Why use three syllables when one works just fine?"

"You act like you've done it before," Gabriel grumbled.

"Whaddya say, Mr. Angel?" Chris asked.

"Alright fine, let's make it quick."

They found a janitor's closet and squeezed in so no one would see them do it. Seconds later they'd ported into another small janitor's closet in the Commons.

When they stepped out, Taylor was beaming. "Un-freaking-believable!" she said. "That was wayyyy better than walking, although flying does have a certain thrill to it."

"Glad you liked it," Chris said.

Gabriel walked Taylor home and Chris went back to his room. When Gabriel dropped her off, he asked, "You ready?"

"As ready as I'll ever be, I guess," she said. "See you at six o'clock sharp."

He kissed her deeply and then hugged her like he'd never see her again. "Goodnight, beautiful," he said, shutting the door.

"Back at you, angelboy," Taylor said to the door.

Forty-Four

It was three o'clock in the morning. Taylor rubbed her eyes and looked at the shining numbers on her iPhone. Sleep came and went. Her body and mind were restless. *Three hours to go*, she thought.

She needed to get some sleep, but every time she closed her eyes, vivid scenes from the last three months of her life flashed by. How had things gotten so out of control? She was just a normal teenager who wanted to have a normal college experience, and now here she was, dating an angel, hunted by demons, a potential midnight snack for some gargoyle.

If only she could tell Sam—that'd change everything. They'd make bad jokes about it, talk to each other about how they were feeling, and just generally be there for each other. The only ones she could talk to about it, Gabriel and Christopher, were the ones causing the problems to begin with.

She rolled back over, trying to tell the thoughts in her head to "Shut up, for the love of God!" when she heard a soft tapping on her window. Glancing at Sam to make sure she was fast asleep, Taylor kneeled on her bed to see what'd caused the sound. It was Gabriel, his wings fully extended and slowly undulating, allowing him to hover outside the glass.

Over the time that she'd been dating him, he'd appeared outside her window countless times. She loved it when he did that. It usually meant going for a midnight flight around campus, or gazing at the stars and talking about fantastical creatures, like angels and demons, or better yet, feeling his lips against hers, their bodies close.

She knew this was not one of those kinds of visits, but still, her heart leapt in anticipation, until she saw the troubled look on her boyfriend's face. His face was panicked, his eyes wide and his facial expressions jerky.

Ever so slowly, Taylor lifted the window a few inches, praying it wouldn't betray her with a squeak. "What's wrong?" she hissed.

"He's onto us," Gabriel growled.

"Chris?"

"I wish. No, it's Jonas. He doesn't know the real plan, but he knows the one where we escape with Chris. Maybe Chris told him."

Taylor said, "Chris wouldn't do that."

"Look, we don't have time to argue. Jonas and his boys could show up any second!"

"Okay, one sec." Taylor crawled across her bed and plucked the small overnight bag she'd packed from the floor, slid the note she'd written Sam onto her desk, slipped on and tied her sneakers, and clambered back to the open window.

Thinking ahead, Taylor had decided to sleep in her jeans and a tank top, so that she was able to leave quickly if necessary. It made her feel like she was a spy or fugitive in some movie.

She'd wanted to bring enough clothes for a few weeks, but Gabriel insisted he wouldn't be able to fly very far with that kind of load on his back and that they'd be able to acquire more clothes along the way if necessary.

Taylor swung her legs out the window and ducked her head, so her entire body was in the open air. Positioning her hands to either side of her hips, she propelled herself forward and onto Gabriel's back, instantly feeling his warmth and the gentle rocking as his body levitated above the ground.

Gabriel soared into the night. The area around Taylor's building was deserted, and even if some insomniac was watching out a window, they'd likely think it was a dream and no one would believe their story anyway.

Once they were away from the campus, Taylor spoke. "How'd you know Jonas was coming for me?"

"It's really not the time to talk about all this…," Gabriel said.

"It's exactly the time," Taylor said, unable to prevent a hint of irritation in her voice.

"Okay, I've been watching Jonas all night. Twenty minutes ago, he left his building and met his buddies and I was able to overhear part of their conversation. They somehow knew we were leaving tomorrow, as we'd agreed with Chris."

"Was Chris with them?" Taylor asked.

"No, but—"

"He didn't tell them," Taylor said.

"I don't know how they found out then. If neither of us told them, that leaves only Chris."

"Maybe they overheard one of our conversations with Chris."

"Maybe," Gabriel said, "but it seemed like Jonas had just found out."

Taylor didn't respond. She didn't feel like talking anymore. Just a few weeks ago she'd felt betrayed by Gabriel, when she found out he'd lied to her, and she really didn't want to think about the possibility that another one of her close friends had betrayed her, too. She rested her head on the upper portion of Gabriel's left wing, using it as a pillow, and slipped into a restless sleep. Early on in their relationship, Taylor had helped Gabriel fashion a harness of sorts that clamped on his retractable wings, which she could strap herself into, so that while she was on his back she could sleep without falling off.

A couple of hours later Gabriel landed near a 24-hour gas station so they could get something to drink and use the bathroom. It almost felt like a road trip. If that's what it was, it was a very strange kind of road trip.

After they got back "on the road", Taylor felt like talking again. The endless silence was deafening, somehow.

"Where exactly are we going?" she demanded, making no attempt to hide her bad mood. "You told me it was a safe place, but that you'd give me the details later." Taylor realized how foolish she sounded.

She wondered how her dad would react when she told him that she was skipping the last part of the semester to go on vacation with the boyfriend he hadn't even met yet. It wouldn't matter that she had a plan to e-mail her assignments to Sam to turn in for her, or that she planned to find a way to make it back for her exams. He'd be furious. She wondered if he'd try to pull her out of UT and transfer her closer to home. Or threaten to not pay for her education altogether.

These thoughts were swirling around her head when Gabriel replied, "We're going to the front lines of the War."

"Wha…What?" Taylor was dumbfounded. "We agreed that I'd stay out of the War! That our lives together and our friendship with Chris and Sam were more important than the politics of angels and demons!"

"Look, Taylor," Gabriel growled, "you act like making these decisions is so easy and that there are no consequences, but there are. If you don't help one side or the other, you'll be hunted for your entire life. The War is bigger than either of us, bigger than our friendships. I know you're going to hate me for having to lie to you again, but you left me no choice. The right thing to do is to help the angels win the War, or else there may not be any world for us to live in. It's a hard decision, but it's what we must do."

Taylor wanted to scream at Gabriel, to hit him, to leap from his back and try her luck skydiving with no parachute, but instead, she just seethed quietly, trying to regain control of her emotions. Eventually, she said, "You could've told me you felt differently. I was willing to listen." Taylor's teeth were clenched, making her words sound slurred.

"I didn't see it that way. And while I know lying to you isn't a good habit, I *will* do it to prevent you from destroying yourself."

"And how will taking me to the front lines of a violent war protect me!" Taylor shouted over the wind.

"Look, I was exaggerating when I said I was taking you to the front lines. We're going to the where the majority of the War is being fought. However, we'll go to the angel command center and training grounds, which is well back from the front lines. That's why it's literally the safest place on earth for you. You'll have the strength of the entire angel army between you and the demons." Gabriel said the last part proudly, like she should feel privileged to be granted such protection.

This sucks, Taylor thought, making the understatement of the year. *I'm a hostage to an angel and to a war.* Not to mention that the angel who abducted her was her boyfriend.

"What do I have to do?" Taylor asked evenly. All she could do with roll with things until an opportunity arose where she could make a move.

"Thanks, Taylor. This is the right decision."

"It was never my decision," Taylor snapped, fury rising once more in her chest. "Just tell me what you want from me and I'll do it."

"Taylor, I—"

"I know, you're sorry, blah, blah. Heard it all before. Just get on with it." Taylor realized she was gripping Gabriel's wings so hard she could feel hard muscle and bone beneath her fingertips. She relaxed her squeeze, took a deep breath, waited.

"Okay," Gabriel said, sounding stung. "Remember when I enhanced my powers by being near you?"

"Yeah…"

"I was really close to you then, which made the effect much greater than if you were say…two miles away."

"How close is the command center to the battlefield?" Taylor asked.

"About a mile," Gabriel replied. "We'll need you on the actual battlefield, close enough that a few of our best soldiers can see you and gain as much strength from your aura as possible."

Taylor sighed loudly, not trying to hide her disgust.

Gabriel added quickly, "But don't worry, you'll be safe. I'll be right next to you, protecting you. If anything manages to get close to you, I'll use your aura to blast them away."

"That's comforting," Taylor said coldly. Even still, she felt her stomach drop, but not from the thrill of the flight. *Wow!* she thought. *She'd actually be in the midst of the battle!* While frightening, there was a certain excitement to it as well. And she knew that regardless of whether Gabriel was near her, she'd be very well protected. After all, she was the most valuable weapon the angels had. But only if they could control her.

"It sounds like it could be fun, in a weird, twisted, thrill-seeking kind of way," Taylor admitted grudgingly. She was only half serious, but Gabriel didn't need to know that.

"I'm sorry I lied to you again," Gabriel said. "But this is the right decision."

"Whatever," Taylor said.

She went silent for a while, thinking about the craziness of the last three months. She even pinched herself a few times to make sure that it wasn't all an exceptionally long dream. Taylor managed to convince herself to brush aside any anger she had towards Gabriel for his lies—they were a problem for another day. Now, she had to focus on the task at hand: pretending to play her role in the Great War. While her mind wandered, they made steady progress towards their destination.

Only one thing was certain: she wouldn't cooperate willingly, not if it meant hurting Chris—and Sam at the same time.

Their destination was about a seven hour flight from UT and in a completely different direction than Mount Olympus, where the angel leaders were located. Located three thousand miles south and two thousand miles east from UT, the equator had to be crossed to reach the front lines of the War.

There was one thing that both the angels and demons agreed on: that the War needed to be confined to a standard location until one side was victorious. In order to keep their existence a secret, which all parties agreed to be necessary, they had to contain the violence in a place that no human would be likely to stumble upon.

All battles were scheduled in advance, so that proper surveillance of the area could be conducted to ensure that a lost or backpacking human didn't find themselves in the middle of a nasty skirmish. When there was a rare human sighting, all planned battles were rescheduled until the *battle-blocker*, as they called the humans, had exited the fight zone.

Both sides maintained a command center and training ground behind the front lines. Taylor and Gabriel were headed for the angel command center.

After he had, unbeknownst to Taylor or Chris, formulated the real plan two weeks earlier, Gabriel had phoned Dionysus to inform him of the change in circumstances. Dionysus was extremely happy with the plan. They did, however, have a slight disagreement on where Taylor should be flown to. Dionysus wanted her to come to Mount Olympus first and then the Council would travel with Gabriel and Taylor to the command center. Gabriel disagreed and eventually was able to convince Dionysus that any delay could allow the demons to stop them.

The full Archangel Council of the Twelve would leave Mount Olympus and meet them at the command center. It was the first time that the entire Council had left their haven simultaneously. Gabriel didn't know whether any Council members would want to participate in the battle in the hopes of gaining glory during the victory, or if they all just wanted to be there to see the end of the War.

As Gabriel thought about introducing Taylor to the Council, a pit formed in his stomach. He felt ill. He'd told so many lies that he was starting to lose track. Jonas hadn't found out about any plans and Chris certainly hadn't told him anything. But he said what he had to say to convince Taylor to go along with him, to convince her that she was in great danger. He didn't like lying to her, not anymore, but he didn't have a choice. Although she seemed to forgive him, something about it had felt less sincere than the last time. He hoped he could contain the remaining lies and get Taylor through the rest of the ordeal alive with their relationship intact.

Once again, they flew in silence as Taylor drifted off to sleep.

§

Hours later, Taylor was awakened by a gentle nudge from the wing she was curled on top of. "Hey, sleepy head, we're here," Gabriel said.

Taylor pried her eyes open and peered groggily over the edge of her flying bed. Below her she saw a massive valley, set between two long, bluish mountain ranges. The sky was crystal-clear and blue, not a cloud in the sky.

"It's awesome," Taylor marveled.

"We ensured you'd arrive on a rest day. There's always at least one day per week that's free from fighting, to allow each side to recover and plan strategies. If this were an action day it'd typically be very dark, as the demons like to control the weather to gain an advantage. They cover the sky with mountains upon mountains of filthy black clouds, blocking out any trace of the sun, moon, and stars. They attack us with lightning, tornadoes, and powerful winds. They can easily see us shining in the dark and it's difficult for us to see them hiding." Gabriel said all of this with a heavy degree of contempt in his voice. It was clear that he had fought many times against the demons.

"If they block the sun and stuff, then how can you fight them at all?" Taylor asked.

"We have to generate light from weaker, artificial power sources, rather than the natural strength of the sun or moon. We try to use floodlights, spotlights, or even flashlights when we are really desperate, but the demons can generally disable them pretty quickly, which puts us at a major disadvantage. That's where you come in." Taylor was sitting higher up on Gabriel's back now, her cheek gently touching his over his shoulder. She saw the edge of his lips curl into a smile. Her heart beating wildly, she pulled away sharply. Damn him for being so good looking even when he was being a jerk.

"Is there anything else I need to know?" she asked flatly, as they closed in on the center of one of the mountains.

"Not really, you'll be involved in all of the strategy meetings so you can ask as many questions as you want. Once we land, let me do most of the talking, I know the angels around here pretty well." Gabriel paused, and seemed to consider whether to say whatever was on his mind. Thirty seconds passed and he said, "Tay, are we…okay?"

Without a hint of emotion in her voice, Taylor said, "We can talk about all that later. Let's focus on the War." They were nearly on top of the mountain now; they appeared to be heading for the highest peak. In an artificial attempt to temporarily get things back to normal, Taylor said, "One more question: Are we allowed to act like…you know…boyfriend/girlfriend?"

Gabriel laughed loudly at her question. "Of course we can. I never planned to fall for you, but it happened and I'm glad it did."

Riiiight. "Okay, is anyone from your family here?"

"You said only one more question, that's two," Gabriel joked, but he answered anyway. "My little brother's here. He just finished his first year of training and is starting his second. My youngest brother is still too little for training and is at home with my parents, going to school."

Over the last few months Taylor had learned that Gabriel had an angel mother and a human father. He also had two younger brothers, David and Peter, aged fourteen and eight. Despite her many questions, he didn't give her a lot of detail about his family, but she could tell he was very close to them; he always had a misty-eyed look or a twinkle in his eyes when he spoke of them.

"Cool, so I'll get to meet David then. It'll be nice to have someone who can tell me embarrassing stories about you."

"Oh, don't worry about that," Gabriel said. "You'll get plenty of dirt from my friends. We grew up together and now most of them are soldiers in the army."

Taylor realized how cold she'd become as they'd gained altitude. Grudgingly, she nestled herself further into his wings as he landed on the circular crest of the mountain. There was a bit of snow on the peak, which measured around thirty feet across.

Trying to stay warm, she clung to him, letting him carry her across to the approximate center of the area. "Close your eyes," he said.

Taylor shut her eyes tightly and was aware from the warmth that he was resonating light by using the bright sun to create energy. When she could tell that he was back to normal, at least for an angel, she opened her eyes and saw that he'd melted away the snow where they were standing.

Hidden beneath the snow was a small metal hatch. Gabriel set her on the ground and reached down, opening the portal. Steep metal stairs descended. Taylor expected to see only darkness in the hole, but instead she discerned a soft glow and felt a blast of warmth from the opening. Despite the fate that lay inside, she had a strong urge to move into the light.

Grasping her hand, Gabriel began the descent. After only twenty steps they reached a large landing, from which the light originated. Overhead were panels that emanated light from within. The light created a heat that Taylor swore felt like a cozy fireplace in a log cabin.

On one wall was a row of elevators, each with a different marking on them. The symbols reminded her of hieroglyphics. "What do they mean?" she asked.

"They're locations," Gabriel explained. "Each elevator takes you to a different place within central command. They have a unique security system built into them to prevent unwanted visitors from descending into the caverns." He pressed his index finger to the metal surface of one of the elevators. From the exact point where he touched the door, an orangey-yellowish light began to form as if the metal had been superheated. The light then radiated in concentric circles until the entire door was pulsating with heat. Gabriel pulled his finger away from the door and it opened.

"The doors only respond to the touch of an angel," Gabriel explained.

They went inside. The compartment was the size of a standard elevator, but very different in appearance. Every surface shimmered with white light, including the floors and ceilings. When the doors closed they sealed so perfectly that it appeared as if they'd never been open. If Taylor had closed her eyes and spun herself around a few times, she wouldn't have been able to tell which wall contained the doors. *Or maybe they all did*, she thought.

There were no buttons anywhere and Gabriel didn't seem too concerned with where it would take them; there seemed to be only one possible destination. At first she wasn't sure if they were even moving, but then she felt her stomach drop, evidence that they were descending rather rapidly. The movement was noiseless; the elevators seemed to be well-maintained.

The drop ended and her body weight was forced backwards slightly, as if they were moving forwards now, like in a car. "Are we...?" she started to ask.

"Yes," Gabriel replied, guessing her question. "We're now moving forward and still partially down, kind of diagonally. The transporters move in all different directions so they can reach all parts of the facility."

The elevator dropped again and then seemed to curve forward, like going down a quarter-pipe at a skate park. Their movement flattened out and then ceased altogether. Taylor waited for the wall in front of her to open. Gabriel motioned towards the one to her right and, as if on his command, it opened from bottom to top, like the door on a Ferrari.

Gabriel stepped out with Taylor gripping his hand and following from behind. Opening in front of them was the most expansive cavern Taylor had ever seen. Growing up, her father had taken her caving a few times and they had seen some magnificent caverns, complete with stalactites, stalagmites, and bats, but none of them came close to what she was seeing now.

The space had to be ten times the size of the football stadium at UT. In a normal cavern it would be difficult to take in the full breadth of the cave with only small helmet lights and flashlights to provide visibility, but this grand hall was brighter than being outside on a perfectly sunny day, like the one they'd just come from.

Taylor tried to look around to take in all of the different types of light sources, but saw immediately that there had to be thousands of them. She'd need at least a week to catalogue them all.

Farther into the "room" she could see hundreds of glowing figures in various groups. There were flashes of light intermittently from each of the groups. Some were flying, others running, and some watching. Taylor knew she was watching angel training.

"Do you know why I brought you here first?" Gabriel asked.

"Because your brother is here," Taylor replied.

Gabriel nodded and motioned towards a bright figure that'd broken off from one of the groups. The boy leapt high in the air, his wings spreading effortlessly, and raced towards them. Taylor backed away as he got closer and closer without slowing down, on a collision course with them.

Gabriel stepped in front of her protectively. At the last possible second, the white figure stopped in midflight and dropped directly in front of them, putting one hand on the ground and landing in a crouch.

Gabriel released Taylor's hand, and without a word, embraced the boy, hugging him hard. From behind them, Taylor wasn't able to see the boy's face because Gabriel's body eclipsed it.

Gabriel spoke as he released his brother from his arms. "It's good to see you, David."

"Aw, don't get all mushy on me, Gabriel," David whined. Taylor could see past his façade. He was trying to act cool, but in his voice he sounded pleased that his brother was back. "So, is this the girl?"

"This," Gabriel said, sweeping his hand in a dramatic gesture, "is Taylor."

The boy stepped around him and Taylor's eyes lit up in awe. The boy was the spitting image of his older brother. David was somewhat shorter than Gabriel, having not hit his growth spurt yet, and every part of him was smaller, but his features were nearly identical, as if they were twins that just happened to be born years apart.

"It's very nice to finally meet you, David. Gabriel has talked so much about you," Taylor said.

The fourteen-year-old beamed proudly. "Nice to meet you, too. Yeah, I taught him everything he knows," he joked.

"I wouldn't go that far," Gabriel said, "but I was very impressed by your pinpoint stop in midflight just then. I remember the last time you tried that, you just about flew straight through me."

"Aw, bro, that was ages ago. I mastered it in Year One of training. They used to wait until Year Two to teach flying skills, but our class of angels was so talented they decided to teach us some advanced skills."

Taylor continued to stare at David, marveling at his resemblance to her boyfriend. Interrupting the brothers' conversation she said, "You look so much like your brother, David."

"Yeah, sadly it's a curse I'll just have to live with," David joked.

Taylor laughed and said, "Yeah, true. Gabriel is a bit awkward looking. But I bet you still have girls lining up for you."

David blushed at the compliment and looked down at the floor. "Well, uh, there's this one angel back home that thinks I'm kind of cute."

Taylor could tell that Gabriel was trying to contain his laughter at Taylor putting his little brother on the spot. Coming to his rescue, Gabriel said, "So, D, how's Year Two treating you so far?"

David quickly regained his composure at the chance to show off. "Fantastic. I'm the lead angel in most of my courses: Flying II, Hand to Hand Combat, Light Effects, and Fire Defense." He counted them off on his fingers. "The only one I'm not the lead in is Spy Games."

"Yeah, I struggled with that one as well," Gabriel admitted.

"What do you do in Spy Games?" Taylor asked.

David replied, "It's all about sneaking around, reducing your inner light so you can move undetected, living amongst humans, that sort of thing."

Taylor laughed. "That explains why I could immediately tell that Gabriel wasn't a human."

"Really, Gabriel? She knew you were an angel?"

"Because of her exceptionally strong aura, she could see my inner light, but she didn't know what I was," Gabriel said.

"So it's all true then," David said. "She is *the one*."

Taylor rolled her eyes and said, "Look, David. I'm not the chosen one you guys keep talking about. I'm just a human girl who happens to be able to help out your kind. I'm nothing special."

"Except that our people have been talking about you for decades, and even from across the training center I couldn't tell that you were human, because your aura was shining so brightly," David replied.

Taylor didn't know what to say or think. *The angels had been talking about her for decades!* When nothing came to mind, she just shrugged.

David's eyes squinted as he focused on something behind Taylor. When she turned to see what he was looking at, he said, "Is that a tattoo of *the* snake?"

Gabriel said, "Yeah, but she got it before she even knew exactly what the snake was a symbol of."

"Wow!" David said. "Wicked."

Before either of the angels had a chance to say another word, a third angel flashed up the ramp to them, moving at angel speed, only a blur of light giving away the movement.

"Heyyyy, Gabriel! How are ya, buddy?" the angel said, screeching to a halt beside the group. He was shorter than Gabriel, but looked as sturdy as a tank. His hair was fully white and curled up slightly at the front.

Gabriel was all smiles. He reached out his hand and clasped it with the newcomer's, pulling him towards him in a manly embrace. "I'm good, Sampson, how are you?"

Sampson replied, "Not bad, man, I'm teaching a couple of training courses in between strategic attacks on the demons' outer defenses. I heard you found yourself a wifey, is this her?"

Gabriel ignored his friend's jab. "Taylor, meet Sampson. Unfortunately, he's been my friend since I was three."

Taylor replied sweetly, "Nice to meet you, Sampson, but for your information, I'm no one's wifey."

Sampson threw his hands up innocently. "Whoa, no harm intended." Turning to Gabe, he said, "I like her, man. She's got spunk. And geez, she is cute, cute, cute."

Taylor laughed. "Are all angels so forward?" she asked.

Sampson said, "No, mostly just me. I always say that if you've got something to say then just say it. There are too many angels around here who are sweet as pie to your face and then talk nasty behind your back. Better to keep everything out in the open I say."

"I'm glad you haven't changed a bit, Sampson." Gabriel laughed. "I'm about to take Taylor to the command center to meet the generals and the commander. You guys want to come along?" he asked, motioning to David and Sampson.

David's eyes lit up. "Can I really, Gabriel?"

"Sure, bro, today I've got a VIP pass wherever I want to go and can bring whoever I want to bring. You in, Sampson?"

"Sure, let's do it. Plus, you might need back up when we get to the command center and Cassandra sees you with Taylor."

Gabriel made a face.

"Who's Cassandra?" Taylor asked.

Gabriel hesitated a beat too long. Sampson jumped in. "She's Gabriel's ex-girlfriend who still has a massive crush on him. Just a warning, she's not going to like you."

"She was not my girlfriend, Sampson. Taylor, it wasn't like that at all."

"So you had a thing with her, I don't give a crap," Taylor said. "As long as it's in the past."

Gabriel continued to deny it. "There was no *thing*. We were just friends and then she wanted to be more than

265

that, it got weird, and I told her we couldn't hang out anymore. She refuses to let it go and is constantly trying to find ways back into my life."

"Okay, no need to get defensive, I believe you," Taylor said.

"What kind of drugs has this joker been feeding you, Taylor?" Sampson said as he landed a light punch on his friend's ribcage. "I wouldn't trust a word that comes out of his mouth."

"I've already found that out," Taylor said dryly, remembering sharply why she was here. Amidst all the relative normalcy of meeting David and Sampson, Taylor had almost forgotten her anger at her angel boyfriend.

Gabriel lunged playfully at his friend, hitting him back and starting a lighthearted angel fight. Before long, Gabriel had his friend pinned to the floor, his superior speed and strength serving him well.

"Say it, Sampson," Gabriel instructed, pushing his entire body weight onto Sampson's chest.

"Alright, alright, I can hardly breathe." Gabriel released a bit of pressure and Sampson said sarcastically, "You can trust everything Gabriel says, he is the coolest, most perfect angel in the world."

"Damn right I am," Gabriel said, releasing his friend. "Now let's head to central."

Forty-Five

It was Wednesday night and Christopher was getting worried. He hadn't seen Gabriel or Taylor all day and wasn't able to reach Sam on her cell phone. With Jonas controlling the operation there were a million things that could've gone wrong.

At six o'clock his phone finally rang. It was Sam.

"Hey, babe," she said.

"Hey, how was your day?" Chris asked casually.

"It was a killer. I had three exams and a pop quiz. Sorry that I had to turn off my phone, but I really needed to study in between classes. I saw you called a few times, is anything the matter?"

"I'm not sure. I'm just getting a bit worried that I haven't seen Gabriel or Taylor today and they were supposed to meet me for lunch. And they aren't answering their phones either."

"Oh, sorry, Chris. No need to worry, I know where they are. I was a bit surprised about it, because it was so unlike Taylor."

"What was unlike Taylor?" Chris asked.

"Skipping a couple of weeks of classes to take a random vacation. I mean, we're getting close to the end of the semester, but she said she'd e-mail me her assignments and asked if I'd hand them in."

"She went on vacation? You talked to her?" Chris's heart sank. He'd been duped by the angel.

"Yes and not exactly. She apparently snuck out this morning. There was a note on my desk that said she decided to take a long trip with Gabriel to the Bahamas. She said something about him having airline miles that were going to expire and the trip would be free."

"Did she say where they'd be staying?" Chris asked.

"Hmm, no, she didn't. But I just figured if I needed her I could call her on her cell or e-mail her. Why all the questions, Chris? As long as she's with Gabriel she'll be fine."

Christopher had been thinking about his secret life a lot lately, as his relationship with Sam had grown stronger and stronger. Regardless of whether Gabriel or Taylor agreed with him, it was as much his decision to make as theirs.

Now was the right time. "There's something I need to tell you," he said grimly.

"What is it, Chris?"

"I should do it in person. Can I come to your room?"

"Sure. But, Chris?"

"Yeah?"

"Should I be worried?"

"No, no, don't worry. There are just a few things you don't know about me that I really want you to know."

"Okay, see you soon."

Chris pressed END and immediately called Jonas's phone. He picked up on the first ring.

"What the hell is going on?" Jonas asked angrily.

"I was hoping you could tell me," Chris replied.

"I don't freakin' know, man. My scouts haven't caught a whiff of that pigeon or the girl all day."

"So you had nothing to do with their disappearance?" Chris asked, probing for information.

"Well...," Jonas started.

"What is it? If you did something, you need to tell me or the entire operation could be compromised!"

"I kinda tried to scare the girl to make sure she'd cooperate. I guess it didn't really work."

"What did you do?" Chris said accusingly.

"Nothing much, I just brought Freddy along to freak the girl out and then the bird man swooped in and saved the day, but look, I never thought it'd cause them to skip town."

"You did what? Are you out of your mind? What did you think they were going to do, bow down and worship you? Wait until the Elders hear about this one."

Jonas's voice quivered on the other line, all toughness shattered by Chris's threat. "You're not going to tell them are you?"

"Oh yes I am. I want them to know that the moron they sent to spy on my operation screwed it all up when I had things perfectly under control." Chris spat out the last few words, his voice laced with contempt.

"What do we do next?" Jonas asked.

"*We* don't do anything. *You* will go back to the front lines with your cronies and tell the Elders what happened. And don't even think about lying, because when I show up I'm going to tell them *everything*. It's crucial that you get there as quickly as possible because the attack could come any day now. I have something to take care of here and then I'll catch up with you. Remember, no lies." Chris hung up without waiting for another word from the goon.

He'd been jogging while he was talking, moving at demon speed whenever he was out of sight of any humans. Now he approached Shyloh Hall. Not wanting to call Sam to let him in, he took a peek around, and seeing no one, scaled the wall like a spider and crept onto the fifth floor through an open stairwell window. He could've just teleported in, but was afraid of appearing somewhere that someone would see him.

Seconds later he knocked on Sam's door. The door was thrust open; Sam's face was riddled with concern.

Christopher wanted to put her at ease so he said, "Everything's fine, Sam, I promise." Then he took her chin in his hand and kissed her passionately.

After their embrace, she pulled back from him, studying his face. "Okay, I guess that rules out the possibility of you breaking up with me," she said, seeming relieved.

"What?" Chris said, shocked at the thought. "Of course not, Sam. Is that what you thought? I'm so sorry, I didn't mean to give you that impression. I mean, what I have to tell you is very important, but I really care about you and will stick with you as long as you'll have me."

Sam put her arms around him and pulled him close. "Thanks for saying that, Chris. I've never been with anyone that cared about me this much."

He hugged her back and then closed the door. They sat down on her bed. In a rare display of restraint, Sam waited patiently for him to speak.

Christopher had given this a lot of thought and decided on complete honesty, but wanted to ease her into the idea that demons could be good. He knew that everything that'd ever been instilled in her, from church, to her parents, to movies like *The Exorcist*, would give her the instinct to push him away and not believe him. He needed to back his way into it.

"I have certain powers," he said, waiting for a reaction.

Sam stared at him, waiting for the punch line. When it didn't come, she said, "Well, you are a damn good kisser."

Chris smiled. "Thanks for that, but I'm talking like superhuman."

Sam didn't know what to say to that and stopped a handful of jokes from tumbling off her lips. Instead, all she said was, "Like…what?"

Chris sat up straighter. "I can make things darker. Some of it I can control and other things I can't. For example, have you ever noticed that I look darker than most people from far away or that a room gets slightly darker when I enter it?"

Sam laughed. "I had noticed it, but I just thought it was just part of your mystery, your allure. I kind of like it."

"I'm glad you do, but it's not something I can control. What I can control is how strong the darkness is around me. If I show you, will you promise not to freak out?"

Sam wanted to laugh again, but decided against it because the look on Chris's face was so deadly serious. "Uh, sure, no problem."

Chris closed his eyes as if concentrating hard, and then a veil of darkness swept over him, partially obscuring him from her sight, even though she was sitting right next to him. Astonished, Sam reached through the veil to feel that he was still there. She felt his arms, his chest, his face.

"How'd you do that?" she asked, her hand pulling away sharply, as if she'd been burned.

The fog lifted and she could see him again. Chris smiled. "It's a gift. It's part of who I am, just like your ability to make people laugh in a tense situation. That's just the first one though, I have many powers, but maybe I should tell you more about how I have these powers first."

"No," Sam countered, her brow furrowed into a mess of unnatural wrinkles, "first show me another power."

"Okay, hold my hand," he instructed, reaching for her.

She hesitated, but only briefly, before grabbing his hand tightly. Her vision instantly went dark, although her eyes were still open. She cried out. And then she could see again. She looked at Chris. They were still holding hands, but something was different. She couldn't quite put her finger on what.

"What was that?" Sam asked.

"Look where we're sitting."

Samantha glanced to her right and her left and then down before it finally dawned on her. They were sitting on a bed with a *blue* comforter. *Taylor's bed.* She was sure they'd been sitting on her own bed. They always sat on her bed when he came over. Even though she'd lost vision for a moment, she was certain she didn't feel any motion or him grabbing her to carry her to the other bed.

"How'd you do that?" she said, releasing his hand and backing away.

Chris smiled. "What does it feel like?"

Uh, magic, witchcraft, hallucinogenic drugs... The answer hit her. "Did we just.............*teleport?*" She felt nerdier just saying the word.

Chris was grinning. "Yes. Whaddya think?"

Sam's head was spinning. Her boyfriend had powers? What was she supposed to think?

She stood up, moved clear of Chris, eyed the door. Her only way out. "Honestly, I'm a little freaked out. Okay, a lot freaked out. I think I should go now."

"Please, Sam," Chris said. "Let me explain. Plus, it's your room, so if anyone should go, it should be me. Just say the word."

Sam stared at him. There was no violence in his dark eyes, no danger. He was just the same old Chris. Sweet and beautiful, inside and out. But what about the powers? What he could do, it wasn't natural. "You have five minutes and then I want you out of here." The words tasted bitter on her tongue.

"Have a seat," Chris said, motioning across from him.

"I'll stand."

Chris shrugged. "Okay. "Let me give you a little background that might help you understand. The first thing you should know is that Gabriel has powers, too, and Taylor already knows all about them."

Sam's eyes widened. "Gabriel can teleport too and Taylor knows about it?" Impossible, she would've told her.

"Well no, Gabriel mostly has different powers than mine and so he can't teleport, but he can fly. So when Taylor's note said he has frequent flyer miles, Taylor really just meant that he was going to fly her wherever they went. But yes, she knows all about his powers. And mine too," he added.

Her legs feeling wobbly, Sam sat down on her bed, leaning forward on her toes in case she needed to make a break for it. She said, "None of this makes sense. So Taylor knows you can teleport?"

"Absolutely. I've teleported her and Gabriel once before."

Sam's frown deepened. She was going to need a good moisturizer to prevent the wrinkles that this conversation would surely leave her with. "Why'd you tell Taylor before me?"

"A fair question. People like me and Gabriel like to keep our abilities a secret from humans because people don't understand us sometimes. Well any of the time, really. But Gabriel insisted on telling Taylor about what he can do and he told her about me at the same time."

Sam's head was swimming as each piece of information led to ten other questions. "What do you mean, 'a secret from *humans*'?" she quoted. "Are you saying you're not human?"

"I think it's time I told you a story." Chris checked his watch. *Eight o'clock.* "This could take a while so I hope you're not too tired."

"I'll be fine."

Chris proceeded to tell Samantha the history of angels and demons, hiding nothing from her. While many of the facts were the same in his story, there were a number of important details that were quite different from the story that Gabriel had told Taylor. The main difference was that Chris's story was the truth.

He watched her face carefully when he explained how and why his people were referred to as demons. She didn't seem scared or angry, so he went on to explain that his race had no relationship to the devils or demons spoken about in the Bible or Quran.

When he asked her whether him being a demon scared her, she said, "The thought scares the crap out of me, and maybe I'll freak out and have weird nightmares later, but you're one of the kindest, gentlest people I know, so if you're a demon then I wish I knew more demons."

Chris's heart soared. Elated, he continued with his story. After he'd finished telling her the history of both angels and demons, he recounted everything that'd happened since they arrived at school. He left nothing out, including why Taylor had become involved.

Sam's face had turned white with shock upon hearing about her friend's extra-strong aura and that the angels wanted to use her against the demons. When he finished by telling her about the gargoyle attack and why Gabriel and Taylor had suddenly left, Sam's astonishment turned to worry.

"If they didn't go to the Caribbean, where do you think they went?" she asked.

"I'm scared he may have taken her to the angels' headquarters, near the battleground. The Archangel Council wants to use her to fight against the demons."

"But why would Taylor agree to help the angels destroy the demons?" Sam asked.

"I'm not sure she knows what she's doing. It's not her fault," Chris said. "Gabriel hasn't been fully honest with her. He was sent on a mission to attract her to their cause and get her to cooperate."

"So he doesn't really care about her?" Sam asked.

"I think he really did fall for her, but he's really confused now. He's trying to protect her the best way he can. If he didn't bring her in, the Archangel Council would've hunted her down and taken her by force. Or the demons would've gotten to her first."

"What would the demons have done to her?" Sam asked, accusation in her tone.

"Sam, my people are not perfect, I'm the first one to admit that. But we're not murderers. We want to co-exist with humans, while the angels want to destroy the human race. If they'd taken Taylor, they would've brought her back to the demon Lair and allowed her to live there safely. Just so you know, I think that decision would be against everything that we believe in. We need to find a way to protect Taylor *and* my people, without sacrificing Taylor's chance at a real human life."

"The demon Lair, huh? That sounds welcoming." Before Chris could respond, she looked at him seriously and asked, "Why're you telling me all of this?"

"Because I think you deserve to know and...and because I think I need your help."

Sam froze, stared unblinking into his eyes. "What can I possibly do?"

"I want you to come with me to the Lair. From there we'll devise a plan to get Taylor back once we've confirmed that she's with the angels. I think you could be important to any plan we come up with because we'll need someone there that she trusts to convince her to abandon the angel cause."

Sam stood up, marched towards the door, and for a moment, Chris thought she'd had enough and was going to leave. But she stopped, raised a hand to her forehead, massaging it gently. "What a headache," she said. "Could any of this be real?"

"It's all real, Sam, I swear." All Chris had left in his arsenal was getting on his knees and pleading with her.

"Seems like something out of a sci-fi movie—and not a good one," she said.

Chris sat in silence, never taking his eyes off the back of Sam's head. She turned, a grimace on her face, as if she'd just been punched. "I can't believe I'm saying this, but I'll come with you. When do we leave?"

Chris felt a lightness in his chest. He didn't know what would come of all this, but at least she hadn't left. "Immediately," he said.

Forty-Six

In the Lair, it looked like the floor of the New York Stock Exchange. Demons were running about everywhere, making preparations to defend their strongholds. Jonas had arrived shortly before and had, to his credit, laid it all out on the line, so to speak.

He'd told the Elders everything, including his blunders, bad decisions, and misuse of the authority granted to him. The Elders were harsh in their rebuke, but in the end they gave him credit for his honesty. Then they sounded the alarm.

This was not a drill and everyone knew it. The rule in this situation was to get where you were instructed to be as quickly as possible. While no one, other than Jonas and the Elders, knew for sure why the alarm had been sounded, there were rumors flying around already. People were saying that the angels had a new weapon, like nothing they'd ever seen before, and that they were planning to use it very soon. One of Jonas's goons had probably leaked the information.

The demons wouldn't go down without a fight.

Forty-Seven

Samantha packed lightly, but still managed to scrunch three or four changes of clothes into her overnight bag. When she asked Chris how long the trip would be, he said, "A couple of seconds, we'll teleport."

She cringed, still trying to come to terms with the fact that her boyfriend was a demon with incredible powers.

"Are you ready?" Chris asked.

Ummm, no? Never. Maybe. "I think so," Sam said instead, trying to block out her run-for-the-hills instincts.

She held Chris's hand, but then released it. "Wait, wait...I forgot my toothbrush!"

"You're about to go on what'll likely be the most thrilling adventure of your life and you're worried about your teeth?"

She stood up, putting her hands on her hips. "Christopher Lyon, above all I'm still a human and I'll not be getting cavities while on this little excursion of yours, regardless of whether it's a 'great adventure' or not." She made quote marks with her fingers. She sighed. "Sorry, I'm just a little flustered. It's all a lot to take in, and in the back of my head I'm still hoping you're all just playing a particularly elaborate prank."

"It's okay," Chris said, raising a hand to touch her face. She felt warmth on her cheek. "I wish it were a prank, but this is real."

She touched his hand and then pulled it away, sighing again. As she grabbed her toothbrush, she said, "Do demons even have to brush their teeth?"

Chris chuckled. "I brush my teeth and even floss sometimes. I also eat, shower and sleep, too."

Sam was happy they could both laugh a little before leaving for the unknown. She tried to remember that she was doing it for Taylor, which made her less scared and more determined. With all the essentials packed, she said, "Okay, now I'm ready."

Chris concentrated and then she experienced the same temporary blindness as before, but this time, she felt a pulling motion as well, like her body and mind were twisting in tandem. The sensation was longer than before, but only by a few seconds.

She could tell that her vision was restored, as the absolute darkness became a murky black, but she still couldn't see. Chris said, "Sorry about that, I didn't have time to tell the command center that we'd be arriving, and it seems that unlike Motel 6, they *did* not leave the lights on for us."

Sam groaned at the bad joke and then asked, "Where are we anyway?" With the question came a sinking feeling in her stomach at the certainty that there was zero chance she was being pranked.

"The teleport room in the Lair. All teleporting is controlled through this room to prevent the chaos there'd be if demons were appearing and disappearing constantly throughout the facility."

Sam was still clutching his hand, afraid of getting lost in the dark. She squeezed harder. "Oww!" Chris said.

"Oops! Sorry, Chris, I didn't realize I was squeezing that hard."

"It didn't really hurt, I was just messing with you." Sam could feel him massaging his sore hand in the dark.

"Didn't hurt, huh?" she said, grabbing his hands to show him she wasn't fooled.

"Well, maybe a little."

"That's what I thought. So, how do we get the lights on?"

"If I show you another demon power, do you promise not to freak out?"

Sam rolled her eyes in the dark. "Seriously, Chris? You just teleported me who knows how far and I didn't freak out, so I think we're past all that."

"More than three thousand miles," he said.

"What?" Sam asked, confused.

"That's how far I teleported you, more than three thousand miles."

She gasped. "Wow, really? That's amazing! And you said Gabriel had to fly Taylor here?"

"Yep, it would've taken them at least seven hours, so even though they probably had more than twelve hours head start they'd have only arrived a couple of hours before us. Aren't you glad your boyfriend's powers are way cooler?"

Even with her world spiraling out of control, she couldn't stop joking. "Hmm, I don't know, being able to fly is pretty sexy. It's got that whole Superman vibe, and he was a total stud."

Bright flames suddenly leapt up in front of her face, blazing with heat. Sam jumped back, ready to stop, drop, and roll if her clothes caught fire. The fire dwindled down to a small flame. It looked like Chris was holding the fire in his hand. She crept closer to him again, peering into his palm. The fire was literally coming out of his skin, as if he was a human lighter. *Well, not exactly human*, she thought.

Chris grinned. "Can Superman do that?"

Sam smiled back at him, admiring her boyfriend. This couldn't be happening. Could it? "No," she murmured. "Why doesn't your skin burn?"

"I have no idea, but it's cool, isn't it? I can make my entire body into a torch if I want to, but all of my clothes would burn away."

A seductive smile crossed Samantha's face. "Ooh, I want to play that game," she said, the words melting off her lips. She knew her flirting was perhaps a bit misplaced for the situation, but being herself was the only way she could cope with everything that was happening.

"Later, baby," Chris said slyly. "Right now we need to find the Elders and figure out a plan."

He grabbed her right hand with his left, while using his right hand as a torch, the fire increasing until they were able to see the entire room. It was a rather small room and they were standing directly in the center of it.

Chris pulled her towards the outline of a small door in the corner. There was no handle. He raised his flaming hand towards the door and touched it. Upon contact with the flames, the door swung open, moving outwards. They stepped into a hall and Chris closed his right hand, instantly smothering the fire in his palm.

Torches lined the walls, burning brightly and lighting the way. He led her in silence down a short path to another door, this one much bigger. Again, no handle. Sam expected him to perform the same trick with his fiery door opener, but instead he reached down and pressed a button she hadn't seen on the wall.

A voice spoke from the wall. "State your name."

Chris spoke confidently. "Christopher Lyon. The Elders will want to see me immediately."

Without another word, the stone door rotated open from the center, creating two smaller openings on each side. They entered through the gap on the left. The next room was much larger, with many doors lining the walls. One of them stood open.

Chris explained, "The security team opened the door we need to travel to the Elders' Chamber. It's just a short trip from here."

"Good, because I'm really tired after a *long* day of travelling and could really use a latte and a bubble bath right now," Sam joked.

Chris gave her a wry smile. "Teleporting's the only way to travel. However, I *will* show you to your room after this meeting's over, so that bubble bath may be a possibility after all."

"Only if you join me," she said flirtatiously, once more cringing inwardly at how misplaced her banter was. *Why can't you be serious?* she asked herself. *Because I've been teleported by a demon into a mountain to save my best friend who's been brainwashed by an angel into fighting in a crazy supernatural war*, she answered herself. Good point.

Chris's eyes were misty. His confidence was gone. He seemed…exposed, naked, like she could see into his soul.

"Sam," he started. She looked at him expectantly. "I...I," Chris stammered, unable to get the words out.

"You've never felt this way before," she finished for him.

"Exactly, how did you know?"

"Because I've never felt this way either, Chris," she stated matter-of-factly. "Whether you're a demon or now. Now let's go get that latte." She headed for the open door, pulling him behind her this time.

She led him through the door and into a pod-like vehicle that looked like something from *Star Wars*. Not knowing what to do next, she waited for him to operate the machine.

"This will take us to the Elders," Chris said, breaking the brief silence.

The doors closed automatically and the pod accelerated through the tunnel. The vehicle was glass on all sides, allowing passengers to appreciate the thrill of its speed, as it twisted, turned, dipped, and dove through the rocky passage.

Soon after it started moving, Chris sat on the large seating platform at the end of the capsule. He tugged Sam onto his lap, and said, "Hang on!" He held her tightly. She twisted her head backwards and kissed him deeply on the lips, lingering for as long as she could before the motion of the ride forced her to turn back around. *I'm kissing a demon*, she thought devilishly.

In minutes, the transporter began to slow down, eventually coming to a stop at their destination. The door opened and Chris released Sam from his embrace. They stood and exited into a beautiful foyer.

Sam's breath was taken away by the room and the contrast to the dimly-lit, rocky rooms and tunnels from which they'd come. The walls and floor were shiny marble and large pillars rose like sentries along the sides. Fireplaces were cut into the bottoms of the walls in at least ten places, each with warm healthy fires burning, sending wisps of smoke up chimneys that disappeared into the ceiling.

Sam's first thought was that the room would be a nice place to curl up and read a book, but she noticed that there was nowhere to sit except for a desk in the far corner. At the desk sat a dark man, patiently waiting for the visitors to approach him. When they neared him, he said, "Hello, Christopher. The Elders are waiting for you, but they were not expecting you to bring company." He looked curiously at the strange girl before him. Sam wondered if he could tell she was human.

Chris replied with authority. "She's critical to our current situation. I'll take responsibility for any consequences of bringing her here."

The demon stared at Samantha, probably wondering what use a human could possibly have to the Elders. He shrugged his shoulders. "As you wish." He picked up the phone and said, "Sir, Mr. Lyon has arrived, I'm sending him in." As he hung up the phone, the oval door next to his desk opened from the center, both doors swinging away from them, like flower petals opening in the Spring.

Chris had dropped Sam's hand when they left the transporter. They now walked through the door side by side, but separate, the gulf between them feeling like eternity. Chris whispered, "Let me do the talking," as they entered the room. Sam took a deep breath when she saw the many old and wise-looking faces staring at her, regarding her with interest. She steeled herself, determined not to look nervous or scared.

Oddly enough, she observed, many of the faces were smiling at her, their kind eyes welcoming her to the assembly. During the history lesson, Chris had explained to her that 'the demon Elders were comprised of any demon over the age of forty, unlike the Archangel Council, which had only an elite group of twelve.

The demons were sitting on benches in a U-shape, the way you might expect an English Parliament from the 1800s to look. The benches rose five levels high on each side. Sam quickly estimated that there were ten demons on each bench so there were approximately one hundred and fifty Elders surrounding them as they walked into the center, towards a podium.

At the stand was a particularly old demon, whose bushy eyebrows were raised in amusement at the sight of Samantha. His dark beard was short and well-trimmed— had his facial hair been longer and if he wore a pointy hat he could've easily passed for the wizard Merlin or perhaps Gandalf the Grey from *The Lord of the Rings*.

"Good day, my dear," he said, speaking slowly only to Sam. "I'm Clifford Dempsey, the head of the Eldership of the demons."

Ignoring Chris's command to let him handle things, Sam replied smartly, "And I'm Samantha Collins, head cheerleader at Savannah High School and now attending the University of Trinton with your little worker bee here, Christopher. We've been dating since the beginning of the semester."

Sam could tell that Christopher had frozen when she spoke. Maybe she'd gone a little too far.

But to her surprise, Clifford looked amused by her introduction. "Nice to meet you, my dear. Why have you...," he started to say.

Samantha suddenly remembered why the name Clifford sounded so familiar. Interrupting, she said, "You said your name is Clifford? Are you the first demon? But Christopher said it all began more than a century ago?"

"Ah, my dear, so you've had a full history lesson. I know what you're thinking, but unfortunately demons don't age at a slower rate than humans. Clifford was my great grandfather and I was blessed with the same name by my mother. Now, as I was saying, why have you come with Christopher?"

Sam hadn't expected such a question to be directed at her, but because it had, she felt obligated to answer it. So far, Chris hadn't said a word. "I want to help my friend, Taylor Kingston. Oh, and the demons, too, I guess, by default," she added.

"A noble cause," Clifford murmured. Finally he turned to Chris. "And, Mr. Lyon, why do you feel Miss Collins can be of assistance to us?"

Finally opening his mouth, Chris replied, "Taylor's the girl that we've talked about in our legends. For the angels she's the ultimate weapon and can be used to destroy us all. Gabriel Knight, the angel, has brainwashed her into thinking we're the true enemy and she's fallen into their hands. I fear she may already be here, at the front lines."

He continued, his eyes scanning the faces on the benches as he spoke. There was something attractive about the way he commanded the attention of the audience. "We're going to need someone that Taylor trusts—to help us convince her that she's been deceived. Samantha's been Taylor's best friend most of her life and she'll trust her above all others, even Gabriel. In short, I believe Samantha's our only hope."

The head of the Elders stroked his gray beard thoughtfully. He seemed to be considering Christopher's words. "I agree with you, but first we must figure out how to get close enough to Taylor to allow Samantha to talk to her."

Forty-Eight

The group made their way to central command. As they travelled, many angels wanted to stop to talk to Gabriel, saying things like, "Gabriel, long time no see, how are you?" or "Hey, Gabriel, who's the girl?" Many of the angels were females and Taylor didn't like the way they looked at her boyfriend. First, they were all stunningly beautiful, making her look even more ordinary than usual. Second, he didn't shut them down the way she'd hoped. His responses were typically, "Later, Rose, we're in a hurry," or "We'll catch up soon, Sandra, gotta run."

Taylor did *not* want Gabriel "catching up" with any of these beautiful women. She was relieved when they finally reached their destination. The only one with clearance, Gabriel punched in a code on the door and it opened, twisting like a pinwheel from the center. Looking inside, Taylor could see a bustle of activity, as angels diagrammed attack strategies on whiteboards, looked at security feeds, and shouted orders into headsets. She tried to pick out which one was the mysterious Cassandra, but she didn't see anyone that might fit the part.

When they entered the room, the flurry of motion, as well as all conversation, stopped abruptly. Then she saw her. Initially her back was to them, but then, with a whirl of perfectly smooth blond hair, she turned, and with her perfectly blue eyes, gazed upon them from across the room. She smiled a perfectly white smile and walked to meet them with perfectly graceful strides. *Crap*, Taylor thought. *I don't stand a chance.*

"Welcome back, Gabriel," Cassandra said, kissing him on the cheek and generally ignoring Taylor's presence.

"Cassandra," Gabriel said coldly, turning his cheek away from her.

He put his arm around Taylor and pulled her close to him. "This is my girlfriend, Taylor. Taylor, meet Cassandra."

Despite how angry she was with Gabriel for all his lies, it still felt good to be the object of his affections in the presence of the goddess standing before her. She said, "It's nice to meet you. Gabriel has told me what a good *friend* you've always been to him."

"Oh, how nice," Cassandra sneered, "you've found yourself a human pet." She looked Taylor up and down, inspecting her ripped jeans, tattoo, and punkish styling. "And how lovely she is…"

"Get over yourself, Cass. Taylor has more power within her than you could ever hope to have. Now step aside, we need to see the Council," Gabriel ordered.

Clearly outranked, she turned sideways to let them pass. Her angry eyes never left Taylor's, but Taylor stared right back at her without blinking, determined to maintain the upper hand that she'd gained when Gabriel defended her. For the moment, she even considered forgiving Gabriel for his second round of lies, just to spite Cassandra by keeping him off the market.

The other angels in the room had watched the exchange with interest, but now, seeing that the action had ended, went back to their planning and strategizing. When they reached the far end of the command center, Sampson said, "Man, you really handled her. It was fun to see someone put her in her place for once."

Gabriel smirked and said, "She's a stuck-up, obnoxious little know-it-all, and I'm sick of her crap. Don't listen to her, Taylor, everyone else here realizes that you're special."

Yeah, special enough to lie to, Taylor thought, but she kept her thoughts to herself. "If you say so," is all she said.

Gabriel said, "This is the War Room, where the key strategic decisions are typically made. Usually it's used by only the generals and the commander, and the Council participates by video conference, but this time the full Council's here in person."

"This is awesome, Gabriel, thanks for bringing me," said David, in awe of the command center.

"No problem, bro, but unfortunately, only Taylor and I will be able to meet with the Council. However, under my authority you guys can stay in the command center and observe for as long as you want."

"Cool, thanks!" David said enthusiastically. "My friends are never going to believe this!"

"Good luck, man," Sampson said, giving him another man-hug.

"Thanks, we'll see you all later." He pressed his glowing finger to the door and it opened for him. Taylor took a deep breath.

They moved past the door and it closed automatically the instant they were inside. Now they were in a tiny intermediate room, separating the command center from the War Room. Gabriel strode confidently to the next door and repeated the finger trick. It opened with his touch.

Walking into the next room, Taylor ignored the thirty-four eyes that watched her from the long table. Gabriel pulled out one of the two remaining chairs for her to sit in and then pushed her closer to the table. He sat in the last open seat.

Gabriel spoke first: "Dionysus, Councilmembers, meet Taylor Kingston, the girl whose arrival I'm sure you have all been anxiously awaiting."

The angel at the head of the table rose from his seat and the other sixteen angels followed his lead. He began clapping and soon the other angels joined him, a full applause to welcome the lady of the hour and the angel who'd escorted her. Taylor was speechless—it wasn't the reception she'd expected from the very angels that hoped to use her in a war.

Dionysus walked around the table. Taylor stood as he approached her. He took her hand and kissed it gently. "I'm Dionysus, the Head of the Archangel Council," he said. "We are forever in your debt for your willingness to help us."

Taylor felt awkward. Not only was she not willing, but she didn't know how to address him, so she said, "Thank you, your majesty."

There were a couple of snickers around the table at her use of a pronoun typically reserved for royalty. She glared at the offenders, who seemed taken aback by her boldness.

"You can call me Dionysus, for I'm not royalty. The Council is a democracy that, by necessity, needs a head to ensure protocols are followed."

"Thank you, Dionysus," Taylor said, correcting herself.

As Dionysus walked back to the head and sat down, Taylor scanned the room. Sitting at the table were some of the most stunning people she'd ever seen. Any one of them could be photographed and placed on the cover of national magazines and look completely natural. There were five women and eleven men.

Upon sitting, Dionysus folded his hands and placed them on the table in front of him. "Now, gentlemen and ladies, we have some work to do. Thanks to Taylor, we now have the ability to finally win the Great War and defeat the greatest enemy that mankind has ever seen, the demon army. Commander Lewis, have you come up with a proposed strategy?" When Dionysus said *demon*, Taylor could only think of Chris. She couldn't be the one responsible for his death. She'd never be able to live with herself. But what could she do to stop it?

A sturdy man with short white hair and a white goatee was standing in front of the longest wall in the room. Except for his hair color, his features were remarkably young looking; Taylor guessed he was between thirty and thirty five years old. His finger glowed as he touched the wall. A large screen appeared. On the screen was what appeared to be a satellite view of the valley they'd flown over when they arrived at the mountain.

Motioning to the screen, he explained slowly for Taylor's sake. "This is the battlefield and our forces are here." He pointed to the left side of the map. "Tomorrow we have a large-scale battle scheduled with the demons. It's estimated that at least two-thirds of their forces will be exposed in the valley. The width of the battlefield is less than two miles wide, so based on the estimations we've been given, we should be able to impose mass devastation on the majority of the demon army within a few minutes. Would that be accurate, Gabriel?"

Gabriel spoke confidently. "Based on our tests," he said, looking at Taylor, "if a single angel harnesses her aura, we can, without question, vaporize anything within two miles."

Commander Lewis smiled and rubbed his hands together greedily. "This is exactly the opportunity we've been looking for. The key will be to avoid killing our own forces with friendly fire. We'll need to have our entire army out on the field to lure the demon forces into combat, but the Generals and I propose a synchronized maneuver, where at the exact moment that we fire the weapon our troops fly high in the air and out of the line of fire."

"That could work," Gabriel commented, "but the timing would need to be perfect. Too early and the demons will flee, suspecting the trap, and too late…well, I think we all know what that would mean."

Dionysus stroked his chin. "Hmmmm," he murmured. All eyes waited for him to speak. "I think it's the best plan we have at this point. We'll separate the attack strategy from the defense strategy for voting purposes. Council, let's put the attack strategy outlined by the Commander to a vote. Those in favor…" All of the Council members' hands went up.

"Unanimous. Excellent. Thank you, ladies and gentlemen. Back over to you, Commander, for the defense strategy." Dionysus motioned to Lewis, who'd remained standing during the first vote.

"Thank you. While our primary goal is the complete obliteration of the demons, we have a secondary goal which is to protect the gir...I mean Taylor, from harm." He paused for a moment to collect his thoughts.

Secondary goal, Taylor thought. She squirmed uneasily in her chair. Gabriel noticed and grabbed her hand, holding it tightly under the table. She kicked him hard and he released her hand.

Lewis continued. "Now, we must do everything in our power to protect her, as without her, we cannot achieve our primary goal. She is our most valuable resource."

Taylor was getting dizzy now. After the standing ovation, Dionysus kissing her cheek, and the "thank you's", she thought the angels' at least respected her as a human. *Cannot achieve our primary goal. Most valuable resource.* All they really cared about was killing demons! Protecting her had nothing to do with caring about her human life; rather, it had to do with killing demons! She was pissed off and considered speaking her mind, but her dizziness was becoming unbearable. Gabriel seemed to sense the change in her body language and leaned close to steady her.

Gabriel interjected, "Sir, if I may. We've had a long trip today and I think it'd be best if Taylor lies down for a while. Once the decisions have been made, Commander Lewis can fill us in on the details."

Dionysus's silky smooth, tender voice was back and he spoke directly to Taylor. "Certainly, my dear, how thoughtless of us to not think that you'd be fatigued from the journey. Please go, have a rest and we can talk later as Gabriel suggested."

Taylor didn't think she'd be able to speak without throwing up all over the War Room table, so she just nodded and pushed her chair back, standing up. Gabriel held her arm, trying to provide support if she needed it, but she shrugged him off. Noiselessly, they left the room, strode through the command center and then cut a path through a maze of six or seven twisting and turning hallways.

Taylor's legs eventually failed her and Gabriel had to catch her from falling—she let him touch her this time. She felt weak. He swept her legs out from under her and picked her up, carrying her around a few more bends before taking her through a door to the left. Through her half-closed eyes she could see they were in a large, brightly-lit room with a king-sized bed, small kitchenette, and sitting area, complete with couch and love seat. Gabriel said, "We're alone, you can rest now."

"Bathroom," she managed to groan.

He carried her into a lavish and sparklingly clean bathroom.

"Down," she mumbled and he set her back on her feet. She immediately fell to her knees and vomited, desecrating the shiny white toilet.

Gabriel wet a washcloth and brought it to her, kneeling. "Are you okay?" he asked.

She coughed once, twice, and then snapped, "Do I look like I'm okay?" She snatched the wet cloth from him and wiped her mouth. Scrambling to her feet, Taylor unzipped her overnight bag, which was still hanging diagonally from her shoulder, and removed her travel toothbrush and a small tube of toothpaste. Ignoring Gabriel, who was hovering over her, she thoroughly brushed her teeth, thankful that the awful taste in her mouth and pangs of nausea had subsided.

Upon finishing, she pushed past Gabriel, moving out of the bathroom. She sat on the edge of the bed. Gabriel sat next to her, barely touching. They sat unspeaking for a minute. Gabriel seemed afraid to talk after the harsh response he'd received the last time.

Finally, Taylor said, "They made it sound like I was a piece of meat in there, to be used up and thrown to the dogs!"

"I'm sorry about that, Taylor. They aren't used to having humans around, especially in strategy sessions," Gabriel replied, weakly defending his leaders.

"You told me that I was going to *help* the angels, not be *used* by them; there's a major difference!" Taylor shouted.

"I know, I know, you're right. Let me talk to them about it. They've got their priorities mixed up. Their primary goal should be your protection and attacking the demons should be secondary."

"No! I want to talk to them and tell them how repulsive their behavior was. How I didn't want to help them in the first place, and how one of my best friends is a *demon*. Let me talk to them or I won't help you," Taylor demanded, eyes flashing.

"I don't think that's a good idea, Taylor. The Council will respond better to me. They know and trust me."

"I don't care if you think it's a good idea, that's what we're doing!" Taylor raised her voice again, practically shrieking.

Gabriel shouted back. "It doesn't matter what you think, Taylor! You're going to help destroy the demons either way!"

With her boyfriend's true colors exposed, Taylor's face blanched, all heat drawn from it. She threw herself to the side, her arms covering her face. *Don't cry, don't cry, don't cry*, she though, gritting her teeth. *Don't you dare cry for this— this—despicable angel!*

§

As soon as he'd shouted the awful words, he knew he shouldn't have. The funny thing though, was that it was probably the truest thing he'd ever said to her. Their entire relationship had been based on lies and half-truths. He realized that he hated it, and had hated it for a long time. Because he cared about her. A human.

Fearing the damage he'd just caused, Gabriel shifted towards her, placed his hand on her back and said, "Taylor, please, I swear I didn't mean it the way it sounded. I'm so sorry. I need you in my life. Please, Taylor. Please…" He trailed off. He continued to rub her back, tracing the curves of her slithering tattoo with the tips of his fingers.

Her body was shaking gently, as if she was cold, but he didn't hear her crying. Dry sobbing. Eventually though, her breathing slowed to a gentle rhythm and her body melted into the bed. She seemed so peaceful that Gabriel began to wonder if she'd shaken herself to sleep.

Suddenly Taylor sat up and looked at him, her dry face clenched with anger. "Has it all been a lie? You say you care about me and yet you're willing to let them put me in harm's way? You've been using me the entire time. My mom wouldn't have approved of you." Taylor spat out the last few words, spit bubbles flying from her lips.

Gabriel knew the last sentence was the most terrible of all. Taylor had told him all about her mother and the relationship that they had before she died. To not have her mother's approval was equal to not having Taylor's approval. The pain of her words ripped through him, causing an ache in his chest. "No, Taylor, I swear that's not true. I do care about you, with all my heart, and I'll do everything in my power to protect you."

"Okay, then take me away from this damn place," Taylor demanded.

Gabriel's mind spun, as he tried to solve a problem with no solution. There were an endless number of potential methods of escaping from the complex; however, each of them would result in a dead end or capture. Getting out of angel headquarters without proper clearance was just as difficult as getting in. And as much clearance as he had *within* the mountain, the one type of clearance he needed—Exit Clearance—he didn't have. The only way out would be with the army, when they marched out onto the battlefield.

"I can't do that. If there was any way I could, I would," Gabriel said, "but there's no way out now. We have no choice but to follow the Council's plan."

"What if I refuse?" Taylor said between clenched teeth.

"They'll make you. You can't stop them."

"Dead," she said.

"I promise you, Taylor, I'll die to protect you if I have to. I'll prove my feelings for you."

"You idiot," she said, her words like poison darts. "Are you so blind? I don't care if I die. I care that I'll be a part of the killing. Chris could die because of me." And with that statement, her shoulders slumped and she covered her face with her hands.

Everything clicked into place for Gabriel at that moment. Demons were going to die, and not all of them bad. Chris definitely wasn't bad, Gabriel knew that firsthand. In fact, he suspected many of them were far better than the angels. But what could he possibly do? One thing was certain: if he tried to break Taylor out, Dionysus wouldn't sleep until they'd been hunted down. He didn't know what to say. "I'm sorry, Tay," he said.

Evidently, Taylor wasn't in a forgiving mood, not that he blamed her. "If you cared anything about me, you'd never have brought me here," she said accusingly.

On hearing Taylor's words, Gabriel's thoughts darkened. Even if he was able to protect her, and the angels defeated the demons, she'd never give up her heart to him again, especially considering that Dionysus's next move would be to enslave the human race. She'd hate him forever, even if he was able to negotiate a relatively normal life for her family in the New World. What was stronger, his devotion to the cause of his people or his commitment to the girl who'd stolen his heart? But was it really the cause of his people or just the cause of a few madmen who wanted to dominate the earth? Yes, he'd been taught that humans were inferior to angels and maybe they were in some ways, but in other ways they were equal or even superior to angels. They had an incredible capacity to love and to forgive, as well as a willingness to help each other in times of need. Wasn't it worth reconsidering whether angels could live alongside humans like the demons suggested? Why had he been so *stupid*, so blinded by his own ambition? What kind of monster had he become? His parents had surely not raised him this way. They were kind, loving people, who only supported the supposed "angel cause" because they believed they were protecting the world from the evil demons, the gangsters of the underworld.

Gabriel knew the Council would never change their plans, so he had a decision to make. Sacrifice his own feelings and rededicate himself to The Plan, or follow his heart and find another way out of this mess. Seeing Taylor's anger towards him solidified his decision. He couldn't live without her.

This meant three things: he needed to protect her; he needed to prevent her aura from being used to destroy the demons; and he needed to get her the hell out of there.

All of these thoughts spilled through his mind in less than a minute with Taylor staring at her palms, unable to even look at him. He finally said, "Well, I did bring you here and now we at least have a chance to help mankind by winning a war that's being fought on their behalf. I'll do what I can to protect you and then I'll return you to school once it's over. I'll go check in with the Council to finalize the plans and then I'll bring some food back for us. We can go through the plans together and then get some sleep. I'm sorry I let you down, I hope someday you'll forgive me."

He said all of this with as little emotion as possible, afraid that his shaky voice would betray him. Gabriel thought it was best if he told one final lie for her own good; it was better if she didn't know what he was planning. Later, once they'd escaped, he would tell her everything, the full truth. If he was lucky, she'd forgive him and take him back.

Forty-Nine

Back in the Lair, the Elders had finalized a strategy. Of course a lot was dependent on whether Taylor was already on the angel front lines and when the attack would eventually come. The Elders agreed that the strategy would have to be in place for every battle going forward, as the angels could decide to use Taylor's power any day they chose. Given his knowledge of Dionysus, Clifford believed the attack would likely come sooner rather than later.

The plan was to first locate Taylor's position using an infrared scanner—due to the strength of her aura she'd show up as a brighter image on the map. Once located, the demons would send all of their troops to her location. The troops would teleport as close to her as they could and draw the attention of any angels defending her. They expected her to have the strongest angels protecting her, including Gabriel.

With the defending angels in front of her distracted by the ferocity of the demon attack, Chris and Sam would attempt to teleport in behind Taylor and get her attention. Ideally, they hoped that if Sam called to her, Taylor would be more willing to come to them without raising an alarm. Chris would then teleport them all back to the Lair.

In the event that Taylor refused to run to them, Chris would do everything in his power to get to her. If he was just able to touch her, he could teleport her to where Sam was waiting and then get them all out safely.

A condition of the entire plan was that Taylor could'nt be harmed in the process. The attacking demons would be given the strictest instructions to not lay a hand on her and to merely act as a diversion for Chris and Sam.

The meeting adjourned and Chris grabbed Sam's hand. "You were great in there, I think Clifford really likes you. From now on, if I tell you to let me do the talking, just ignore me. You handled yourself far better than I ever could have."

Sam smiled at the compliment. "Thanks, I was nervous when I walked in and all those old people were looking at me, but for some reason I always feel the most comfortable when my mouth starts moving."

"I haven't noticed," Chris joked.

"Very funny. Now how 'bout you give a girl a tour of this crazy place?"

"I'd love to, but aren't you tired yet? It's nearly midnight."

"Midnight? I guess I lost track of time being underground. What time do we need to get up tomorrow?" Sam asked, hoping for a chance to sleep in.

"The good news is that the battles are generally scheduled at around two o'clock in the afternoon, but the bad news is that those participating have to start prepping at nine o'clock in the morning, so if you want time to shower and eat breakfast we'll need to get up pretty early."

"Ugh. I guess I can sacrifice some of my beauty sleep to help save Taylor. Wake me up at seven because I definitely want enough time to get ready. A girl's got to look good if she's going to be out there saving the world!"

Chris laughed and said, "Sam, you'd look good if you rolled from bed and walked straight out the door."

"Why thank you, Mr. Lyon, you're such a gentleman. Would you mind escorting me to my room?"

"Sure, but once we get there I hope you'll allow me to stay for a few minutes, just to make sure you're okay," he said mischievously.

"I was hoping you'd say that," Sam replied with a sly grin.

Fifty

Gabriel had been busy. He left Taylor in her room after warning her not to do anything stupid, because there'd be guards stationed outside her door for "protection". Then he left and went back to the War Room. Everyone was gone except for Dionysus and Commander Lewis. They were deep in conversation when he entered unannounced. Dionysus motioned for him to join them.

"Ahh, Gabriel. We've been worried about the girl, she seemed quite upset when you left."

Gabriel knew better than to lie too much to the Head of the Council, so he ensured his response had at least some truth to it. "To be honest, my lord, she didn't appreciate the fact that her safety was being given second priority in the plan. She feels like she's being used by the Council. I was able to calm her down and she's still agreed to help us, but we need to be a bit careful how we speak about her when she's around."

"I guess I see her point although it doesn't change the fact that our primary objective will be to use her power to destroy the demons. Anything regretful that happens as a consequence of us trying to achieve that goal will just have to be considered necessary collateral damage.

"However, I think we can easily calm her fears by apologizing and simply lying to her when she's around— perhaps tell her that our primary goal has changed to keeping her safe. How does that sound?"

"I think that could work," Gabriel said, although he wasn't sure it would. He didn't really care either way as he was going to formulate a different plan. "Why don't you come back with me when I bring her dinner and you can apologize on behalf of the Council."

Dionysus smiled wickedly. "Excellent. Commander, are we done here?"

"Yessir, we can finish the briefing in the morning."

"Very good, let's go pay the girl a visit."

§

On the way out, Dionysus pulled Gabriel aside to explain the strategy that'd been approved by the Council.

313

Gabriel seemed satisfied with it, although Dionysus left out some of the key points. He didn't need to know.

After collecting some food from the kitchen, Dionysus and Gabriel knocked gently on Taylor's door. When there was no answer, Gabriel pushed the door open and said, "Taylor—Dionysus and I are coming in."

Dionysus glanced around the room. Everything appeared to be in order. As they approached the bed, he could see a slight bump about the size of her body. The sound of heavy breathing came from the bump.

Gabriel got to his knees and touched her shoulder. "Taylor, we've brought some food."

Taylor rolled over and took the food. She began eating greedily, ignoring them completely.

When she finally looked up, she frowned at Dionysus, her eyes narrow and piercing. "How is it?" Dionysus asked.

"Delicious," she mumbled, her mouth still full.

"Good, we have a fine chef indeed. Taylor, I'm here because Gabriel told me you were somewhat distressed earlier." Taylor's face was like stone. "He also told me why you were upset and I've had a long think about it. I've realized how terrible we must've sounded and it really pains me that it's caused you any emotional distress. I want to apologize on behalf of the Council. We were out of line and we've since changed our objectives for the mission, with your safety being our number one priority. Will you please forgive us?" He made his voice as gentle as he could muster, saturated with an obnoxious dose of kindness and caring.

Taylor looked at him thoughtfully and then asked, "That depends, are you only saying all of this because you're afraid I won't cooperate?"

Dionysus's face went white. How dare this *human* girl accuse him of lying? He counted to ten, allowing his blood pressure to return to normal before responding. "My dear, we've been trying to save humankind from the demons for decades and now that we're so close we're just afraid something will go wrong. However, my apology *is* sincere, because if we don't protect you, then everything we are working for will be for naught."

Taylor stared at Dionysus emotionlessly for so long that even the Head of the Council began to feel uncomfortable. Then she suddenly broke eye contact and said, "Okay, I forgive you, please don't let it happen again. I'll do whatever you think is necessary to win this war." She put down the empty plate and said, "I'm pretty tired now so I may just have Gabriel explain the strategy to me in the morning if that's okay?"

Dionysus replied, "Of course, my dear…and thank you. Sweet dreams." He turned on his heel and walked out the door, an evil smile forming on his beautiful face.

♫

When Dionysus was gone, Gabriel looked at her curiously and asked, "Am I forgiven, too?"

"Not even close, Gabriel. How can you expect this to work when we only met because you were on a mission to recruit me to your cause?"

"Because I—I want it too," Gabriel replied simply.

"That's not enough. We can talk about that after this is all over. Now tell me the plan."

Wondering how she'd figured out that he was making plans of his own, he stammered, "The...the plan? But how? What do you mean?"

Taylor looked at him like he was mad and said, "What's wrong with you tonight? You sound crazy. You know, the big plan, how we're going to defeat the demons?"

The blood rushed back into his face. "Oh yeah, *the plan*. But you told Dionysus that you wanted to sleep."

"I also told him I'd forgiven him, which I haven't, nor will I ever. That was just to get rid of him," she said, motioning to the door that Dionysus had recently passed through.

Now Gabriel was truly amazed. She'd just out-lied one of the world's best liars. He wondered what else she might've lied about. "Okay, no problem."

Over the next hour Gabriel took her through the detailed strategy. She wouldn't have to do much at all, except to act as the conduit for her aura to be used by four specially chosen angel attackers. These attackers were the most powerful in the army and were also considered to be the best marksmen, able to destroy targets from great distances. The four angels would be elevated on platforms so that they'd always have a clear line of sight to draw on Taylor's aura.

The remaining angel forces would be spread out on the field to avoid drawing attention to Taylor's location. However, as Dionysus promised, Taylor's safety would be a major concern and the twelve largest angels would be responsible for creating a wall around her. On Gabriel's recommendation, he was charged with standing next to Taylor as the last line of defense, just in case the main protectors were killed.

When Gabriel finished, Taylor gave no indication as to whether she approved of the plan. Instead, she just thanked him and wished him a goodnight. Gabriel considered asking her whether she'd like him to sleep on the couch, but he already knew the answer, so he just left, promising to wake her for breakfast in the morning.

He went to bed, drifting into a restless sleep filled with dreams about what might happen the next day, which was potentially the most important day of his life.

Fifty-One

"Dammit, dammit, dammit!" Taylor mumbled to herself. The ill feeling had morphed into anger, then into sadness, and now she was back to anger again. She was seething. How could she have been so stupid? She felt like one of those idiot, big-boobed air-heads from high school—the ones who were so easily sweet-talked by the horny, hormone-driven guys. Now she knew it was all a brilliant act, by a brilliant actor. She'd been used. For something she didn't even know she had until a few months ago: her aura.

But she was tired of feeling sorry for herself. She stood up and looked at the back of her shoulder in the mirror.

That's why she'd gotten the tattoo. As a sort of *screw you* to those that tried to make her unhappy—like the snake.

She *would* make it through the next twenty-four hours, do everything in her power to escape, and then, if she ever saw Gabriel again, she'd have to end things; if there was anything left to end. And hopefully go back to being herself, rather than some guy-obsessed, love-craving, needy, uncomfortable-in-her-own-skin twit that jumped from boyfriend to boyfriend because of some insecurity handed down from generation to generation. Her mom had taught her better than that, had shown her a better way to be, had shown her how to love herself, to be herself. She was Taylor again, not Gabriel's girlfriend, or Taylor-and-Gabriel. Just Taylor. And that was good enough.

Fifty-Two

The next day Gabriel arose from bed early, having slept off and on for six hours. He got ready quickly, clothing himself in a comfortable white shirt and loose-fitting white pants. His outfit looked similar to hospital garbs, but it was what he always wore on the day of a battle. The soft clothing was comfortable underneath the armor he'd typically wear out on the battlefield. Some angels chose not to wear armor, but Gabriel was taught from a young age that just because your skin was tougher and healed faster than humans, didn't mean you shouldn't protect it from harm. Gabriel always wore armor, but today would be an exception.

Ready in minutes, he left his room and went directly to Taylor's room, expecting her to still be sleeping off the long day of travel and stress. He knocked and no one answered so he pushed the door open like he had the previous night. He walked in, softly calling her name, but didn't receive an answer. The bed was made so he peeked into the bathroom. It was empty. Walking through the room once more, he noticed a small note on the pillow that he'd missed when he first glanced at the bed. It read:

Hope you don't mind, got up early and was hungry so I had one of the guards show me the
way to the kitchen. See you there. Taylor

Assuming the note was the truth, Gabriel was relieved she hadn't tried anything stupid, like attempting to escape, but his fears were not completely allayed until he saw her sitting with Sampson and David at a table in the dining area. Her plate had apparently been full of eggs, bacon, and toast, but was now half empty.

He watched her for a moment before approaching. As strained as she seemed to be when he'd left her the previous night, she was the complete opposite this morning. She was laughing at something one of them had said, Sampson most likely. Her face seemed relaxed and free of stress. What a difference a good night sleep made. Or was it all an act? After her brilliant display of lying the previous night, he just wasn't sure anymore.

As he approached the table, Taylor saw him. The smile remained on her face as she said, "Some warrior you are. We thought you'd never get up."

Delighted that the "old" Taylor had returned, Gabriel decided to keep things light. "I like to sleep in on fight days. It prevents me from falling asleep when I'm supposed to be marching, isn't that right, Sampson?"

Sampson looked at him sharply and rolled his eyes. "It only happened once, man, it could happen to anyone!"

Taylor looked at Gabriel, clearly confused as to what they were talking about.

Gabriel explained. "One time Sampson was supposed to be marching with the 4th Quadrant of ground soldiers, but he was so tired that he fell asleep just outside the battle doors with his head against a rock. Despite the epic battle that occurred that day, he slept through the entire thing. He almost got kicked out of the army because of it."

Taylor and David were both laughing hard at Sampson's expense, neither of them having ever heard the story.

"Ha-ha, very funny. Let's all laugh at the screw up," Sampson said. He acted like he was annoyed, but they could all tell he was pleased the story had been so amusing to everyone.

Still chuckling to himself and glad that things appeared to be better with Taylor, Gabriel grabbed a plate of food from the kitchen and rejoined his friends. Taylor had finished eating.

"Hurry up, Gabriel, Sampson's going to show me around the joint," she said.

Ignoring her taunt, Gabriel woofed down his food in less than two minutes and said, "Alright, let's go!"

§

Sampson led Taylor along a path through the complex, pointing out various items of interest along the way. As she listened, Taylor was proud of how well she'd managed to convince Gabriel that everything was okay and that she was prepared to carry out the plan that'd been discussed.

"Here you have the armory," "on your left is the central power plant," and "just beyond that door are the training grounds you saw yesterday," were some of the tour guide-like things that he told her.

Being himself, Sampson told a lot of jokes, too, so his three followers were constantly cracking up. He was telling one when they passed by a massive door with a "Strictly Authorized Personnel Only" sign on it.

Sampson was saying, "Did I ever tell you about the time when Gabriel got his wings stuck in between the fence posts at the angel elementary school?"

Taylor was about to reply that she'd love to hear the story, when she saw the large metal doors. "What's in there?" she asked.

Sampson said, "Ah, one of my favorite places. Those are the gargoyle paddocks. Typically I couldn't get in, but since we're fortunate enough to have such an *important* angel with us, we can get in anywhere we want, right, Gabriel?"

Taylor looked at Gabriel. "What does he mean 'gargoyle paddocks'? I thought only the demons used gargoyles, like the one I saw."

Before Gabriel could answer, David's eyes widened and he exclaimed, "You've seen a demon gargoyle, Taylor?"

"Yep, damn near killed me until my hero swooped in and rescued me from its evil clutches."

Gabriel jumped in quickly, trying to set the record straight. "She was never in any real danger, the demons were just trying to play a trick on her. You know, give her a bit of a scare."

"Tell that to its claws and razor sharp fangs," she retorted.

"Wow, Taylor," David said, looking at her in awe. "Even I've only seen pictures of them."

Sampson answered her original question. "The gargoyle you saw was bred from two demons, whereas the gargoyles we have are bred from two angels. They're fairly similar in basic appearance except that ours are light and theirs are dark, kind of like the difference between angels and demons."

"I want to see them," Taylor demanded.

"I'm not sure that's such a good idea," Gabriel replied.

"C'mon," Sampson urged, "she's going to see them during the battle anyway, so you might as well give her a taste of what to expect so she's not surprised."

"Fine, but just a quick peek."

"Awesome!" David exclaimed.

Gabriel touched his finger to the door and there was a loud creak, as intersecting panels of metal moved either up or down to reveal a wide passage beyond them. The passage was unusually dark for the angel complex, giving it the appearance of a dungeon.

Gabriel led the way with David right on his heels. Sampson and Taylor followed closely behind. They passed two, then four alcoves on each side. Each space was closed off by thick, heavy iron bars. The spaces were empty. As they approached the next two sets of bars, Gabriel slowed his stride.

The heavy sound of breathing broke the silence.

"Hey, little buddy, just coming to say hello," Gabriel said when he reached the cell.

David gasped. "Wow, it's incredible! I've never seen one in person!"

As the interior of the cell came into Taylor's view, she saw a massive white animal with a body very similar to the one that'd attacked her. Sitting on its hind legs, it resembled a dinosaur, except for its head, which looked human, in a strange, mutated way.

The main differences between the angel and demon gargoyles were cosmetic in nature: the angel version was a pure white color, with blue eyes and spots of white-blond hair, versus the black eyes and dark hair of the demonesque monster she'd encountered in the forest.

She stared at the creature, unblinking. Interestingly, the gargoyle ignored its other three viewers and stared right back at Taylor. To get a closer look, the beast sauntered up to the bars, its giant legs crashing with each step.

"I wonder why it's so interested in you, Taylor," Gabriel said. His face looked puzzled, confused. Suddenly his eyebrows arched, as he came to some sort of realization. "Oh freakin' hell, it can see your aura, Tay!" Things suddenly seemed to move in slow motion as Gabriel yelled, "Ruuuunnn.....Taaaylllorrrr!" As he screamed he dashed towards her, his arms outstretched. He was too late.

The gargoyle lifted a single clawed finger towards her and instantly she felt a tingling sensation like she'd felt when Gabriel had first accessed her aura. She began to shine brightly and then, just as Gabriel's streaking form collided with her, there was an explosion of light and the cell's metal bars were vaporized. *The gargoyle was free.*

Taylor felt the wind fly from her lungs. She wheezed, trying to catch her breath, while lying face down on the ground with Gabriel partially on top of her. She pushed with her arms to try to free herself, and heard Gabriel roar in pain as he rolled off her. Evidently, he'd not been as lucky as the others, and although he'd been able to knock Taylor out of the way of the blast, his foot had caught the edge of it. Taylor looked down at the mangled stump at the end of his leg and could see a stream of bright white blood flowing freely from where his foot should've been.

Luckily, the gargoyle seemed confused by what'd happened and was standing still, clawing at the empty air where the bars used to be; it seemed to be trying to work things out in its brain.

Despite his injuries, Gabriel yelled, "Sampson, David— can you handle it?"

Sampson and David had managed to avoid the explosion, rolling to the opposite side of the gargoyle's cell. Sampson replied by lifting his fist with his thumb up. He barked orders to David, who looked ready for action, almost eager for it. "You distract it from the front and I'll go for the wings, got it?"

David nodded in understanding.

Taylor clambered to her feet and helped pull Gabriel up after her; he was hobbling on one leg. Taylor headed for the door with Gabriel hopping along beside her. "We've got to get out of here quick," Gabriel instructed.

Taylor was unable to reply as she was still having trouble breathing, but she picked up the pace upon hearing his command. Just as they exited the door and turned the corner, a powerful spout of white flame shot through the doorway, licking the rocky walls. The gargoyle had finally moved from its cell.

They continued to move down the hall, as behind them they heard sounds from the fight they were missing.

Agitated, the gargoyle was groaning in protest, and the roar of fire escaping its lips echoed through the passageways. They heard someone, presumably Sampson, shout, "Now!" and then a ripping sound, followed by a loud *thud!* The beast had fallen.

They stopped and turned around. Gabriel shouted, "Everything alright, guys?"

"No problem," Sampson announced, exiting the dungeon with David close behind him. David was wearing a wide smile, the adrenaline from his first close gargoyle encounter still pumping through his veins.

Taylor touched Gabriel's arm and said, "Thank you for saving my life again." A mix of emotions flooded through her. In a lot of ways, Gabriel had been good to her, and sometimes he seemed so sincere. But then again, it was his fault she was there in the first place.

"It's my fault, we should never have gone in there," Gabriel replied.

"No, it's not—I wanted to go in. No one could've seen that coming. It doesn't matter now, we need to get you to a doctor." Taylor cringed as his tattered leg hung in the air. There was so much radioactive blood, like liquid light.

Gabriel laughed. "It's a mere flesh wound. You forget that angels have incredible healing powers. It's rare to have an injury that requires our healers to get involved. Let's go back to your room to rest and you can see it in action. Sampson, David—not a word to anyone about what happened. Can you take care of the mess?"

"Sure, buddy," Sampson said. David looked frustrated that he wouldn't be able to tell his friends the amazing story.

Taylor and Gabriel made their way back to her room via rarely used paths to avoid being seen. As a temporary fix, Gabriel took off his shirt and wrapped the bottom of his leg in it, so he wouldn't leave a bloody trail behind him.

Taylor couldn't help but to admire his toned body and had a sudden longing to be back at college with him, young and together and normal. She wished he wasn't an angel, with all the agendas and missions and bullcrap. She wondered if she could ever forgive him for all of this. He *had* saved her life twice now, which seemed to warrant a second chance. *No!* she thought. Not again, no more being stupid. *Dammit!* She wished she could turn off her brain.

Back at the room, Gabriel slowly unpacked the wound, which was already looking better than it had down in the dungeon. What was previously just a stump was now a fully formed ankle. Taylor watched in amazement as within minutes, his heel reformed in front of her eyes. The hole was still bleeding and she put a finger into the liquid, gathering a drop onto the tip. She put it up to her eye, inspecting it closely. The liquid was as white a substance as she'd ever seen. Whiter than milk, it shimmered and glowed like the ooze in a glow stick.

"The blood of an angel can heal many human ailments," Gabriel explained. "Just a drop on your forehead can cure a headache faster than Tylenol. A few drops on a broken leg will repair the bone fragments within hours. Putting angel blood into a gunshot wound will actually extract the bullet and then seal off the hole."

"Why don't angels try to help injured humans?" Taylor asked.

"Because we're still trying to keep our secrets. At this point we don't want to upset the balance of nature."

"That's BS and you know it. Stop giving me the 'right' answer. You sound like a robot." Ugh. Taylor was sick of the lies. And even sicker of believing them. No more.

Gabriel frowned, but nodded. "You're right. The real answer is that I don't know why we don't use our blood to help humans. We should."

Satisfied with his honesty, Taylor said, "Why did that gargoyle attack us? If it was created by angels, shouldn't it be loyal to you?"

"Excellent question. You're correct that angel gargoyles usually won't harm an angel. This is especially true on the battlefield, where there are plenty of demons to command their attention. However, in such close quarters, when a gargoyle is distracted by a human like you, they can become less predictable. I should've thought about that before I took you in."

His foot was completely reformed now. He flexed it up and down to test the mobility and then stood up, putting his full weight on it. "Good as new," he said. "How are you feeling?"

"I'm perfectly fine," she lied, feeling nervous bubbles in her stomach and chest. "Let's get this over with."

Fifty-Three

Similar to Taylor and Gabriel, Samantha and Christopher awoke early. Sam got ready in record time, which gave them a chance to have a long breakfast together. She was dressed in her workout clothes: a bright red tank top and her favorite black Lululemon pants. Chris wore a simple pair of black shorts and a black hoodie.

At breakfast, the dark male and female demons at the other tables looked at her curiously, which made her uncomfortable. "Maybe you should introduce me so they stop staring," she grumbled.

"There'll be plenty of time for that later. Anyway, they already know who you are because you were named in the briefing papers they received this morning. You're essential to the mission today. Let's just eat and then I can show you where we'll be positioned during the battle."

Sam shrugged, finished her food quickly, and they left the dining room. Chris had a sneaky smile on his face as they walked up a steep incline.

"What are you grinning about? Are you trying to give me a workout on these hills?" Sam said.

"Nope, just excited to see your reaction to something," Chris said secretively.

Sam liked surprises and opted not to question him further as they hiked higher and higher. They reached a set of stairs that seemed to rise forever. More than a thousand steps later—Sam lost count after ninety-six—they reached the top. Sam could see light coming from a small hole in the rock wall.

Chris led her to the hole and climbed through it, disappearing. Having no other choice, Sam crawled after him, annoyed at having to get dirty in the process. Emerging from the crevice, Samantha's mouth fell open, in awe of the sight that opened before her. The view was breathtaking; they were near the top of a mountain and looking out into the valley below. In the distance, she could see another set of mountain ranges on the other side of the valley.

Pointing directly opposite their current position, Chris said, "Taylor is probably somewhere within that mountain and the angels are making plans to use her against us."

"Thanks for putting a damper on the beautiful view, Debbie Downer," Sam joked.

"Sorry about that," Chris said.

"So, did you just bring me up here to show me the sights or what?" Sam asked.

Suddenly full of energy, Chris said, "Actually, no. This is where we'll be today when the battle commences."

Moving towards the edge of the cliff, Chris drew Sam's attention to a large gate thousands of feet below their current position. "That's where our army will march out to meet the angels. We'll remain up here with a couple of technicians who'll scan the angel forces for infrared anomalies, which'll hopefully allow us to determine whether Taylor is outside the mountain and if so, where she's located."

"What if she's not there?" Sam asked.

"Then we'll just watch the fight from the best seat in the house and then do it all again for the next scheduled battle, until she does eventually appear. Any other questions?"

Sam shook her head.

"Good, because I'm tired of talking about all this war stuff. I've cleared it with the Elders and we can stay up here until the skirmish begins." Reaching behind a large rock, Chris extracted a large wooden basket that was hidden from view. "I've taken the liberty of stashing a picnic lunch for us."

Samantha put her arms around her boyfriend and rested her head on his muscular chest. "Thank you for trying to make all of this so comfortable for me," she said. And she meant it. "I meant what I said earlier, I really do feel crazy feelings for you."

With her head on his chest, she could feel Chris's heart rate speed up, likely due to the exhilaration of her words whirling through his chest like a tornado. You too, Samantha."

They held each other for a while, happy to be close to each other. Then Sam raised her head and kissed him once, then again, and then she couldn't stop. They moved to the ground, enjoying each other and the much needed reprieve from the very long day that lay ahead of them.

Fifty-Four

When they arrived at the armory, there was already a buzz of activity. Angels were strapping on tight-fitting breastplates, leg armor, and helmets. The armor was thin and reminded Taylor of S.W.A.T. team bullet-proof vests.

"What do you think?" Gabriel asked.

"It's not what I expected," she replied.

"What did you think, that we'd be wearing medieval knight's armor?" Gabriel laughed.

"Actually, yeah, that's exactly what I was picturing."

"The thin, moldable armor is fitted to each angel's body so that they have the highest level of mobility," Gabriel explained.

"That's pretty awesome," Taylor admitted. It was also pretty scary watching everyone get ready, like they were about to play in some full contact sporting event, rather than a fight to the death.

Gabriel led her to the back, where a short, odd-looking angel was cutting and shaping armor. He was the first angel she'd seen that didn't look like a cut-out from some glossy magazine.

Gabriel greeted him. "Hey, Jonesy, we need to get some armor fitted and cut for her asap."

"Ahh, Gabriel. I'm glad you're back," Jonesy said. Then turning to Taylor he said, "You're about the size of some of the students in Year Three training, so I'll probably have a piece that won't need too much alteration."

He went into a large room in the back while they waited outside. After a short silence they heard, "Hmmm, yes....yes, I think this'll do just fine."

Jonesy returned carrying a white suit made up of eight or nine pieces clipped together to look like a single suit. He began unclipping each piece and handing them to Taylor as he went. "Here, try these on for size."

Not always knowing which piece went on what part of her body, Taylor relied on Gabriel to make sure she didn't end up with a leg guard on her arm or a foot flap on her elbow. Concentrating on getting the armor on correctly, Taylor wasn't paying attention to whether it fit until she had everything assembled.

When she strapped on the last piece, the helmet, she took a minute to stretch out her body, moving her arms and legs. "How does it feel?" Jonesy asked.

"It feels…It feels like I'm not even wearing any armor, like it's an extension of my body," Taylor said, her eyes wide with excitement. "That's wicked!"

Gabriel congratulated Jonesy. "I gotta hand it to you, man, you've got one helluva eye for these things."

"Just doin' my job," Jonesy said modestly.

Taylor thanked him and waved goodbye as they headed through to the next section, leaving the racks of armor behind. As they were leaving, Taylor stopped and said, "Wait, Gabriel, you forgot your armor."

Gabriel said, "I'm not wearing any today, Taylor."

"Why not?"

"If a spare shot gets through our defenses and hits me, I'll heal quickly and it'll be fine. If you get hit, you'll be killed if you aren't wearing protection. On the other hand, if our defenses break down and the demons get through to us, we'll both either be dead or captured anyway, regardless of whether I have any armor on."

"Thanks for the grim details," Taylor said. She detected something in his words that didn't make sense. She knew there was something he wasn't telling her, as usual, but she kept it to herself, knowing that arguing was a waste of time. Plus, she had her own plans anyway. Instead, she just nodded once and they continued into the next room: the weapons cache.

"Now, I *will* grab something from here," Gabriel said, licking his lips. He explained as they walked along the shelves of weapons: "Each of these weapons has been designed and built to use the angel's inner light as its power source. As a result, they're quite a bit more powerful than human weapons."

He picked up something that looked like a cross between a machine gun and a bow and arrow. "This'll do just fine," he said.

Taylor wasn't interested in the angel weaponry and just wanted it to all be over. She stayed quiet while Gabriel inspected the gun, clicking different pieces off and back on. Once satisfied with his choice, they left through another door, moving forwards.

The next room wasn't really a room; it was more like an empty warehouse, with high ceilings and lots of floor space. Gabriel explained that this was where the army assembled into the designated formation before heading out into the open air.

At the end of the warehouse were massive metal doors, wide enough to allow at least fifty angels, walking side by side, to exit simultaneously. Gabriel headed to the far left side instead.

"We'll be going out a less visible entrance," he instructed. "Our protectors are already waiting. Are you ready to do this?" he asked, his face tight and serious.

All of the events of the last two weeks tumbled through Taylor's stomach and she suddenly felt sick again. For part of her there was a certain exhilaration, like the feeling right before you get on a rollercoaster, but the other part felt ill, like the feeling just before you get up in front of a lot of people to give a speech. She grabbed Gabriel's arm to steady herself, readying herself for the task at hand.

"Breathe, Taylor," he said.

She took a large breath, and then another. The color returned to her face and the sickness passed. It was now or never. Trust her instincts. No fear. Do or die, literally.

"Okay, I'm ready," she said.

Gabriel opened the small door for her and she passed through into a path between the rocks. She breathed the open air deeply, enjoying the warmth of the sun high overhead. Not far along the path, she heard the dull sound of conversation. Reaching the end of the rock walls, she peeked out into the open.

Four platforms had been raised and were already manned by fully-armed and armored angels standing on them. Twelve other burly angels were standing shoulder to shoulder in a circle, eyes looking out. They were chatting as if it was just another day.

"I heard the entire Council's in the mountain," one of them said.

"C'mon, man, everyone knows they never leave their little hideout," another one replied.

"Think what you want, but I know a guy who knows a guy that saw Dionysus himself wandering the halls," the first one said.

Gabriel stepped past Taylor and out of the rocks and said, "I've seen the entire Council and can confirm that they're all here."

A couple of the meaty angels appeared to know him. One of them said, "Yo, Gabriel, I heard you were mixed up in all of this somehow."

"That's right. I'll be standing next to Taylor in case any of you guys can't do your job."

"Who's Taylor?" another one asked stupidly.

"She is." He motioned for her to step out and she did. "She's only the one that you idiots are supposed to be protecting."

One of the quieter angels decided it was appropriate to bow as Taylor walked up. "We'll do our best to serve you," he said.

"Uh, thanks," Taylor replied awkwardly.

Gabriel took charge. "Okay, here's how it's gonna work." He glanced at his watch. "In exactly ten minutes the army will march out. Taylor and I will be hiding back on the path, and once half the army is out of the gates, I'll run her out and through a small opening in your circle of protection. As soon as we're in the circle, close it off. After that, it's as simple as not letting any demon attacks through the circle.

"The attackers on the platforms will do the rest and if all goes according to plan, we'll end this war forever. Any questions?"

They shook their heads in unison.

"Good, stay in position until the fight."

Gabriel led Taylor back onto the path, just out of sight of the battlefield. They waited.

Fifty-Five

Sam and Chris enjoyed the picnic lunch he'd prepared and were now sunning themselves on the ledge, high above the valley. Chris had brought two pairs of binoculars, so that they'd be able to see the action better when the battle commenced. The binoculars were hanging around their necks, useless for the moment, as the valley was completely free of activity.

The technicians arrived and began setting up their equipment. They tested the equipment on Sam and could make out the location of her body by picking up the heat coming from her skin. Satisfied that everything was working properly, they locked the infrared scanner into position and set it to continuously scan the base of the mountain in the distance.

In only a few minutes they received a positive heat reading. Frederick, one of the technicians declared, "We've got something!"

Sam and Chris came around to look at the screen. Sure enough, there was a clear red blob on the screen, moving ever so slightly. It was off to the side and away from the angel gates, a good distance from where the angel army would typically emerge.

"It might just be an animal," Chris suggested.

"Maybe...," Frederick said. "Wait, look!"

Another red form appeared, then another, then another.

Frederick started counting, "Four, five, six....fifteen, sixteen." Sixteen red circles were now clustered in the same area. They were moving around, but it was hard to make out any pattern, like lottery balls in a canister, waiting for the winning numbers to be announced.

Then a clear pattern emerged. "Are they...in a circle?" Sam suggested.

Frederick replied, "Yes, twelve of them are, but the other four appear to be outside of the circle and might even be at a higher elevation, like they're flying or something." The equipment was pretty sensitive and could accurately detect differences in altitude and distance to within a few feet.

Frederick continued. "We can keep an eye on it, but it might just be a distraction to divert our attention away from where she'll really be. The infrared forms appear to all be about the same size, which indicates they're all angels. We expect her to show up as a heat source that's at least twice as large as the angels."

Chris suddenly seemed to remember that he had high-powered binoculars around his neck. He pulled them up to his eyes, and Sam, noticing what he was doing, did the same. They panned across the mountain, past the massive doors, until they reached the spot from where the infrared scanners had detected the heat images. They could see the bright outlines of angels.

"I see them," Chris said. "They're standing in a circle, just like we thought, and there are four that are out in front of the rest, situated about ten feet in the air, on platforms."

"Oh my gosh!" Sam suddenly exclaimed. "There's Taylor! She's there!"

Sam watched as Taylor and Gabriel emerged from the mountain; they appeared to have walked directly through the rock face. *There must be a small path*, Sam thought.

"I see her too," Chris said.

"We can now see a heat form on the infrared that's significantly larger than the others," Frederick confirmed.

Sam and Chris watched intently, as Taylor and Gabriel approached the angels, stood there for a few minutes and then walked right back into the rock wall, out of sight.

"They've dropped off our scan again," the second technician noted.

"They moved behind some rocks, but I think they're still there, waiting for the battle to begin," Chris guessed.

"We generally can't get a reading behind large rocks, but if this is the point of attack, which it appears to be, it will at least give us a small advantage when it all goes down. Radio it in, Howie!"

The previously nameless technician grabbed his mobile radio and spoke into it urgently: "This is Tech 49 calling all team leaders. We have an infrared and visually confirmed location for the *package*. Please communicate the following coordinates to all resources immediately: seventeen, ninety-nine, two. I repeat: one-seven, niner-niner, oh-two. Over!"

Chris grinned. "Looks like we have a job to do, Sam. We'll wait until the battle begins and all hell breaks loose, and then I'll attempt to teleport us behind one of the large rocks near where we spotted Taylor.

"It looks like they're going to try to encircle her to protect her, but when our forces get close, they'll be forced to break formation to fight. I'll throw a small stone to get her attention and then I'll rely on you to motion her to come over to us so we can all teleport out together. If she ignores us or is unable to get to us, then I'll try to get to her. You will NOT move towards her regardless of what happens, is that agreed?"

Sam nodded, impressed by the firm, in-control tone in her boyfriend's voice. Butterflies invaded her stomach. Was this really happening?

"Okay, now we wait," Chris said, bringing his binoculars back up to his eyes.

Fifty-Six

The waiting was unbearable. Taylor felt like a child playing hide-and-go-seek, waiting anxiously to see if someone would find her. Except the someone was trying to kill her. It made her have to pee. She tried to hold it. She couldn't see the battlefield, which made it even worse. All she could do was listen to the sounds and Gabriel's commentary on what he thought was happening.

She heard a loud groan, as presumably the giant doors were cranked open. Then came the sound of many marching feet, thumping in rhythm.

Gabriel commentated: "First, the light infantry will march out—that's what you're hearing now. Next will be the gargoyles and gargoyle masters, and last will be the heavy artillery. The battle will begin the old fashioned way: we'll sound a horn and then the demons will answer with another horn and then the fighting begins. As soon as we hear the second horn, we go."

Taylor's heart battered around in her chest with each second that passed.

Fifty-Seven

Unlike Taylor, Sam and Chris had perfect seats for the battle. While not close to the action, with their binoculars they could see everything. The angel army emerged from the mountain first, with brilliant white flags flapping in the breeze. They looked beautiful, in perfect formation, each step synchronized like a dancer with his partner.

Hundreds upon hundreds of soldiers marched through the door and with each line, Sam expected it to be the last, but they just kept on coming. Finally she saw a large gap in the advancing legions. What came out next would be burned in her memory forever. She saw huge creatures, breathing bursts of curling light and roaring so loudly that

Sam could hear them, despite being almost two miles away. The gargoyles were ready for action.

Their masters either walked a distance behind them or rode them, depending on how tame the beasts were. They were a magnificent—and also frightening—sight to see. Sam counted them and noted there were thirteen. She tried not to think about what it might mean for their luck.

When the last gargoyle appeared, she heard another sound from much closer. She peered over the edge of the cliff and saw that an opening had appeared in the demon mountain and that their soldiers were now moving into position. It was a very different sight to the angels' tight formations, but equally beautiful. With no particular structure to their ranks, hundreds of dark demons passed under them, looking fierce and threatening. Soon after they emerged, there was a loud clap of thunder and dark clouds rolled in.

Sam looked at Chris expectantly. He explained: "My people can control the weather and we much prefer the dark, so that we can easily see the angels and they have more difficulty seeing us. Fighting in the rain is no fun so we simulate a thunderstorm, except without the rain."

Sam gazed upon the battlefield, wondering if she would suddenly awake to find out that it had all been a dream. Teleporting? Controlling the weather? Gargoyles? Might as well add in unicorns and leprechauns while they were at it.

A loud roar from below drew her attention, as the demon gargoyles stomped out into the rain-free storm. After the gargoyles came the heavy artillery on both sides. Huge angels and demons wheeled large, powerful-looking weapons out behind the soldiers and animals.

Abruptly, all activity ceased and the only noise was the intermittent sound of thunder.

"Time to go," Chris said, grabbing Sam's hand.

She closed her eyes as a horn sounded. Another horn sounded in response and she felt the feeling of being transported, as if by magic, through time and space.

Fifty-Eight

When Taylor heard the second horn she didn't even have time to think, as Gabriel was already carrying her towards the circle. Once inside, he set her back on her feet and she tried to see through the cracks between the burly protectors that surrounded her. They were meant to keep danger out, but inadvertently they were also keeping her in. How the hell would she escape? She looked up and saw the four attackers raised above the field; they each had one eye on her and one eye on the battle.

Then, as Chris had predicted unbeknownst to Taylor, *all hell broke loose.*

The initially distant sounds of the battle were suddenly much closer and she saw orbs of light flying overhead and lightning crashing all around them, and heard cries of pain from injured soldiers.

A cry of, "They know we're here, fire the weapon!" came from one of her defenders. She looked up and made eye contact with one of the attackers as he stretched an arm towards her, opening his hand as if to invite her up with him. She knew he was preparing to absorb her aura.

If she was going to run, now was the moment.

ॐ

Unbeknownst to Taylor, Gabriel was watching things carefully from her side, waiting for the right moment to launch his own plan. When he saw the attacker point to her, he started to grab her, his wings already extending in anticipation of a flying escape from the melee.

Unexpectedly, someone grabbed him from behind, whispering in his ear. "I wouldn't do that if I were you."

Gabriel spun around and saw that Dionysus had snuck up behind him, anticipating his plan.

"Let go of me, Dionysus," Gabriel demanded.

"You know I can't do that," Dionysus replied, gritting his teeth as Gabriel struggled to wrench himself free.

Calling upon all of his strength, Gabriel twisted his body and swung his arms to try to dislodge Dionysus's hold. Dionysus's grip held strong and so, instead of separating them, Gabriel's maneuver caused them to both tumble hard to the ground, rolling several feet and smashing into the back of one of the protector's legs. The circle of defense was partially broken.

§₹

Before Taylor could even consider running, her body was struck by the connection between the first angel attacker's inner light and her own aura. This time there was no tingling. Pain shot through her body and she cried out in agony as she fell to one knee.

She was confused by the pain. When Gabriel had harnessed her power, it'd felt good, had made her happy, but this felt like torture. She looked up at the attacker and could see him laughing, as he enjoyed the god-like power that now coursed through his veins. His body began to glow brighter and brighter in preparation for his attack. With each second that passed, Taylor's pain grew exponentially.

As quickly as it started, the pain ended. Taylor collapsed in a heap, her body exhausted from the ordeal. She lifted her head to see what had happened and saw that the angel was no longer on his pedestal. *A demon must've hit him*, she thought.

She forced herself to one knee, then to a standing position, gasping for breath. She took a step towards the edge of the circle, prepared to push her way through if she had to. *Fight, Taylor,* she commanded herself. She took another step, gaining hope that she might be able to get out of the situation after all.

But her relief was short lived as the second angel attacker locked onto her and began to draw energy from her aura. Immediately the pain returned and crept up her legs, into her spine, and finally into her skull. Her head felt like it would split in two if he didn't stop soon. Once again, she collapsed, writhing in pain, her eyes locked on the angel.

The second attacker learned from his predecessor's mistake and didn't linger at the point of full power. As soon as he was charged, he fired the weapon straight ahead, not caring what was in its path.

The destruction was instantaneous. Many angels lost their lives in the blast, not expecting it to come when it did, but the angel deaths were nothing compared to the legions of demons that were wiped out by the massive beam of light.

At first glance it appeared that at least a third of the demon army was vaporized, but upon further review, it was somewhat less than that, as many of the demons in the direct path of the attack had seen it coming and were able to teleport out of harm's way.

Seconds after firing his weapon, the second angel attacker was crippled by another well-aimed demon artillery round. Seeing the fate of their comrades, the remaining two angel attackers scoured the battlefield for signs of attack, before locking onto Taylor's aura simultaneously. Her head began to ache as knives of pain assaulted her skull. There was no escape now. This was it. She was done for. She'd be used to kill again. Probably Chris, probably many others, and she'd be killed too. All for what? For some secret war over territory?

While Taylor struggled to maintain consciousness, several large demons were able to teleport close to the circle of defense around Taylor, causing her protectors to spring into action, breaking the wall around her. Bodies thrashed, bodies crashed, and Taylor blacked out.

Fifty-Nine

Chris and Sam watched anxiously from their hiding place behind a large rock. Sam wanted to rush out to try to help Taylor when she first screamed in pain, but Chris wisely held her back and told her that they'd be able to best help her if they were patient; they'd only have one chance to rescue her.

Even when the weapon was fired, Chris held his ground, waiting for the perfect opportunity.

When the wall of angel defenders crumbled and they began fighting the demons, Chris sprang into action, charging out of hiding at full demon speed. Reaching her in seconds, Chris touched her and instantly teleported back to where Sam remained hidden.

He scooped up Taylor's limp body and reached his hand out for Sam to grab, which she did, and the three disappeared. The rescue took all of three seconds and all but two of the angels were oblivious that anything had even happened.

♫

Gabriel was grappling with Dionysus when they heard the yells from the attacking demons. They were right on top of them. They both saw the circle around Taylor open up to reveal her lifeless body on the ground. They were both about to rush to her side—Gabriel to try to protect her and escape with her, and Dionysus to ensure she was still alive enough to be used against the demons—when Chris appeared out of thin air and was gone even quicker than he'd come.

"Noooo!" Gabriel yelled, dropping to his knees.

Dionysus glared at him. "This is your fault, you'll be charged with treason. Guards! Arrest Gabriel."

The demons fell back, rushing towards their mountain in retreat. They were likely already aware that the girl had been rescued. Many angels and demons had been killed during the battle, but most of the casualties had been from the single death blast. There was no evidence that they'd ever even existed, their bodies having been disintegrated.

Two of the angels that'd previously been defending Gabriel and Taylor, responded to Dionysus's command by grabbing Gabriel and lifting him to his feet. He didn't struggle. There was no point. He'd failed the only person that he'd ever truly wanted to protect and if by some miracle she was still alive, she'd never forgive him.

Sixty

Chris had a license to breach the normal teleportation rules within the demon complex, and so he reappeared with both girls in the midst of the medical corridor. "I need medical assistance NOW!" he yelled.

Before Chris said a word, the staff were already rushing a cart over and preparing a room. They quickly, but carefully slid Taylor's limp body onto a backboard and then moved her to a rolling cart.

Sam was hysterical, tears rushing down her face. "Oh God, I don't think she's breathing, please save her, please…" She passed out in mid-sentence, but Chris was there to catch her before she hit the ground.

He set her gently on another bed and asked a demon nurse to take care of her while he checked on Taylor. He went into Taylor's room, where the doctors were performing CPR on her. Sam was right, *she wasn't breathing.* "Her pulse has stopped," one noted. "Charge the panels."

They applied defibrillator panels to her chest and her body convulsed when they shocked her. Nothing happened. "Prepare for a second charge!"

After the second shock, Taylor gasped, her eyes opening wide.

"We've got a pulse. It's weak, but she should be just fine."

Chris breathed a sigh of relief. Taylor's eyes closed again, her breathing slow and steady. "Can she hear me?" he asked the doctor.

"Probably not, she really just needs to rest."

"Please let me know if anything changes." Chris left Taylor's room and rejoined Sam, who was now awake after receiving a heavy dose of smelling salts from the nurse.

"Is she...?" Sam started to ask, her body tensing as if preparing for bad news.

"She's fine," Chris said. "The doctor thinks she'll make a full recovery."

"Thank God." Her body relaxed and she hugged Chris tightly, her head pressed against his shoulder.

Sixty-One

Ten days later, Taylor, Samantha, and Christopher were lounging in the recreational room in the Lair. Taylor *had* made a full recovery in only three days and the girls had had a week of recovering, exploring the caves, and talking about what had happened.

However, no one talked about Gabriel, and Taylor could tell that Sam and Chris were avoiding the subject. She could also tell that they were trying not to look too much like boyfriend-girlfriend, clearly afraid that it would upset Taylor. Eventually, she had enough of avoiding the hard topics.

"I can't believe that Gabriel was lying to me all this time. He was just a puppet for the Council. I don't think he ever really cared about me," Taylor said.

Sam looked at Chris. Chris replied, "I think what he did to you is despicable and awful, but he was in an impossible situation and in the end, he tried to do the right thing."

Taylor's voice rose quickly. "The right thing? The right thing? He served me up on a platter to those angels who tried to suck the life out of me!"

Chris put his arms up in surrender. "Whoa, hold on, Tay, there's something you should know. We saw the whole thing. Gabriel had another plan in mind and he tried to save you. He was about to grab you and fly you to safety, but Dionysus stopped him. While they were fighting each other we saved you."

Taylor was confused. "What? But I didn't see...He was right next to me when my aura was being used."

"Did you see him?" Chris asked.

"Well, no, but that's because I was too busy being torn apart by those damn sadistic angels."

"Tay, what Chris is saying is true. I saw it too. I think he really does want to be with you," Sam said. "He was about to betray his own people when Dionysus grabbed him."

Taylor's face softened. "He does want to be with me," she repeated. "What'll happen to him?"

"Our lookouts saw him being arrested and taken back into the mountain. He'll likely be charged with treason and executed."

Taylor's head was a whirlwind of emotion. He'd hurt her so deeply, his lies and half-truths cutting deep into her heart, but she didn't want him to die, especially not if he tried, in the end, to try to save her. A rush of happy memories of Gabriel flew through her mind. The next thing she knew she was curled up in a ball on the couch, sobbing uncontrollably, letting out all the emotion she'd been holding inside. She let out tears of anger at Gabriel and herself, tears of sadness for the demons dead at her hand, tears of fear for what would happen to the angel she once cared about. Sam was by her side, rubbing her back.

"It will be okay, Tay. Chris will think of something. We'll get him out, I promise."

After ten minutes, Taylor had exhausted herself from crying and the tears finally dried up, as if someone turned off the faucet. She sat up and hugged her friend, so glad that she was with her and that she didn't have to keep secrets from her anymore. They held each other for a long time.

Taylor tried to make sense of it in her head. Before the battle, she'd vowed to be true to herself from now on, even if it meant staying away from Gabriel. Her heart said that she needed him, but her head said that she was being a stupid little girl and that everything she liked about him was a lie. The truth might be somewhere in between, she reasoned. In any case, if the demons couldn't rescue him, then it wouldn't matter. *Not knowing whether it could've worked would be the worst*, Taylor thought.

Chris, who'd apparently left when the crying started, came back. "We have a plan," he announced. "But first we have to get you girls back to college."

"What?" Taylor and Sam both said at the same time.

"I'm not leaving until we've tried to save Gabriel," Taylor said.

Chris sighed. "I understand why you'd think that way, but please just hear me out. Do you trust me?"

Taylor thought it odd that she was actually considering trusting a demon. It was difficult to change her thinking after everything Gabriel had told her about demons. Maybe that's why it was so difficult for Gabriel to go against the angels. But she *did* trust Chris. "Yes, I trust you," she said.

"Thanks, Taylor. That really means a lot. Okay, we can't just ignore the fact that you have normal human lives outside of all of this. You have families—people that care about you—and if you skip classes and final exams, they'll demand real answers that make sense. So we need to get you back to do all that."

Taylor frowned. "Two questions: First, won't I be a sitting duck for the angels to just come and kidnap me again? And second, won't Gabriel be dead before the semester is even over?"

Chris replied, "Both good questions. The demon Elders have put into immediate effect a protection order for both of you no matter where in the world you are. They take this very seriously so you'll have top-notch bodyguards around at all times who will ensure the angels don't try anything. Trust me, the Elders didn't go through all of that trouble to rescue you just to give you right back to the angels.

"On your second point, we have some inside information that Gabriel's life is not in immediate danger and that there's some contention within the Archangel Council about what to do with him. It seems they don't all necessarily want to kill him straight away, at least not without a proper trial. It's been agreed that he'll remain in prison until January, at which time he'll be officially put on trial for his 'crimes'."

The girls fired additional questions at Chris for a few more minutes, slowly coming to the same conclusion that he was right. Arrangements were made for them to be teleported back to the campus as soon as possible to ensure they didn't miss any more classes.

Sixty-Two

The next few weeks were torture, as neither of them were able to concentrate on assignments or studying for exams after all that'd happened, but miraculously, they were both able to get by with reasonably good grades in all of their classes.

It had already been arranged for them to return to the Lair shortly after the end of the semester. They'd each tell their parents that they were going away to a beach house in Florida that they'd rented with a group of friends for Christmas break. The demon budget paid for the beach house, but no one would ever set foot in it.

Taylor's dad arrived early on the first day after final exams. He honked his horn in greeting as he pulled up. He'd arranged with Sam's father to drive them home and then Mr. Collins would return them after the four week break. She and Sam were waiting with their bags. Sam had said goodbye to Chris earlier, worried that Taylor's dad might ask too many questions if he saw her kissing the darkly handsome boy before they left.

"Hey, princess, how was your first semester of college?" her father asked, stepping out of the car.

"Interesting, Dad," she said. "Very different than what I expected."

"How so?" he asked.

"I'll tell you all about it on the drive home."

He shrugged, firing off another question in his normal style. "So, where's this Gabriel fellow I've heard so little about? I was hoping to meet him."

Pangs of pain shot through Taylor's chest. "Oh, sorry, Dad, he left yesterday. Perhaps you can meet him next semester."

He looked disappointed as he loaded the girls' luggage into the trunk, but once in the car he turned to Taylor and said, "I'm just glad that you'll be home for a few weeks."

Taylor glanced at Sam in the backseat who was trying not to laugh. Now was not the time to tell him about their little vacation. "Uh, yeah. Me too, Dad...Me too. I'm even excited about seeing James, believe it or not."

Her father smiled. "That's good, because we're going to pick him up now."

Taylor smiled back as he started the engine and headed for the apartment blocks off campus. Taylor stared out the window, but didn't even see the lecture buildings flashing by. She was wondering if she would ever see Gabriel again.

Sixty-Three

He stared at the dark, damp stone wall in misery. Gabriel had been in the angel prison for fourteen days, but with no sunlight, it could've been one hundred and fourteen days for all he knew. Not that he cared.

He had lost everything. If Taylor was dead he'd never see her again. If she was alive and in the hands of the demons he'd never see her again. Bottom line: he'd never see her again.

He'd never experienced this kind of sadness and it had sent him spiraling into a deep depression. His only hope was that the Archangel Council would charge him with treason and sentence him to a quick and painless execution. It's what he deserved. Death would be a relief.

These were his thoughts when a ray of hope pierced through the gloomy dungeon. It was in the form of a crumpled up piece of paper that an invisible hand slipped through the air hole in his cell door. It was written in block letters to hide the handwriting. It read:

DO NOT DESPAIR
SHE IS ALIVE AND HASN'T GIVEN UP ON YOU
HELP IS ON THE WAY
INSTRUCTIONS TO FOLLOW
DESTROY THIS MESSAGE

Gabriel read the note three times, faith and hope entering his heart for the first time since he lost her. Determination coursed through his veins as he pledged to himself that he'd never give up, that he'd fight to see Taylor again, and that he'd hold her in his arms once more before he died.

About the Author

After growing up in Pittsburgh, Pennsylvania, David Estes moved to Sydney, Australia, where he met his wife, Adele. Now they travel the world writing and reading and taking photographs.

21362633R00201

Made in the USA
Lexington, KY
16 March 2013